# RIVERS AND SEAS

Printed in Australia

Cover and internal design by New Found Books Australia Pty Ltd
Images in this book are copyright approved for New Found Books Australia Pty Ltd
Illustrations within this book are copyright approved for New Found Books Australia Pty Ltd

First printing: OCTOBER 2024

New Found Books Australia Pty Ltd
www.newfoundbooks.au

Paperback ISBN 9781923173699
eBook ISBN 9781923172739
Hardback ISBN 9781923172852

Distributed by New Found Books Australia and Lightning Source Global

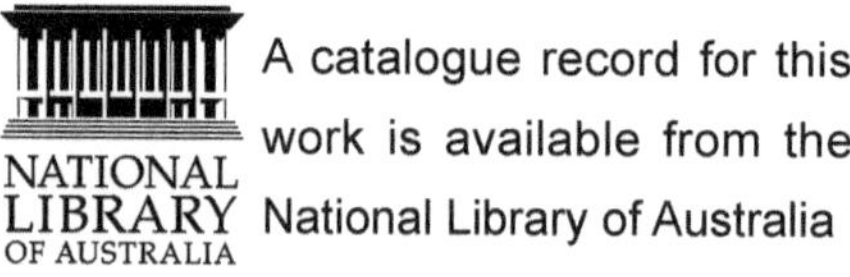


A catalogue record for this work is available from the National Library of Australia

More great New Found Books Australia titles can be found at:
www.newfoundbooks.au/our-titles/
*We acknowledge the traditional owners of the land
and pay respects to the Elders, past, present and future.*

# Rivers and Seas

## Timothy Gerrard

# Acknowledgements

I owe debts of thanks for assistance, advice, opinions and expertise to the following people for their support on this journey with Ippolito and Ruth; Vicki Smith, Bill Legge, Chris and Nina Legge, Liz Drysdale and Wendy Dimond. My thanks to all of you.

Thanks must also go to the great teams at Malua Bay Foodworks and The Moorings Resort for their ongoing promotion and marketing of my previous novels

Finally, special thanks to Graeme Fletcher. You have been on a four-year journey with me, Ippolito, Ruth and Raymond. We would never have made it to the end without you and your input.

Thank you dear friend.

*To Andy.*
*Deep peace, dear brother. I miss you.*

# What Went Before....

During the crusades, the young king of Jerusalem, Baldwin IV, had leprosy. A rumour reached his court of a cure for the disease to be found in India. Hadar, a court physician, and his two apprentices, Ippolito and Ruth, are commissioned to travel to India. The trio are accompanied by two Hospitaller knights, Godfrey and Caspar, a sergeant, Edward, a young squire, Raymond and Benedict, a priest.

Their journey sees many adventures but, most significantly, the rape of Ruth by Benedict leaves her mute with trauma. Benedict is slain by Godfrey who also dies of his wounds. With typical ingenuity, Ippolito and Ruth soon develop a sign language which sees their relationship develop further. Caspar also teaches Ruth the skills of the throwing knife at which she soon becomes a lethal adept. Edward dies in a sandstorm saving the life of a young boy.

Accompanied by Kali, a magician entertainer and sole survivor of a shark attack on a stricken circus troupe ship, the party arrive in southern India only to discover that India is rife with leprosy and there is no cure. All hope is not lost, as Kali informs Hadar and his companions of the holy men of the Himalayas who are supposedly possessed of certain skills and knowledge unknown elsewhere.

As the party travel north, they become embroiled in the Muslim invasion of the north India kingdom of Gujarat where the mentally unstable queen, Naiki Devi, has plans to utilise Ruth's knife throwing ability, disguising her as a blue demon riding an elephant. Ruth becomes emotionally attached to Narmala, a female horse guard captain who is charged with Ruth's training. The Muslim army is defeated but Ippolito falls across the great sabre attached to the elephant's tusk. He is ripped open from neck to foot and sure to die. It is only the return of Ruth's voice in the crisis that allows her to issue instructions on the battlefield that saves Ippolito's life.

As Ippolito recovers in an Indian hospital under Ruth's care, the queen falls under her own delusions and comes to believe Ruth and Ippolito really are demons and plots to kill the pair and their party. It is only Narmala's intervention that saves them and allows them to escape the queen's madness.

During their escape, Ruth finds and adopts a snow leopard cub she names "Whisper". Eventually the party reach the Himalayas and are near an underground Buddhist monastery known as 'The Buddha's Smile' when Hadar falls down the side of the mountain sustaining head injuries that will see him in a coma for over a year.

Rescued by the monks of the monastery, Ippolito, Ruth, Raymond and Caspar learn not only the unique unarmed fighting skills of the warrior monks but also aspects of eastern medicine, in particular acupuncture, to compliment what Hadar has already taught Ruth and Ippolito. During this time, a young monk, Darma, befriends the group also acting as an interpreter where needed.

As Hadar emerges from his coma a year later, with some loss of speech and weakness down one side, the monastery comes under threat from migrating hordes of steppe horsemen. With Whisper's assistance, Ippolito and his companions delay the horsemen's advance on the monastery. An arrow in the spine renders Caspar a paraplegic and a battle for the monastery ensues which is narrowly won by the warrior monks.

Both Hadar and Caspar realise they will never be able to return to Jerusalem but are adamant that Ippolito, Ruth and Raymond must return to bring the valuable knowledge of their hybrid medicine to the west and establish a free hospital for the poor and disadvantaged. Ruth is distraught about leaving Whisper behind but with Darma acting as a guide, the four depart down the Indus River to reach the sea and find a ship for home.

# 1

'Oh. The Bells of Hell. The damned beasts are all around us,' exclaimed a fretful looking Raymond.

The setting afternoon sun was casting its orange warmth across the lazily running water of the Indus River. The raw sienna light both highlighted and reflected in the dozens of pairs of bulging eyes that were sitting just above the water line. Occasionally, very long snouts with impressive jaws and rows of numerous long teeth also broke the surface of the water. The hideous monsters appeared to be maintaining a guarding vigil, either accompanying alongside, or circling, our small river punt. Were they simply curious or, were they herding us?

We had ceased poling our way down the river and were letting the gentle current of the Indus take our small punt along with it. This allowed all hands in the punt to grab a weapon with which to fight back should the giant reptiles try to attack or overturn our vessel. The punt was old but watertight. We had bought it just a week before so our small party of four could hopefully make an uneventful downriver voyage to the northern coast of Hind. From there, we intended to take a trading vessel to the Red Sea and then travel with a caravan overland and onto Jerusalem. It did not look like it was going to be an uneventful voyage right now.

The previous weeks had been tinged with sadness and sorrow as we had left two of our companions, Hadar and Caspar, behind us. They had been our friends, our mentors, our guardians and protectors. Injury and debilitation had seen them unable to make the return journey from the Buddhist monastery and they had opted to stay behind to embrace the contemplative life, along with the peaceful ambience of the Buddha's Smile Monastery, in the time that was left to them. The pain of this separation still brings tears to my eyes and are in them now as I write.

For Ruth, the pain was twofold, as she had to leave behind, not just two beloved colleagues, but also her unique feline companion, Whisper, a Himalayan snow leopard she had rescued as a cub. Sadly, Whisper would have sickened and died in the heat and humidity of the lower Hindi plains and needed to stay behind in the colder climes of the Himalaya mountains.

Never have I known a more intelligent, intuitive and capable animal than that snow leopard. Like the monks of the monastery and local villagers, I was quite ready to believe Whisper was indeed some kind of messenger from the gods. They believed she had the ears of the gods and was serviced to assist the shamans, wisemen and healers of this world in their work. Whisper had saved my life and those of others in our party on more than one occasion. Her job now was to care for Hadar and Caspar in their monastic retreat. Our other companion, Kali, had remained behind and returned to his home village after an absence of more than three decades.

Still, the grief and pain of separation was abating, particularly right now as we waited for what appeared to be a massing crocodile attack on our small punt.

'These are not like crocodiles I have seen before,' said Darma grasping the punt's pole, ready to use it against any of the reptiles that might try to board or capsize our little boat. 'I would have expected they should have swamped our boat and swallowed us all by now.'

'They do look different,' I agreed. Their reptilian snouts and jaws were longer and slenderer, while their actual heads seemed smaller in comparison to other crocodiles I had seen on our travels. But they were still just as big as the largest I had ever seen as well.

'What are those bulbous knobs on the tips of their snouts on half of them? Is that buzzing, humming sound coming from them?' asked Ruth, ever more attentive to more than just the visual aspects of her surroundings, 'They seem to blow bubbles through them under the water before they surface.'

We had had two whole days of observing these creatures as they slowly gathered in twos and threes around the punt, initially frightening us all to the point where we feared an imminent and grisly death between snapping, long, white teeth. Fortunately, the creatures had remained docile and seemed merely inquisitive. Hopefully, not just for the time being. Only one terrifying incident had occurred when two of the monsters rose from the water a few yards from our boat and began gnashing, snapping and biting at each other. They rose high in the water and we feared their crashing into the boat and capsizing it would send us into the river and into their mouths. Despite this, none of us had slept for more than a few snatches of exhausted slumber for fear of the beasts finally turning on us.

The reptilian monsters were not just in the river, they were also lazing in scattered groups along the banks and watching us with what seemed keen eyed attention. It was their presence along the banks that presented us with what was becoming a bigger problem for us as time went by – we had nowhere to cook, eat, sleep and worse, nowhere to pass water or waste with any privacy or safety. None of us were going to stick our backsides over the side of the punt only to have it, or anything dangling nearby it, bitten off by a hungry monster. Consequently, we were all over tired, dirty, hungry and cranky with constipation.

It was as the sun was doing its last rapid descent below the horizon that we saw in the distance a lone washer woman by the riverbank, placing the last of the day's washing in a basket.

'Oh my God,' cried an alarmed Ruth, 'She'll be attacked for certain. We must warn her.'

Immediately, we all started yelling and waving our arms around and soon caught her attention. Raymond swung the pole into the water and steered the punt to the bank.

'Crocodiles. Run. Get away,' we yelled in the northern Hind dialect.

To our surprise, the woman just stood there and as we drew closer, she began to laugh.

'Not crocodiles,' she said cheerfully, 'Gharials. Only eat fish.'

Despite feeling silly and having endured two days of privation, fear and hunger, we pulled onto the bank, quickly found a bush with broad leaves and then separated to dig our own privy holes. Oh! What a relief it was.

The washer woman, who introduced herself as Indra, invited us back to her village for a meal and a night's sleep under a roof. We were happy to accept the offer after our two-day ordeal and followed her over the riverbank and across a field to her village a short distance away. As we entered the village, the four of us were surprised to see another large gharial, nearly 20 feet long, lazing by the door of a small temple. The creature looked less threatening than its colleagues did along the river, largely because it was decked out in colourful flower garlands and had been decorated with numerous dots of different coloured paint along its reptilian spine.

'Do not be scared of Makara,' Indra reassured us, 'He is the village guardian. You do not have to be afraid of him as on land, like all gharials, he has weak legs and can only drag his big fat belly along the ground. It is when he is swimming in the river that he becomes a hunter and a killer. But only fish and small animals like turtles and frogs.'

The beast seemed to yawn and opened its great mouth wide revealing dozens of long, sharp, glistening white teeth. Fat bellied, fish eating or weak legged, I decided I would still keep my distance.

A few weeks later in our voyage, other more concerning news reached us. Mohammed of Ghorr was on the warpath again. After his defeat by Queen Naiki Devi and the Gujarati forces, he had re-entered India and was invading the Punjab region, instead of Gujarat, through which we were then travelling. Fortunately, he was still far to the north and we were travelling away from his advance.

We were definitely in warmer climes now and the time came to discard our heavy winter mountain clothes and purchase lighter cotton wear as spring was turning into summer. The river was changing too. As we traversed the Punjab, the Indus was joined by other rivers, some of considerable size and it swelled to over a mile wide. We kept our raft to the western bank where we could safely pole it along, rather than risk the uncertain currents in the deeper parts of the river.

Eventually the river began dividing itself into branch after branch and Darma informed us we were nearing the coast as we had entered the delta region of the Indus River. Darma had insisted we always take the northern fork as he said when we reached the coast we would be nearer a small local trading port called Kharak Bandar. It was only two days later that I heard the first sounds of waves crashing upon a shore and knew that after nearly two months of rafting down the Indus, we had finally made it to the sea.

2

We may have made it to the sea, but we still had 20 miles or more to trek to cross the vast swathes of sandy coastline and dunes that led to Kharak Bandar, and it was very hot and humid. I was grateful we could make our way through the shallows, splashing playfully at each other to stay cool. Even Darma, who had previously professed that discomfort and pain were only an illusion arising from desire, looked heat stressed and seemed happy enough to splash in the water with us as well. Ruth, in her sari, was perhaps more conscious of her modesty and did not involve herself in the dunking and horseplay that Raymond, Darma and I did. It was fun but it was silly, as it slowed us down when we should have been trying to set a faster pace.

Darma called a halt to our progress about an hour before sundown and suggested we prepare our campsite and see what we could put together for a meal, meaning rice again. While we set about our tasks, Darma took one of our now empty food sacks and made his way over to a rocky spit where he poked around with his knife. An hour later, as we were rolling our rice into balls, he returned and emptied the sack into the cooking pot, depositing a variety of crabs, small shellfish and different seaweeds within it. Ruth wanted to add the last of our spices, but Darma maintained the different seaweeds would give it a unique taste without the extra spices.

Along with the rice balls, Darma's seafood concoction proved to be the best tasting meal we had eaten since staying in Anhilwarra Patan nearly two years before. After we had all complimented Darma on his cooking, he confessed to having grown up in a seaside fishing village further south and that his own path to enlightenment had often been slowed or led astray by memories of meals of the kind we had just enjoyed.

It was around mid-morning the next day when we crossed over a headland and looked down onto the small harbour that constituted the trading port of Kharak Bandar. Ruth, Raymond and I recognised the bay at once from our earlier sea voyage to India from Rey Shah by the long mole that acted as a breakwater and dock for the port. There were a number of vessels moored beside the dock; one in particular was a very large two masted dhow with red and black striped sails. From atop the mainmast flew a pennant with an insignia unknown and unrecognisable to any of us, suggesting the vessel was the property of some further afield regional potentate or magnate. Men, in similar red and black livery to the sails, were busy either guarding against any approach to the dhow along the mole, re-rigging ropes and lines on the deck or lading goods. Others were engaged in the final repairs of what looked like damaged timbers on the portside forward hull. The damage suggested a collision between two vessels. Many of the workers appeared to be the black-skinned people I had heard were called Aethiops in the ports and harbour towns we had seen on our way to Hind. I suspected that most of these Aethiops had been castrated as they had the soft, fatty and fleshy appearance of eunuchs I had seen in other places. Their voices, when they spoke, seemed to be higher in tone than most men's voices.

We made our way past the mole-side dock to what was obviously one of the local marketplaces. Around us, we could hear Persian, Arabic, Hind and other languages being spoken.

'At least one of us will be able to make ourselves understood around here,' commented Raymond upon hearing the gaggle of languages filling the air.

'First things first,' said Darma, 'we need food, some suitable accommodation and shipping information to get you three travellers back home.'

'Agreed,' I concurred.

Belted beneath his tunic, Raymond still carried our small purse of Persian dinars, courtesy of the Emir of Shiraz, and our first stop was a street food vendor who also provided us with the locations of the two caravanserais of Kharak Bandar. Once we were settled into one of the caravanserais, finding the details of ships travelling and trading to the Red Sea, would not be too difficult.

As we made our way through the market crowds in the direction of the first caravanserai the vendor had recommended, I could not help but notice the glances many of the locals were casting in Ruth's direction. In particular, two of the Aethiops we had seen earlier in more ornate red and black livery seemed to be following us from a distance.

'Ruth,' I said with some concern, 'I think you should don a veil for your hair and perhaps one for your face as well. I'm not sure I like the attention you are attracting.'

We all agreed this was probably a good idea and, wisely, Ruth donned two veils and adjusted her clothing to an appropriate modesty so only her hands, ankles and feet were showing bare skin. I knew that beneath her robes, Ruth would have her belt of six throwing knives securely sheathed and unobtrusively strapped across her upper chest. Also belted to her waist, would be the small packet of fine healing needles given to her by Master Do.

Two hours later, we were throwing our packs onto the cots of our appointed bungalow within the caravanserai and settling in. Within the safety of the caravanserai we all felt a greater sense of safety and security, thanks to their long tradition of providing places of safe haven to travellers and merchants.

'Well, I am for having a look around this place,' said Raymond, 'There is always something new or of interest to be seen in these places.'

'I think I would like to join you,' said Darma with interest, 'I have never stayed in a caravanserai before.'

'I'm for a look around as well,' I added, 'Ruth. Are you going to come along?'

'No. I want to take a nap and remove some of this stifling clothing. I'll see you when you get back. Take these with you,' she said handing me our now empty water skins, 'and don't forget to buy something for an evening meal.'

Two hours later, we returned to an empty bungalow. Ruth was nowhere to be seen and I suddenly felt very panicked.

# 3

'She has probably just stepped out for some air,' said Raymond trying to reassure me but my sixth sense was raging against this. I knew instinctively that something was terribly wrong.

'She would not have gone outside the caravanserai without at least one of us to go along with her. Let us do a quick search and meet back here before the guards close the gates at sunset,' offered Darma.

We took off in different directions: Raymond to the caravanserai marketplace while Darma enquired of other travellers staying in the bungalows around us.

I went straight to the gates of the caravanserai to speak with the men on guard duty. I explained to them, in broken Persian and Hindi, Ruth's disappearance, what she was probably wearing and her general physical characteristics given that she would have been modestly covered.

Neither of the guards had noticed a single woman leaving the compound at all during the afternoon and sadly shook their heads.

'Has there been any unusual activity or unexpected people come through the gates?' I pressed further.

At this, they both turned to each other and shared a look that suggested they possibly knew something of relevance.

'This afternoon, three of the Sultan of Pemba's eunuchs arrived carrying a roll of carpet they said was being sold to a passing Hindi merchant. The strange thing was they returned later still carrying

14

the carpet. They told us the merchant had changed his mind on the purchase,' replied the more senior of the guards.

'Where do I find this Sultan of Pemba?' I asked urgently.

'Off the coast of Africa. Probably sitting in his palace smoking hashish and surrounded by his harem. That is his royal dhow with the red and black markings on the dock. It is due to sail with the tide later tonight. I do not wish to upset you, but the Sultan is known for his appetites. The immense size of his harem of wives and concubines is well known across the Hindi Ocean. I would wager that Butu, the Sultan's royal captain, has probably been buying, capturing or kidnapping attractive young women for the Sultan's harem again. I am sorry but I think your friend may be a captive aboard the royal dhow. I doubt that you will see her again.'

I thanked the two and at once took off running to find Raymond and Darma. The sun was getting low by the time I had gathered them back in the bungalow and explained what I thought had happened to Ruth.

'We must get down to the waterfront now. Grab your weapons and let us go. We can decide what to do when we get there,' I said.

Raymond grabbed what had been our comrade Caspar's long sword. Darma took his stave and I thrust my trusty stiletto in my belt as we darted out the door and headed to the gates which were about to close. We raced through the town, retracing our steps from earlier in the day and arrived at the mole dockside as the last rays of sunlight lit the docks.

'We need to get on board undetected. Once we have done that we can search for Ruth under the cover of darkness and try to free her,' I suggested.

'There are eunuch guards everywhere,' pointed out Raymond, 'How do you propose to get past them and then on board the dhow?'

'Darma. Can you create a diversion to draw the guards away from the dock and gangplank and attract the attention of those on deck?' I asked.

Darma smiled and nodded that he could.

'Raymond, while Darma creates a diversion, you and I can climb up the forward hawser and take cover in the foredeck storage area.'

With that, we split up, Raymond and I casually making our way along the far side of the mole towards the bow of the dhow while Darma made his slow way to the gangway. He halted as near to the gangway as the large Aethiop eunuch on guard duty would allow him to approach. At being halted, Darma asked something of the guard who simply shook his head with incomprehension and motioned with his sword that Darma should keep moving. Darma then appeared to ask something else at which the guard raised his voice in a language I did not recognise and made a much more aggressive gesture with his sword suggesting 'move on or else'.

Darma took this as his cue to deftly whirl his stave, striking the guard first on his sword wrist causing the weapon to fall to the ground and then a second blow to the side of the knee causing the guard himself to fall to the ground with a great bellow of pain. He tried but was unable to get up. This drew the attention of the other guards and crew on deck, who raced to the side or to the gangway where they descended upon Darma, who stood with his stave at the bottom of the gangplank.

As Darma's stave whirled, knocking guards and crew from their feet and into the water below, Raymond and I made our move to the fore of the dhow and quickly shinned our way up the hawser to tumble quietly over the side and down behind the coils of rope that were stowed there. We could not see what was happening on the mole but the cries of pain and the cracking of wood on bone suddenly changed to cries of outrage and then the sounds of pursuit as Darma made good his escape. The overweight eunuch guards would never catch the athletic monk.

'What do we do now?' asked Raymond in a whisper.

'Cover ourselves up and wait until dark,' I replied, 'And watch everything for any clues as to where they may be holding Ruth.'

We did the best we could to disappear into the coils of rope around us. The rope was prickly and uncomfortable against the bare skin of arms and necks.

As the evening light slowly faded into darkness and stars appeared in the night sky, we scanned the deck. At the stern of the dhow was a high, three-tiered castle of what were probably cabins or cells. Steering boards projected from both sides of the lowest tier. Above them, guards were returning to their positions outside the top two tiers. They were clearly guarding or protecting something and it was there that I suspected Ruth was being held.

On the deck below were three hatch covers that no doubt led down into the hold and the below decks area. Two were quite large and obviously designed for the lading of large bales and objects. The smallest was no more than a man-hole cover and lay just a few feet from where Raymond and I had concealed ourselves within the coils of ropes.

'If we can get below-deck, we may be able to move closer to the stern-castle without being seen,' I whispered to Raymond, 'We just have to wait for the right opportunity.'

The opportunity came when the last of the wounded and beaten guards were being helped back on deck and their captain, Butu, appeared on the deck of the stern castle. He addressed the guards angrily in a language neither Raymond nor I understood but later learned it was called Swahili. While the captain berated the crew, Raymond and I made our move. We slithered on our bellies to the hatch where I was able to quietly and efficiently raise it for Raymond to crawl into and then allow myself to slip in behind him. Closing the hatch as silently as possible, I slid down into the darkness of the hold.

Above us, we heard Butu finish his tirade at the crew and then the slapping sounds of bare feet on the deck as the crew returned to their positions and duties.

'What now?' came Raymond's voice in the pitch-black darkness we had found ourselves in.

'I can't say I'm sure,' I responded, 'I guess we will have to feel our way to the rear of the ship.'

'You lead the way then,' replied Raymond.

I inched my way forward with my hands out in front of me and kept my head lowered as there was not much headspace between the decks. For the most part, we were surrounded by bales of differing goods discernible by their fragrances and odours. They were stacked closely together and piled almost to the ceiling, making progress difficult and slow. From up on the decks, we could hear orders being yelled in Swahili and an increased activity as measured by the increased slapping of feet on deck.

There was a creaking and moaning of the ship's timbers as if it had been released from some restraint and suddenly, I felt the dhow shifting beneath my feet.

'Oh, my sacred God in heaven,' exclaimed Raymond, 'we're underway.'

'Yes. But where to?' I wondered.

# 4

Our first night below decks was a miserable one. Unable to see more than a few dark shapes against even darker shapes we were virtually blind. We managed to make ourselves vaguely comfortable sitting down between two bales but had to keep our knees bent to fit into the space. At least we could rest our heads upon our knees. The sound of scuttling and chittering rats did not help with sleep either. Even so every so often one of us would have to stand to get the blood flowing in our legs again and to cease the irritating pins and needles that came with having our knees bent up for so long.

'I think it must be getting light,' I said to Raymond many hours later, 'I can see a little better and it looks like those tiny flickers of light may be holes or small cracks in the deck.'

I stood up and did my best to stretch out the night's discomfort from my arms and legs before gently lifting the hatch a fraction to peep out onto the deck. Dawn had arrived in the east and was slowly lighting the rest of the sky. Up on the deck, various guards and sailors were rousing themselves from sleep and getting ready for another day's work. I pulled the hatch back down.

'I think we need to secure our position down here,' said Raymond.

'How so?' I replied.

'There is no point in trying to rescue Ruth while we are still at sea, there is nowhere to run, nowhere to go. We must hope she will be safe until we make port somewhere and then we can try to rescue her. What do you think?'

20

I reluctantly did so despite all my instincts wanting me to rescue Ruth right away.

'Once the light improves a little more, we need to find or make a safe bolt hole in case of any of the crew have reason to come down here. We also need to find access to food and water as well as a place we can piss and crap, that will not attract the attention of any sensitive noses on board. Ippolito, we could be weeks down here.'

'You are right. I am as dry as a biscuit and I need to empty myself somewhere,' I replied.

As our eyes became accustomed to the twilight belowdecks we were able to make out much of our surroundings. The first thing we noticed was a narrow walkway that ran the length of the ship between the bales of goods stacked high to the deck above. At regular intervals along the walkway were openings down to the bilge and ballast that lay at the bottom of the dhow. These openings were there to help realign the ballast under different sailing conditions and different trade loads. At the first of these, Raymond and I both raised our tunics and lowered our hose to meet one of the first needs of any day.

'Oh, that is much better,' said Raymond as he readjusted his clothing.

'I'll bet there are water butts beneath the main hatches for easy access,' I said pointing to a lighter area beneath a large hatch situated about mid deck.

Sure enough, we found a dozen or more of easily moved medium sized water butts beneath the hatch. We both slaked our thirst, as our second morning ritual, from one of the butts before replacing its cover.

'Time to put our noses to work,' I said wiping the water from my chin.

'Smelling bales, you mean,' clarified Raymond.

And so, we went to work and very quickly discovered we would eat quite well during our transit. Aside from replenishing the sultan's harem, the dhow was also replenishing the palace's food stocks. There were bales of fruit such as figs and dates, vegetable roots, beans, spices and herbs. Our only problem would be eating our food raw as there could be no cooking below decks. We partially solved this problem with soaking many of the harder food stuffs for a day or so in a water butt.

Raymond and I decided, as there was only a single gangway running the length of the hull, we should try to establish four or five bolt holes along its path so we could readily escape detection anytime members of the crew might choose to venture below decks. This was very hard work as moving many of the bales, even just a few inches, took time and considerable effort from both of us. We did have some luck finding a cavity within the great stack of bales that could accommodate the both of us standing up and lying down. During this time, we were alerted to any crew coming below deck by the heavy grating sound of the hatches being lifted and moved aside. This gave us time to duck down and hide in the nearest bolt hole.

Every so often, we would hear the sounds of different activities coming from the deck above, such as the running out of lines, the reefing of sails, the practicing of drills and other such shipboard sounds. It was as Raymond and I were laying some empty bale sacks as bedding on the deck of our "living area" that we heard some different sounds coming from above. It was the sound of women, their female voices carrying in the way that men's voices don't. There was also the sound of the occasional sobbing and crying.

I bounded down the gangway to the forward hatch and gently lifted it a fraction to give me a view across the main deck. There, about 30 women were being encouraged by their guards to walk around the deck and take some exercise and fresh air. Many were holding and comforting each other while some in small groups talked quietly amongst themselves. I searched for Ruth and finally spied her, sitting at the other end of the deck comforting another young woman. She was too far away to attract her attention without giving myself up. In my mind, I willed her to get up and walk my way but of course this did not happen. After about half an hour the women were shepherded back to the stern of the ship and mounted the ladder, leading to the topmost tier of the stern castle. At least I now knew, with certainty, where the women and Ruth were being held captive.

# 5

I was vastly relieved to know Ruth was actually aboard the dhow, as I had secretly been worried Raymond and I had entered in on a wild goose chase and she could have been in some other place and not on board. I told this to Raymond, along with the other details of what I had observed.

'At least we can take solace that as a harem prospect she will be treated better than if she had been taken as a slave,' observed Raymond, 'No slave gets an outdoor exercise period as part of their day. Given this is our first day out of port, I suspect this exercise will be a daily occurrence. I'm sure we will get the chance to make contact with Ruth before long.'

He was correct.

Three days later, Ruth took her walk and this time she came to the forward deck. There were some other women nearby and I was unsure about attracting Ruth's attention where others might hear and, advertently or inadvertently, alert the guards and crew to our presence below deck.

I opted to try and sibilantly hissed, 'Forsooth Ruth,' doing my best to make the utterance sound like the sea and windblown spray around us.

Ruth's body immediately gave an involuntary jerk before she quickly brought herself back under self-control. She surreptitiously began to slowly look around her as if curious about the dhow's design and structure.

'The hatch,' I softly hissed.

Ruth's eyes turned to look at the hatch without moving her head around in my direction, as this might have given her interest in where I was away. Our eyes met for a brief moment, that I knew gave us both equal joy. She then moved away and leant against the forward mast where she could see me and also appear to be looking forward out to sea in an innocuous way. She placed her hands across her midriff where they were hidden from the sight of anyone standing behind her and immediately began to sign to me in the language we had developed during the period of her mute trauma in Persia and Hind.

She began with our little sign for 'I love you,' then she continued, 'Safe. Unhurt. Dhow go Africa. Island name Pemba. Harem ship of Sultan. Six-week sail. You?'

'R with me. Hide below. Think safe now. Rescue you Pemba. No good here,' and then I too made our little sign of 'I love you.'

She smiled that smile of hers at me before signing, 'Tomorrow,' and then turned away to join the women who were being directed by their guards back to their quarters, their exercise period over.

Over the next week, I was able to learn in bits and pieces how Ruth and the other women were faring on board the harem ship. To my great relief, Ruth and the other women had been left unmolested. Apart from captain Butu and his chief mate, all the other men on board were eunuchs who had been especially selected for this mission. They may have been eunuchs but they were warrior eunuchs, a speciality of the Aethiops or Swahili, as they called themselves. I was pleased Ruth still had her belt of sheathed throwing knives strapped to her chest. They would come in handy when we made our escape. Ruth also had her small wallet of needles that Master

Do had given each of us. She indicated she had been treating some of the women for menstrual problems and other complaints that arise with shipboard life, such as sea sickness and bowel disturbances.

All in all, Ruth and her companions were being fed and treated well. They were definitely having a better time of it than Raymond and I were below decks. As we travelled south, the weather became hotter and more humid and none so more as the space below decks with its lack of ventilation and fresh air. The heat also made the rancid odour of the ballast and bilge water, combined with our own bowel matter, at times over-powering.

Aside from the heat and smell, the animal life of the dhow made our lives barely tolerable. We were constantly on guard against the rats of the ship who had grown large and fat on the contents of some of the bales and were very aggressive when disturbed. Added to this, they were bold enough to come close when we were asleep. I remember waking with the dark brown pellet evidence of their visitations on my chest and around my person on several occasions. Raymond and I agreed to take it in turns to stand guard over each other during the night shooing the horrible long toothed night visitors away.

Along with the rats, we had to contend with the cockroaches. Whilst not as threatening as the rats, in terms of bites and potential infection, they ate more of Raymond and me than the rats. We both had thought the bits of skin peeling from the soles of our feet was due to the heat and humidity, until we discovered the cockroaches were actually gnawing away at the tough skin of our heels, toes and balls of our feet during our sleep. We slept with our boots on after this discovery, further adding to our discomfort.

Ruth and I managed daily short conversations in our sign language being careful not to be seen. Some days, the presence of an idle guard taking his ease on the foredeck prevented or inhibited the communication we might have had with each other. It was hard as we could both see the longing for each other in our eyes and I ached to hold Ruth in my arms and never let her go.

It was some weeks into our voyage when Ruth informed me that one of the guards had told the prospective harem we were less than a week's sailing from our destination – Pemba Island or Jazirat al-Khudrah, "The Green Island".

Raymond and I had some serious consideration to give to our escape plans.

# 6

The plan Raymond and I developed for the escape was simple – set fire to the dhow and, in the confusion, release Ruth from her captivity and flee. Of course, we had some problems and planning that needed sorting out. The first was, how were we going to start a fire? We had no flint, fire steel or tinder. We would have to steal it and that was going to be a problem. The only place on the dhow where a fire was laid was the great cooking stone in the middle of the dhow's deck, surrounded by butts of water. Each morning, the dhow's cook would light a new fire on the stone with his tinderbox and then the fire would be totally extinguished as soon as the meal was cooked and ready for serving. The process was repeated for each meal of the day. Fire is the great enemy of ships and sailors.

The night before we were due to dock on Pemba Island, Raymond and I readied ourselves. I had briefed Ruth on the plan the day before and she knew what to expect and when. There was a good cloud cover and the night was very dark, which was to our advantage. Raymond stole silently up through the manhole hatch and then reached down to grab the sack of vegetable roots I handed up to him. He then quickly made his way to the side of the ship and took cover behind a water butt. At the same time, I made my way to hide behind the main mast of the dhow, a few yards in front of the fire stone. We both settled down to wait for the cook's arrival on deck which was not long.

The cook made his way to the stone and from years of habit and practice, assembled his fire making apparatus. Raymond and I had agreed that the moment he put his tinderbox down beside him, to kindle the fire, was our signal. Sure enough, the cook deftly and efficiently struck flint and steel to spark and fire the tinder in front of him. He put his tinderbox down and reached for the nearby kindling. From the portside of the ship came a startled and distressed, 'Yaahhh,' followed by the sound of the vegetable sack splashing into the water below. All attention went to that side of the ship as the two guards and the cook raced to try and possibly save the crewman presumed to have fallen overboard, probably while having a piss. I dashed forward and deftly grabbed the tinderbox from beside the firestone before turning and retreating to the forward hatch where Raymond was just making his descent. The whole ruse, from splash to final dash, had taken less than a minute.

The steersman called the three men back to order and to their positions and there was some calling back and forth as the cook tried to find his tinderbox. His fire needed kindling up and he set to work doing just that, no doubt expecting to find his fire-starting equipment later.

Raymond and I then settled down to wait, hoping the supposed disappearance of a member of the crew would not generate an investigation, as the crew would need to ready themselves for entering Pemba port and getting dockside with their precious cargo for the Sultan. Over the previous days, Raymond and I had made an inventory of the flammable goods below deck such as bolts of cotton, sacks of dried herbs and some amphorae of oil which we now liberally doused over everything, in and around the forward underdeck.

The sun was now up and from the sounds above, we could tell the dhow was readying to turn to harbour and eventually dock. The crew were busy readying lines, adjusting sails or readying the winches to raise the cargo below deck. Raymond and I waited with bated breath for the dhow to make dockside. We heard the landsmen calling out, the crew responding and the sounds of lines being thrown out from the deck to the pier below. And then we heard it, the gentle thump of wood on wood as the dhow touched dockside.

Raymond immediately struck the cook's flint stone against the steel over the oil-soaked goods below the foredeck. We had used too much oil and the whole fuel load exploded in a ball of flame that sent us sprawling on our backs and scrambling to get away from the conflagration as quickly as we could. We ran as fast as we were able along the central gangway to the aft of the dhow and waited below the stern hatch.

From above and on the docks, came shrieks and screams of fear and panic as the quickly spreading fire threatened, not only the Sultan's dhow but, the vessels around it and the dock itself. We could hear the sound of feet running everywhere above us as crew members raced to grab water butts and pour them down the forward hatch. Pushing the aft hatch up just an inch I was able to observe the stern castle, waiting for the moment when the guards would race to free the captive residents of the harem cabins.

Smoke was billowing across the deck by now, obscuring vision not just for ourselves but for everyone on deck and on the dock. I did not see the guard who unlocked the cabin doors on the stern castle, but I did see the women fleeing and heard their screaming as they fled to escape the flames.

'Now,' I said to Raymond as we pushed the weight of the stern hatch from above us and climbed out onto the deck where we were quickly obscured by more drifts of smoke. We made our way to the steer-board side of the dhow where I glimpsed the smoke-shrouded silhouette of Ruth crouching by the dhow's deck railing.

'Quick! Jump into the water,' I said, knowing Ruth, Raymond and I could all swim.

'Okay,' replied Ruth.

And with that we leapt from the decks into the warm equatorial waters of the Pemba harbour.

# 7

Flotsam was already floating on the surface around us when we surfaced from under the water. A drifting spar gave us a little buoyancy and allowed me time to look back at the damage and havoc we had created.

There were others in the water apart from the three of us, but each was concerned with preserving their own lives and ignored us as they tried to make it to their own safety or went under to a watery death. Looking back, I could see the Sultan's dhow was well ablaze from bow to stern and the vessel to the fore of it was also burning. On the dock, flying embers had set alight what was probably a tariff office and flames were licking their way down two of the dock's piers. Sailors, eunuchs, guards and stevedores were madly trying to beat out the flames or organise a bucket brigade to douse the fire. It was chaos and panic.

'Not a bad job if I say so myself,' said a very satisfied looking Raymond, even if he was missing the best part of his forehead fringe, eyebrows, moustache, and beard from the initial ignition of the blaze.

'I'm not keen to stay in the water,' I said, memories of the voyage to India coming to mind, 'Ports attract sharks due to all the rubbish and waste that is thrown overboard from vessels.'

Raymond and Ruth needed no further prompting and we hastily kicked our spar to the beach end of the docks and brought ourselves ashore where we took stock of ourselves. We all had weapons; Ruth, her throwing knives, Raymond, Caspar's long sword and I had my trusty stiletto. Raymond and I also had the skills we had learned in

32

unarmed combat during our stay in the Buddha's Smile. We were in agreement that it was unlikely there would be any concerted search for us as no-one knew Raymond and I were aboard and Ruth's absence would no doubt be put down as a lost victim of the fire.

Raymond still had several of the Emir of Shiraz's silver dinars in the purse strapped inside his loin cloth. Ruth stated she could earn some coins treating the sick with Master Do's needles, if needed.

'I think we should retire to the jungle at the edge of the settlement and watch for a while, before entering the town. See what we can learn before revealing ourselves,' offered Ruth.

'And dry out a bit,' added a dripping Raymond.

This was a very good idea as the jungle around the town was a virtual garden of Eden where Raymond and I feasted on a variety of fruits and flavours we had not experienced in the weeks of our voyage. Ruth, who had eaten well on the voyage, ate sparingly but appeared to enjoy nature's bounty as much as Raymond and me. It was not hard to understand why Pemba Island was known as the Green Island.

From our hiding place, we were able to observe much about the port and town. The bulk of the people we observed were the very dark skinned Aethiopian Africans we later learned referred to themselves as either Bantu or Swahili; Swahili being the common language. There were also plenty of Arab merchants and officials who we later found out were mostly Persians, known as Shirazis, having come from our friend the Emir's city of Shiraz. Added to this mix, were small groups of Indian people I assumed were probably merchants, as well. I could tell by the many different skin tones and facial shapes that a fair bit of interbreeding had happened in the past between the Swahili, Arab, Persian and Indian inhabitants of Pemba Island.

The call to prayer sounded from the minaret of a nearby mosque at which, virtually everyone stopped what they were doing and unrolled their mats to face Mecca. I suspected they were Sunni Muslims from the prayer format. Pemba Island seemed to be a melting pot of peoples, culture and religion. In this regard, it was just like any other trading port around the Indian Ocean and the Persian Gulf.

We had waited and watched for the best part of two hours in which time the vessel we had sailed on had burned to the waterline. The vessel behind it had been doused and was only steaming, not smoking and the fires on the piers of the dock had been extinguished. Not far from where we were hiding was the dockside market, which we decided to investigate once Ruth had donned her veils as a disguise, in case she was recognised by members of the crew.

The outer buildings of the town were basic affairs of small mudbrick or wooden huts. Each had its own small produce garden and one or two fruit trees growing around it. As we got closer to the market and the docks, the houses became larger and were made of stone, or rather coral blocks held together with mortar. I assumed these were the houses of wealthy merchants lodged not too far from their well-stocked warehouses and storerooms. Others possibly belonged to government officials involved in the taxation of goods in and out of the port. Apart from the mosque and, what I assumed was, the palace in the distance, all the houses were single-storeyed and white, presumably to reflect the equatorial heat of the sun.

The outer stalls of the market were primarily for food produce and appeared to be principally frequented by locals doing their shopping for sorghum grain, rice, yams, bananas, cassava, coconuts, herbs and spices and other vegetable produce. Other stalls displayed bolts of cotton cloth in every colour imaginable, household kitchen and pottery items, animal hides, which painfully included leopard skins, salt and household medicines.

After the stalls came the emporia and warehouses, where commercial quantities of other luxury goods were displayed under the watchful eyes of merchants and paid security guards. Goods available included: precious metal ingots and jewellery of gold, iron and copper, ivory, tortoise shells, luxury timbers, such as sandalwood and ebony, incense and perfumes and rhinoceros horns. Goods such as silks and other fine fabrics, porcelain and pottery, glassware and other types of jewellery were on display in other areas of imported goods. It seemed the Island of Pemba was an international marketplace.

At the far end of the market stood an enclosed pen that held dozens of poor miserable-looking people, destined to be auctioned and sold off as slaves.

8

Our anonymity on Pemba was not to last too long. Whether their blood was up from watching the burning of the Sultan's dhow or they had simply had enough of imprisonment, poor food and degradation, the slaves in the pens chose their moment to rise-up and escape, just as we were passing by their enclosure. The first we became aware of the breakout was the sudden raising of many deep throated voices from the back of the pen and then a concerted rush of men charging at the pen's fence and crashing into it, almost as one body. It was enough. The fence leaned over and then, with a push or two more, it was breached and dozens of dark-skinned men, women and children rushed madly onto the docks causing chaos in the marketplace. Panicked people ran here and there, knocking over stalls, crashing into each other and a few even falling from the dock and ending up in Pemba Bay.

A young slave girl, with juvenile buds for breasts and only a tiny, beaded loin cloth for clothing, tripped and stumbled in front of us landing heavily and hurting herself in the process. Spontaneously, Ruth stopped to render the girl assistance. At the same time, one of the guards stopped running as well, but not to help. He reached the pair of them and raised his sword above them.

'Ruth! Look out,' yelled Raymond as he stepped forward and with one swipe of his long sword sliced right through the guard's sword-arm at the elbow leaving him shrieking in pain and attracting the attention of the other guards.

36

'That's torn it,' I said, 'They will be after us as well. Let us get out of here.'

We took off in the same direction the bulk of the slaves were running, back into the jungle where we had previously been hiding. Ruth and I aided the girl who had fallen and obviously badly sprained her ankle. Raymond held our rear, stopping every so often to engage a closing guard with his sword before, either swiftly despatching him or, causing the guard to stop, reconsider and wait for back-up before closing in on the fugitives. As the jungle got thicker and heavier going, the pursuing guards fell behind and eventually gave up the race.

The four of us kept going but soon realised we had fallen behind the main body of escapees and had no idea where we were or where we should go. This was quite an urgent matter as there would soon be organised search parties for all the escapees which now included ourselves. Eventually, we had to stop as all four of us were exhausted.

'Do you know where we are?' I asked the girl in Persian, Indian and Arabic to which she indicated no understanding.

Ruth then tried some improvised sign language, pointing first to the four of us and then in the four major directions around us and then shrugged her shoulders as if to say, 'I don't know.'

The girl was quick to comprehend and immediately pointed to the north and then made a wavey motion with her hands that seemed to indicate the sea. I wondered how far away that was.

Our progress was badly hampered by our injured companion. Despite valiant attempts not to show her distress, she was clearly in pain and unable to weight bear on her affected foot. It was Ruth who called a halt and sat us down. She pulled the wallet of needles,

Master Do had given her, from her tunic. She turned to the girl and got her attention. Ruth showed her one of the slender needles and then pierced her upper arm with it; the girl showing no distress. Ruth then pointed to the girl's ankle and made an 'Ooo Ooo' sound of pain. She then pointed to a place beneath the girl's knee and showed her the needle. She mimed piercing the girl's skin with the needle, then pointed to the ankle again and made a long relaxing 'Aaaahh' sound of comfort. Then without giving the girl any hint of her intention, she deftly pierced the meridian point beneath the knee, surprising the girl but not distressing her. Ruth then pointed to her ankle with a questioning look on her face. The girl looked perplexed for a moment and then smiled with pleasure and nodded her appreciation of the almost immediate reduction in pain.

As we got up and began to move on, the girl still needed assistance but was able to travel much more quickly, untroubled by her previous amount of pain but not entirely able to support her weight. I suspected more than just a sprain, possibly torn muscles, ligaments or tendons instead. I hoped there were no bones involved in the trauma.

As the afternoon and then the early evening wore on, we were joined in ones and twos by other escaping slaves who had either fallen behind the others or become lost in the jungle. Their joining our company allowed Ruth and me to relinquish assistance to the girl to make her way, as two young men, who appeared to know her, took over from us. One of them, I quickly learned, spoke Arabic.

'Where are we heading?' I asked.

'North to Kigomasha. There is a fishing village with lots of fishing boats. We will take the boats and cross the sea to our homeland,' replied the youth.

'How far to the fishing village?'

'We must walk and run all night. Meet in jungle near village tomorrow morning and then steal boats.'

'How far from village to homeland?'

'Two days, if weather bad and sea strong. One entire day if the weather is good for boats.'

It quickly became dark and the jungle canopy prevented what moon and starlight there was from penetrating the growth to light our way. This slowed us down considerably as, in some parts of the jungle, we were reduced to feeling our way and holding onto each other so as not to become separated.

At last, we came to a vast area of open fields that were under cultivation and we were able to make up for lost time in the jungle. Ahead of us and across the fields, we could see other small groups of escapees making their way north whilst heading in each other's direction to join up. An hour later, we were united with a large party from whom a tall warrior stepped forward and came toward us to take the girl in what was obviously a fatherly embrace.

He said something to his daughter in Swahili and she responded at some length, retelling her story. She then turned and pointed to Raymond with a coy smile on her face, before pointing to Ruth acknowledging her in some way to her father, as a woman worthy of respect given that her father bowed his head solemnly to her. I seemed to rate a third and not as important, introduction.

# 9

He then turned to the three of us and said, 'You speak Arabic. I want to thank you for the life of my only child. My name is Amana the "faithful warrior" and this is my daughter N'sibi.

Amana directed us all to keep moving. He explained to me that speed was everything if we were to make good our escape from Pemba and return to our respective homes by whatever routes.

Amana further explained, 'The Sultan, al–Hasah ibn Talut, will be beside himself with anger right now. First, he loses his flagship and cargo to a mysterious fire and then over 60 slaves escape his custody in broad daylight. He will have his guards and eunuchs force marched along every road to every settlement and village to track us down. We have been slowed by the jungle, whereas he has had the roads to follow. We must reach Kigomasha by morning and steal enough boats to get us home before his forces arrive.

'I would also hazard,' he added, 'that he will put his remaining fleet to service in searching for us at sea as well. He knows that we were captured on the mainland and then brought over land and sea to Pemba. I visited Pemba as a young man under a different sultan and know the northern half of the island well enough to find our way.'

We pushed on through the night over alternating cultivated land and jungle. As the group moved, it grew slowly larger as more of the escapees found our trail and followed to join up. It was about an hour before sunup that we crested a small hill and looked down on a sandy peninsula in the middle of which sat a fishing village of 30 or more rough fishermen's huts. Nets and fishing gear were stored along-side each hut, fish were drying on racks and, pulled up on the beach were not the fishing boats with sails I had been expecting but, 30 or so log canoes.

Amana wasted no time and ordered us down to the beach and into the canoes before the alarm could be raised. Each canoe was long enough to hold between six and eight rowers. Running silently over the sand, everyone found a canoe with paddles stored at the rear and pushed them out to sea before beginning vigorously paddling to the west. Amana and six others remained on shore, to push the remaining canoes out to sea on the conveniently outgoing tide, before jumping in one last one themselves. Not a soul in the village had heard us, stirred, looked out and seen us. The only clue to our presence was the disappearance of the canoes and a lot of footprints in the sand.

Despite our fatigue from the two nights' previous escape from the harem ship and the journey of the night just gone, Raymond and I both grabbed a paddle each and, along with the other men of the boat, began paddling as hard as we could. The paddler at the front of the canoe, setting the pace for the rest of us. Ruth sat between the two us as we paddled. The sea was choppy and waves splashed into the canoe, keeping Ruth busy bailing with her hands, as were the women and girls in the other canoes. I quietly prayed that the sea would not get any rougher.

We paddled and paddled, despite the constant burning ache in our backs, arms and shoulders, keeping the pace up until the island had all but disappeared below the horizon. It was only then that Amana called a loud command and our lead paddler settled down to a more leisurely stroke. Despite the lessening of pace, every stroke of my paddle was agony that my body did not want to experience. I was not the only one affected as I noticed that the faces of all the paddlers were strained and showing fatigue and pain. Amana would have to call a rest before too long. I believe he would have, were it not for the two red and black lateen sails he had spied coming, still hull down below the horizon, in our direction.

To add to my discomfort, the sight of swiftly moving long black shadows under the water trailing our little flotilla brought back horrifying memories of the shark feeding frenzy that had savaged and eaten our friends from the circus troupe on the sea leg of our journey to Hind. The sharks below us were not to be our biggest worry as it was only an hour or so before the red and black sails had devolved into two medium-sized dhows rapidly closing in on us. Amana yelled another command and our canoes began to slowly diverge from their individual courses so as not to be grouped together when the sultan's dhows caught up with us.

An hour later, we watched from afar the two dhows come along either side of the slowest moving canoe. Palace guards in red and black lined the gunnels with spears and arrows ready to rain down on the helpless occupants of the canoe. Shouts were called back and forth between the dhows and the canoe then suddenly, as one, the soldiers released their weaponry slaying everyone in the canoe. The two dhows continued on their course without stopping. The sharks, somehow sensing the blood above them, capsized the canoe tumbling the dead bodies into the sea to be torn apart by their savage mouths.

Their next victims, having seen the fate of their fellow escapees, gave up their attempt at freedom and threw down their paddles as the dhows drew alongside. Ropes were thrown over the side of the dhows and the recaptured prisoners were unceremoniously hauled up and tumbled aboard the dhows. This worked in the favour of the rest making their escape as it slowed the dhows down in the water. Obviously, the price of slaves prohibited too much indiscriminate killing of valuable commodities by the sultan's men on board.

An hour later, the scene was being repeated as the dhows had caught up, under a freshening wind beneath their sails. The wind was also chopping up the sea, making headway more difficult and bringing much more water on board. I could see Ruth was becoming fatigued after hours of bailing water.

A cry from a canoe across the water attracted the attention of Amana who was in a nearby canoe. He turned his head and looked to an area in the choppy sea that had a permanent turbulence around it. There were obviously rocks near the surface. I watched him as he steered the canoe in a direct line toward the turbulence. At the same time, I noticed the rate of paddle strokes decreasing and the canoe slowly losing speed. The dhows took the bait and immediately began a pursuit of what they thought was a disabled canoe or exhausted crew.

'I think he wants to draw them onto the rocks,' observed Ruth.

'It will have to be a closely timed thing,' added Raymond.

Amana's canoe was running a little too fast and they arrived near the rocks while the dhows were still some distance behind them. Amana and his men made a great show of pretending to bail water as the dhows closed in on the canoe. Then, just as the dhows were only 20 yards from them, the crew of the canoe dug their paddles in and swept to the windward side. The dhows had no time to readjust their course before it was too late and the first of them tore onto the rocky outcrop, ripping a great hole in its hull with a fearful tearing sound that carried across the water. The stricken dhow went under very quickly and sailors and soldiers were struggling in the water trying to stay afloat or clinging to spars, crossbars and any other flotsam they could grab.

The second dhow had avoided collision with the rocks but was obliged to lower sails and put out an anchor to assist those in the water. They would be delayed for quite a while, which gave us good cheer.

'I just hope the second dhow does not decide to continue the chase,' I said putting a damper on this brief moment of cheerfulness.

# 10

Unfortunately, the dhow's captain did decide to chase us. Whether it was from a sense of righteous anger or the prospect of returning to the sultan's capital and his accompanying wrath, minus one dhow and only eight recaptured slaves, I do not know. I suspect the latter. In the time that the captain of the second dhow had taken to rescue members of the stricken dhow, we had a chance to draw further ahead. However, it was not long before the second dhow was underway and following fast on our trail.

An idea was forming in my mind about what would happen if the quarry suddenly turned on the attacker. We would have a better chance than being picked off one by one as we tried to paddle our way to the coast without failing from exhaustion. I asked the others in our canoe to steer over to Amana's canoe and put the proposition to him.

'The idea has merit,' he said, 'We are more numerous than they, possibly twice as many, depending on how many of them drowned in the sea back there. There is one huge flaw to your plan. They have spears, swords and bows and arrows, we have nothing.'

'We have around 50 paddles, six throwing knives, a broadsword, a stiletto and four fists and feet that can fight in unarmed combat. Overall, your men are bigger and stronger than those on board the dhow. Plus, we are fighting for our freedom. They only fight for pay and fear of the sultan's displeasure and discipline.'

'How do you propose we get onto the dhow? She sits higher in the water than our canoes. Our men would be sitting ducks to their spears and arrows as they tried to clamber on board.'

'Is not one chance of freedom for all of us better than having it snatched away piecemeal, as we are picked up or picked off, one by one between here and the mainland coast?'

Amana was still unconvinced, but neither could he see an alternative. We were sitting ducks at sea otherwise.

'Okay. Tell me the details of your plan,' he acquiesced.

An hour later, we had managed to bring all the canoes together and Amana loudly explained what was expected of every man on every canoe. After that, our flotilla sat on the water while we rested and refreshed ourselves as best we could before the upcoming battle. The dhow was still a league away but was slowing its speed, no doubt trying to make sense of why we had given up being chased.

'Get over to the steer board side as she comes in close,' I said in Arabic, which was then translated into Swahili so that all in our canoe and those around us understood.

As the dhow approached, she started to lower her sails and reduce speed to commence her turn into our small armada of canoes. The dhow was only 20 feet from our canoe.

'Now,' I said to Ruth and immediately, a knife flicked its way over the water and embedded itself in the steersman's eye, causing him to grab his face and let go of the steer board which swung wildly at first and then turned the ship dead into the wind. It brought the dhow to a sudden stop in the water, causing many on deck to lose their footing.

Amana gave his war cry and immediately the canoes turned on the dhow as Swahilis stood up and leapt to grab the gunnels of the dhow and swing themselves aboard. Ruth continued her knife throwing and took the captain out, who was trying to correct the now limp steer board. He fell with a knife embedded in his jugular. The crew were now leaderless and uncertain of what to do except fight and a vicious but short fight it was.

Those who were last to leave the canoes tossed the last paddles aboard as Raymond laid about him with his broadsword, aiming to take any guards with bows and arrows out as quickly as possible. The paddles were longer than the guards' swords but easily snapped by the swipe of a swift blade. They evened the score just the same. My stiletto was not much good in this sort of skirmish, so I took to the bare-handed, unarmed combat skills I had learned in my year at the Buddha's Smile. I quickly put two swordsmen down and two others over the side. From the water, Ruth was launching her remaining knives judiciously at any guard who appeared to be overpowering any of our men.

Gradually, as more guards were put down, our men picked up their fallen swords and the battle on the deck swung our way. Finally, the last half dozen of the dhow's crew, finding themselves surrounded, threw down their weapons and begged for mercy. They were quickly thrown over the side to make their way back to Pemba in one of the canoes without paddles or water. They would be lucky to make it. Even so, they wasted no time getting away from us, paddling furiously with their hands.

Over 20 guards and sailors lay dead upon the deck matched by an equivalent number of our own. At least the dhow was ours and it looked like the Swahili bid for freedom had been a success, albeit costly in the lives of the 20 men lying dead on the deck. We also had a dozen or so who had sustained serious wounds and injuries who Ruth and I started to treat as best we could with the limited number of the Chinese needles Master Do had given us. For the most part, all we could do was relieve some of the warriors' pain with the needles, that was until a makeshift medical kit was found in the captain's cabin and we commenced sewing up the wounds that we could.

Amana had sent men over the side to turn the dhow into the wind and then quickly haul them aboard as the vessel 's sails filled with the wind and started to move off. No one on board really knew how to sail the dhow. We only knew we wanted to go west into the now setting sun. Whether by good luck or good management, we somehow managed to make the vessel face to the west while the wind remained constant from the east. Nobody had a clue what to do if the wind changed. The warriors were all landsmen. It was Raymond who took the steer board and tried to set a straight course.

N'sibi quietly wandered up to the steer board deck and stood beside him. She placed her arm beneath and between his and snuggled in beside him as he controlled the steer-board. Despite her youth, it looked like she was claiming her man. Raymond had saved her life in the market and defended her against attackers as we escaped through the jungle. I could not help noticing Amana smiling to himself at this.

# 11

Raymond did not want to tighten our sails, instead he was content to let the craft take a leisurely course to the coast. He was quite anxious about being helmsman of the vessel and obviously did not feel the need for any sea speed. Everyone was dog tired from a sleepless march through the night, an arduous paddle and a sea fight. Many simply fell asleep on the deck. I was too wound up to sleep and decided to talk with Amana for a while until I felt ready to go to sleep.

Amana told me a great deal about himself and his people. In the quiet of the night his voice was deep, low and gently sonorous.

'My people live on the shores of a great lake. From the coast it is one cycle of the moon's journey.'

I took this to mean 28 days or about a month's travelling.

'In the time of my distant grandfathers, my people called themselves the Bantu and we still do in places. It was in those distant times that the Muslim men, the Arabs from Oman, came to trade and then to stay. They brought many things that were good for the people and that the people wanted. Things like cloths and silks, glass and beads, new medicines, jewellery, swords and knives and other metalwork. We traded with them. They wanted our ivory, rhinoceros horns,'

'Rhinoceros horns?' I asked, 'What is a rhinoceros? Why would they want the horns? In my mind I had pictured something like an antelope or a bull.'

'The rhinoceros is a very deadly animal. He has a very thick and toughened hide. This makes him hard to kill with just one spear. He is heavy set on short legs but can outrun a man over a short distance. We catch them in pit traps and then we gather to stab and spear them to death. They are tough and hardy and it takes many punctures to kill them.

'In the middle of his head he can have one or two pointed horns with which he can gore his enemies to death or he may simply trample them under his thunderous hooves. It is the horns that are valuable. The yellow men we sometimes see from the eastern seas buy them. They say that if the horn is powdered it can be used by men to make themselves more virile on the bedroll. Just as the horn stands up in the rhinoceros' head so the yellow man's horn stands up in the middle of his bed.'

With this, he chortled to himself before continuing, 'Of course, a true Swahili man never needs the help of a rhinoceros.'

We both laughed before he continued, 'Gradually over time our peoples, our languages and our customs mingled as people intermarried and interacted through business and village life. We became known as the Swahili people. Our cultures grew closer together and we now share many of the same beliefs, rituals and practices, although with some of our own variations. It is the same now that the Shirazi have arrived from Persia. We are growing even more intermingled.'

'How so?' I asked.

'Most of my people have become Sunni Muslims. The clerics want us to have a focus on the afterlife and what we can achieve through worshipping Allah and living the life the Prophet directs us. Yet, at the same time, we keep to some of the old ways of our grandfathers, such as appeasing the spirits of the land, the dead, sickness and wellbeing, offerings for rain and good crops. We still have what the Muslim clerics call "witch doctors" but in fact, are our holy men or medicine men. It is a religion of the life we lead and the one that we live in where we must face the challenges of everyday life – spirits must be appeased to ward off illness, hunger, misfortune and to help us celebrate with feasting, life, fertility and togetherness.

'We believe we will all be together, even in death, and that even as you and I sit and talk, the spirits of the ancestors are with us, watching and listening. If we need to, we can call upon one of our holy men to help us communicate with the ancestors. Sometimes, the holy man will use prayers upon prayers for days or he may enter a trance from which he will emerge with a message or an answer. At other times, some of the holy men cast the bones or message sticks to receive a message. I sometimes think there are as many ways to talk to the dead as there are holy men. Each seems to have his own totem or ritual to assist in speaking with the ancestors.

'Needless to say, the Muslim clerics cast a disapproving eye over our maintaining the ancient rituals and customs. Despite this, trade and intermarriages still go on, particularly in the cities. It is there that the different cultures: Bantu, Arab and Persian, have merged to become one language, one people, one culture – the Swahili.

'Sadly, many of those in the city have forgotten their heritage and view those of us who live our traditional lives in the interior, away from the Arab trading posts, as inferior and only worthy to be slaves of the rich. My people are in a constant war with the slavers. It is a war we are losing. We do not have the long steel swords, the metal they wear on their bodies or the chains they hold us down with.'

'I hate slavery,' I said, 'What right does one man have to own, order about and beat another man? It makes me so angry.'

'Hah,' laughed Amana, 'Spoken like a true free Bantu,' as he gave me a friendly slap across my shoulders. His smile revealed shiny, white teeth, even in the pre-dawn darkness.

Just then, Raymond's voice broke into our conversation, 'I see white water coming up on the horizon and there is a dark line behind it. I think we may be approaching land.'

'We are,' replied Amana, 'Welcome to Africa.'

# 12

Raymond did a hair-raising job of somehow steering our dhow through the reefs that fronted the coastal shore and he simply ran it up on to the beach just as dawn was breaking. We were fortunate the tide was high and we did not have the hull of the craft ripped out on the jagged rocks that had been just below the surface.

Amana ordered everyone who was able, to plunder as much booty from the dhow as could be managed on the long trek back to their ancestral homelands. Rigging was loosened and rolled into long ropey coils, the sail was lowered and cut and folded into neat sections, useful lengths of timber were cut from the hull and masts, food stores and cooking utensils were plundered from the galley. The captain's cabin was stripped of most of its items, which included a bed, two chairs, a stool and a portable desk, along with some chests, one of which contained a great number of coins of different denominations and countries of origin. A cupboard in the cabin provided the greatest treasure: six scimitars, several helmets, a dozen long handled knives and a suit of chest armour. It would only be a matter of hours before the dhow was a mere skeleton of its former self.

While all this was happening, Ruth decided to call a meeting between the three of us. She had slept on the deck for a few hours in the night while Raymond and I were on our third day without sleep and were desperately fatigued and needing slumber.

'You can sleep once we have made a decision about where we go next,' responded Ruth to Raymond's comment about being bone weary.

I suggested that Amana join us as he could enlighten us more precisely on what our options might be. He was more than willing to oblige.

'Your options are limited. The most direct route for you is to go by sea and hug the African and Egyptian shore all the way to your destination in the north. It will be, however, a most dangerous route for you. There is much Muslim sea traffic upon the Red Sea, both mercantile and military. I suspect, before too long, you would be captured and wind up in a harem, the slave market or at the bench of an oar for the rest of your short life. There are also a great number of sharks in the Red Sea who are known for their ferociousness often attacking small fishing boats and canoes.'

Amana did not have to go any further with this option as I could tell the mention of sharks brought back the memories of the frenzied and bloody attack on our friends off the coast of India.

'Your other option is to join us going inland to our country by the great lake. From there, we can assist you to the headwaters of the "long river". I believe it is called the Nile River by your people and it will take you to the great inland sea. There are of course dangers along this route but not so many.'

'What kinds of dangers?' asked Raymond trying to smother a yawn.

'Mostly crocodiles and river horses,'

'River horses?' asked Ruth.

'Very large river animals with huge mouths with great big stumpy teeth. They capture a victim in their jaws and drag them beneath the water to be drowned before being eaten. They are readily seen floating near the surface of the water and can be easily avoided,' replied Amana.

'I guess that makes our choice simple,' concluded Ruth. 'Amana, may we accompany you inland to your country and then take the river Nile home?'

'You have more than earned the privilege of joining our homecoming trek and we would welcome you amongst us for the journey for as long as you care to stay amidst us.'

'So, I guess that is settled then,' said Raymond supressing yet another yawn, 'Time for some shut eye.'

We thanked Amana before Raymond and I headed off to a shady palm to find some desperately needed sleep.

We both awoke simultaneously about five hours later, just after midday and realised we were both ravenously hungry. N'sibi, Amana's daughter, saw we had awakened and brought two bowls of a steaming grain porridge of sorts over to us. It was hot, very filling and left a pleasant savoury after-taste upon the palate.

When we finally finished our bowls, Raymond showed his satisfaction with a rather loud, cheery and satisfying gut felt burp.

'Manners!' I hissed, 'That might be seen as an insult.'

But it was not. N'sibi laughed and clapped her hands at Raymond's eructation. He smiled and blushed not quite sure what he was supposed to say or do next. A problem confounded by not sharing a language.

I put my bowl down and looked around the beach site. The Bantu, of whom I estimated there were about 60, were mostly men with half a dozen women and three or four younger ones like N'sibi. Of the men, six were carrying wounds but were still ambulant. Everyone had obviously been busy while Raymond and I had slept. All the plunder that had been taken from the Sultan's dhow had been neatly divided up into loads that could be individually portered on heads or shoulders. Amana had distributed the scimitars and knives amongst his principal warriors who now carried them proudly across their shoulders or tied to their waists. We were now a small fighting force.

At a command from Amana, everyone moved to where our baggage and supplies were lying on the beach. All that were able, chose a load and hefted it up onto either their heads or their shoulders. Amana waved his hand and led the way into the jungle. He would lead his people back to their Bantu homeland by the Great Lake. N'sibi seemed intent on leading Raymond there herself as she chose to walk by his side.

# 13

The jungle was hot and very steamy once we were away from the cool breezes blowing along the shore. It was not long before Ruth, Raymond and I were perspiring heavily and becoming thirsty. Our Bantu companions did not seem to be as affected by the heat as much as we were. N'sibi disappeared into the jungle undergrowth for some time and then re-emerged with an armful of fist sized fruits. They were various shades of red, pink and orange in colour and had a beautiful sweet and juicy taste that quickly tempered our thirst.

For the first few days of our journey, nothing much changed. The jungle is the jungle. We heard many unusual and different animal and bird calls but seldom saw the creatures. The creatures we did see were the very small ones that buzzed and whined all around us, landing on our skin and either sucking or biting us to the point where the three of us were covered in itchy red rashes and sores. Both Ruth and I were sure the insect bites were making the three of us unwell, mostly with a slight fever, fatigue, a headache and other general aches and pains in our joints. The Bantu seemed unaffected by any malaise that might have been caused by the insects.

During the evening and at night, despite watering and itchy eyes, we sat in the smoke of one of the campfires to avoid the biting insects. We still itched and scratched constantly and our sleep was disturbed as a consequence. N'sibi seemed aware of our discomfort and, early one morning, brought one of the other women in the party, named Mosi, to look at our skin and, using Amana as an interpreter, asked about the various symptoms we were experiencing.

N'sibi and Mosi conferred with each other and then left and went into the jungle. They were gone for half the day only re-joining our trek around midday when we stopped for a break from the heat and to eat and drink a little.

The two were clutching a variety of plants between them, while N'sibi had a dead lizard slung over her shoulders that was a good three feet in length. Mosi set about separating the plants and then breaking them up into what were their therapeutic components. On one side, she might place the petals of one flower, the roots of another, the stalks of yet others while she discarded the rest of the plant. Once Mosi had a small pile of these cuttings and trimmings, she placed them in a pot of water over which she then squatted and urinated into as well. She then set the pot to boil over a fire.

While Mosi was engaged in her brewing, N'sibi had set about preparing the dead lizard. She did so by making long slits into the flesh of the creature, chopping off the head and feet and then cutting the remaining flesh into medium sized chunks which she also put in a pot of water and placed over the fire to bring to the boil.

Ruth, Raymond and I were aware they were preparing some form of treatment to aid the three of us in our discomfort and malaise. It was a little bit disconcerting for Ruth and myself, going from physician to patient and watching the production of a preparation that was totally alien to our knowledge base.

'It is an odd feeling,' observed Ruth of this role reversal, 'but all we can do is have faith that these people will have their own knowledge of healing and that it will be effective.'

'I agree,' I said, 'Africa seems an awesome land and I am sure there is much more that will amaze us but, at the same time, I am acutely aware this country could also kill us, right down to the smallest biting insect.'

Mosi and N'sibi's distillations continued, quietly simmering and boiling away for the next hour. When Mosi's herbs, flowers, stalks, roots and urine had been reduced to a thick, dark green, viscous fluid, she removed the pot from the flame and placed it close by N'sibi's fire pot. N'sibi's lizard must have been a particularly fatty species as she began spooning, ladle after ladle, of the yellowy coloured fat that was coming to the surface of her pot. Once she and Mosi were satisfied that there was enough fatty fluid floating on the top of Mosi's viscous mixture, they placed the fat and green fluid back on a low heat, which they continuously stirred. After a while, the two conferred again and took the pot from the flame and set it aside to cool.

Once the concoction had cooled, it became a soft, dark brown mass with a rather strange and unknown odour that was not too unpleasant. N'sibi then dipped her fingers in the fatty mass and signed that we should allow her to smear it upon our bites and rashes. One by one, we submitted to her ministrations and were amazed at the almost instantaneous relief from the burning, itching sensations that had plagued us for the last few days. Amana informed us the fat would also deter the insects from seeking out our lighter European skin. Within a couple of days all three of us were recovered from the feelings of unwellness that had accompanied our skin discomfort.

At the same time our symptoms and discomfort began to dissipate, so the jungle began to thin out, to be replaced by what seemed an endless savannah of tall grasses that rippled in intermingling waves with the gentle breeze moving across the plain. It was much more pleasant than the heat and suffocating humidity of the oppressive jungle.

Unlike the jungle, where we could hear but seldom see the wildlife, across the savannah there were plenty of animals to be seen. The few trees upon the plain were obviously hardy and able to survive in low rainfall. Their leafy tops attracted the attention principally of two animals: elephants and an unusually long necked animal Amana called a twiga. I suspected it was what I had heard sailors in Acre refer to as a jeeraff. I was surprised by how much larger the African elephants were than the ones I had ridden, in India. Across the plain roamed different herds of horned antelope, large cattle like beasts, packs of what I thought were wild dogs and, sitting lazily under one of the trees, a pride of lions with three cubs playfully frolicking and rolling around in front of their dozing parents.

Away on the horizon, I could just make out the signs of other life by the shape of the line of dust they raised. They were slavers, obviously returning to the coast with their recent catch of newly acquired goods.

# 14

Amana had seen the lengthy line of a dust trail and ordered a halt to the trek. He ordered all of us to keep our heads down below the level of the tall grasses that grew upon the plain. There was a coppice of small, stunted trees nearby and the three of us chose to settle down in the cool of their shade.

'Watch out for the thorns,' yelped Raymond after sitting down on a thorny twig lying on the ground and jumping straight back up in one leap.

We could not help but laugh at the pained look on his face as he said this. They were exceptionally large thorns.

Amana nominated three of his men who immediately dispatched themselves in a low, loping gait toward the line of dust on the horizon. I noticed, from the way the grasses dipped and waved, that the three men separated shortly after departure presumably to gain multiple perspectives on the slavers and to ensure that should one or two be captured or killed, information would still get back to us on what lay ahead. The runners would have a day and night to travel, reconnoitre, return and report. It was going to be pleasant to have the rest, but Amana was firm about no cooking fires or moving unnecessarily around the camp, due to the possibility of raising dust, along with the suspicions of those we wished to avoid.

The scouts returned at separate times during the next morning. All were unharmed, nor had they suffered difficulty beyond the expected rigours of their long marathon and surveillance. As each returned, they went into conference with Amana, relating all they had seen and answering the many questions he asked of them, before going off to get some sustenance and rest.

After his last interview, Amana sat in silence for a while and appeared to be considering his options. He then got up and made his way to the different groups sitting around the campsite or under the few trees. Eventually he wandered over to our little group.

'My men have informed me that they are indeed slavers returning with a new catch of poor miserable wretches destined for the Pemba slave pens,' he said grimly. 'Many of the captives are from my own peoples' land and others are from lands and tribes that live around the Great Lake. The slavers have had great success as there are over 100 men, women and children, bound by neck chains and yokes, being driven along by Arab slavers with whips and canes. There are six Arabs who ride horses. The riders looked to be in charge with about 60 mixed race people with weapons and whips to do the dirty work.

'My scouts report that many of those who have been captured are showing signs of bad treatment. Dozens have wounds, are limping along or being actively supported by their friends or family. This means that despite the crack of the whip, the column is slow moving. This will serve our purposes very well and will give us time to plan.'

Realisation dawned on me.

'You are planning to rescue these poor wretches!' I blurted, 'Not trying to avoid them?'

Amana simply nodded his head and smiled.

'You would be welcome to join us. We have seen the warrior spirit that is in all three of you on Pemba and at sea against the

Emir's dhow. Your arms, assistance and thoughts could help us to save our people.'

The three of us eyed each other questioningly as if to say, 'Do we or don't we?'

Within a second or two "the eyes had it" and, as one, we nodded our assent.

Amana's smile became even wider.

Ten minutes later, we were joined by the three scouts, two others who, like Amana, were clearly leaders, in one way or another, of the group. Mosi was invited to join us as well and she was accompanied by N'sibi. I wondered in what capacity their advice was being sought in the council.

The general opinion of the scouts was that we had two days' grace before the slave train would reach our location. Amana kept up a running translation for us. It was agreed that two further scouts should return to the slave train and try to contact the captives and let them know to be ready for a rescue attempt in two days' time and to be prepared to use their chains and shackles as weapons against their captors when our attack finally came.

Amana called out to two young men and spoke to them in detail about this part of the plan before dispatching them to take their message of hope to the slaves.

The scouts agreed that our two groups were roughly matched in numbers but not in weaponry. Every one of the slavers was armed with either scimitars, knives or whips, while less than half our troop had any weapons of any kind. It seemed there was very little upon the grassy savannah that we could turn to our advantage as a weapon until Mosi spoke up. Everyone listened to what she had to say and then mischievous grins began to spread across the faces of all present. Amana immediately gave Mosi a nod and she and N'sibi got up from the group, grabbed a woven carry-all from nearby and made their way over to one of the coppices around the grassy plain that had trees bright with red berries upon it.

The three of us did not get a chance to ask what the conversation and outcome was about as Amana pressed the scouts for more details of the slave caravan. The scouts reported that around five or six captive slaves were under the direct control of a slaver who carried a whip or cane. It seemed they were not altogether in one continuous line but rather broken up into these small groups as some were able to travel faster while others were slowed and handicapped by the wounded in their company. Amana smiled at this disclosure.

# 15

The council closed shortly after this with Amana issuing orders for the company to gather suitable stones and pebbles to be used in sling shots. Amana mentioned to me that the sling was not a weapon of choice amongst his people, but every boy had learned to use one when hunting fowls and water birds on the lake and those unissued with scimitars and knives from the dhow would be able to use them in the initial assault on the slaver train.

It was not until mid-afternoon that Mosi and N'sibi returned from their excursion. The carry all bag they had taken with them was full of bright red berries from the trees in the coppice. They immediately sat down and commenced squeezing the berries to force the extrusion of the bright yellow seed from within the fruit. The seeds were collected and placed in a cooking pan. Ruth, Raymond and I went over to assist with the task.

With the five of us squeezing the seeds from the fruit, it was not long before the carry all was emptied and we had a pan half filled with bright yellow seeds. Mosi and N'sibi indicated that the task was finished for the time being.

Amana wandered over to inspect the harvest before explaining to us that after sunset and before moonrise, they would light a small fire. He said the tall grass would hide the light of the fire from the distant slavers and no nocturnal sky light would reveal any smoke rising from it. The seeds would then be baked in the pan until totally dried out and could be ground into a dust.

As the sun set, Mosi and N'sibi set about lighting their fire and placing the pan of seeds over it. At regular intervals, N'sibi turned and tossed the seeds over and around the pan with a wooden spatula she had shaped that afternoon. After an hour of drying the seeds like this, Mosi took a seed from the pan and squeezed it between her thumb and forefinger where it faintly popped releasing a small cloud of pale yellowy powder. Mosi looked up and nodded to N'sibi who ceased her stirring and removed the pan from the fire before extinguishing it with a nearby pile of earth. The pan of desiccated seeds was covered with a cloth and left till morning.

That night, as Ruth and I lay beside each other on a bed of savannah grasses, Ruth wondered aloud, 'Do you suppose Mosi is some kind of wise woman or healer and that N'sibi is her assistant or even her apprentice?'

'Mosi was certainly afforded respect by Amana and the other elders at the council and what we witnessed this evening definitely displayed a store of knowledge regarding the use of plants and herbs. I must admit, I am curious about what she intends to do with the pan of seeds out there,' I replied.

'Mmmmh,' said Ruth clearly thinking, 'There may be things we can learn from her while we are here, but the language barrier and our rescue preparations don't really allow the time. I will ask Amana about her tomorrow.'

'Good idea,' I said, snuggling up before sleep overtook us.

Mosi was indeed a wise woman and healer to her people and N'sibi, her acolyte assistant, although, as Amana pointed out, there was quite a rivalry between Mosi and the tribal shaman who had escaped capture by the slavers.

'Amana,' said Ruth, 'Ippolito and I are healers in our own culture. We would very much appreciate the opportunity to converse with Mosi and participate in a sharing of our knowledge and skills. Would you or one of the other Arabic speaking amongst your group be able to help us in this request?'

'I should have realised, when N'sibi told me about your magic needles that took away the pain of her ankle in our flight from the Pemba slave pens, that you were healers. You amaze me. I have never heard of healer warriors. When this current business with the oncoming slavers is dealt with, we will investigate this. There will be plenty of time in the evenings for such discussion. Hah,' he laughed, 'Perhaps by the end of such discussions I may have learned enough to become a healer warrior as well!'

Pleased that we would have the opportunity for an exchange of ideas and knowledge, we left Amana to his preparations for tomorrow's battle and made our way over to where Mosi and N'sibi had started the final preparations of what Ruth and I still did not know exactly what.

N'sibi was gently pounding and grinding the dried seeds with a round stone in the pan. Every so often, she would lick her fingers and gently pick the husks out of the mix with the wet tip of her finger. This was to preserve as much of the ground seed powder as possible.

Mosi was collecting measured amounts of the yellow seed powder in the shell of a nut about half a thumb in size. She then proceeded to pour the contents of the shell on to one of several dozen leaves she and N'sibi had gathered that morning, while the leaves were still soft and pliable. With the powdered seed sitting in the middle of the leaf, Mosi deftly folded the leaf into an envelope arrangement that held itself together with the powder inside it. Mosi then carefully placed the leafy packages in the direct sun to dry out.

Ruth, Raymond and I were mightily intrigued but still had no idea exactly what it was that was being prepared and manufactured.

Later in the day, the two scouts, who had taken the message of a rescue attempt to the captured slaves, returned to report they had passed the message on to several tribesmen who would secretly disseminate the message to the rest of the captives in readiness for the rescue.

Amana then left with two other warriors and disappeared into the long savannah grass.

# 16

It was not until early the next morning that the slavers and their captives came into clear view. Seated upon a magnificent Arabian stallion was the obvious leader of the slavers, directing their path through the long grass. His hawklike gaze was constantly roving over the landscape as he rode, either seeking out the best path to follow through the long grass or any foe that may be lurking – human or animal. Behind him rode two lieutenants on lesser mounts, who similarly maintained a scrutiny of the environment ahead of them. I noted one of the lieutenants was badly scarred on the left side of his face and was missing his eye from there. All three dangled scimitars and long knives from a sash about their waists. Two other horsemen rode within the column while one brought up the rear. All six horsemen were clearly Arab in features and clothing.

Behind them came the first of the captives. As reported, they were in groups of six. Each cohort was accompanied by a guard carrying either a scimitar, whip or cane, most often with one or the other in each hand. Whilst the horsemen were Arabs, the guards were clearly mixed-race individuals of varying skin colour, facial features, hair styles and clothing. Most of the captives were shackled in neck collars. Connecting them to each other was about two feet of chain. Two other groups of six were restrained and joined to each other by a peculiar yoke-like arrangement made from what looked like twisted vines. The necks of these captives were scarred and bloody from the constant rubbing of vine bark against their skin. The metal neck shackles were obviously a little kinder to the skin.

Amana made some last-minute changes to our small force once we had had time to assess the deployment of the slavers and the disposition of the captives from a distance.

'Ruth, Raymond and Ippolito,' Amana directed, 'I want the three of you upfront with me. I am going to need your knives,' he pointed at Ruth, 'Your great sword,' pointing at Raymond, 'and your fists and fighting techniques,' indicating me.

'We are going to take out the three front leading horsemen. Take the head off the monster the way you did on the dhow against the Sultan of Pemba's men. Let us move now.'

As we moved silently in a very stooped gait through the grass, we came across N'sibi and Mosi who were handing out their peculiar, leafed envelopes with their, as yet, unknown contents to the many within our force who did not have a bladed weapon or sling and shot. There was no time to talk.

Amana had calculated the slavers line of advance and the four of us assumed position in the long grass, keeping as low to the ground as possible. Only Amana, perfectly motionless, with his head temporarily camouflaged in leafy twigs, kept his head half above the grass as the slavers drew closer and closer.

Beside me, Raymond had drawn and was clutching Caspar's old broadsword and looked ready to spring into action. Ruth had detached her belt of six throwing knives from around her chest and held it in her left hand. I noticed Ruth had half removed the blades from their sheaves to facilitate a rapid gripping and then throwing. In her right hand, she held a blade ready for throwing. I had the trailing horseman of the three in my sights and was planning just how I would remove him from the conflict with my hands and feet. My stiletto remained sheathed by my side, just in case.

All down our line of hidden warriors was total silence as we awaited the command for attack. Sounds and voices from the slave column reached us as we lay in the grass. At the sound of every crack of a whip or thwack of a cane and the ensuing cry of pain or deep moan, my anger grew as I'm sure it did for the rest of those patiently and nervously awaiting the commencement of our attack.

Then it happened. Amana whipped his facial camouflage away and made a blood curdling yell as he stood up, scimitar in hand and ran at the horsemen. Ruth stood and immediately launched her first blade – too quickly. It grazed the leading Arab's forehead and took his turban off. He was barely phased by the close shave and immediately drew his scimitar and goaded his horse toward Ruth who was drawing her second blade. Seeing the danger, Raymond stepped up beside her with his broadsword raised as a counter to the Arab's scimitar.

Amana was by now engaged with the second Arab on his horse and was having a hard time of it as the Arab had the advantage of height in the encounter. The third horsemen I had my eye on had turned and was taking in the battle going on behind him down the column. He spurred his horse to the nearest group of attackers, scimitar raised, ready to slice down and kill. He singled one of our group out and closed in. With a shock, I realised his target was N'sibi.

I yelled a warning which was drowned out in the chaos and clamour of the attack. N'sibi must have heard the drumming of the horse's hooves coming up behind her and turned around. In her hand, she held one of the packets she and Mosi had prepared the day before. She fisted her hand, breaking the package open at the same time as waving her hand in front of the oncoming horseman. A cloud of pale-yellow powder hovered momentarily in the air as horse and rider charged through it. Almost immediately, the horse reared up, neighing and squealing in pain. The horse's rider was bellowing as well, his scimitar dropped as he balled both his hands to rub frantically at his eyes. He was thrown from the horse and landed on the ground still balling his eyes and screaming in pain. It was only a moment before one of our warriors fell on him with his scimitar and finished him off.

Meanwhile, Ruth had drawn and thrown her second blade taking the leader in the mouth, drawing lots of blood but not slowing him down in his deadly intent. Just as he drew close and was raising his scimitar to slash down on Ruth, Raymond stepped up swinging with his mighty sword and taking the Arab across the abdomen spilling his intestines all over the savannah before tumbling him from his horse, where he received his death blow to the head.

I had no time to take in any more as Amana was in serious trouble battling against his horsed opponent. He bore several wounds and was bleeding heavily from a cut to his forearm. I launched myself toward them, gathering as much speed as I could through the high grass before springing up in a high rolling leap that saw me wrap my legs around the slaver's neck in a scissor hold and using the rest of my momentum to drag him down from his horse with a heavy crash onto the ground. Despite his wounds, Amana quickly and gleefully put his scimitar through the slaver's neck as he lay on the ground.

'My thanks to you. My life is yours, as yours is mine,' he said before turning and heading back down the column.

The three of us followed him.

# 17

The long grass of the savannah obscured much of our view of what was happening down the line of slavers and their captives. At least our little force had taken out the leader and two of his principals. As in any battle, all was noise, dust, the rank smell of blood and intestinal contents and above all, confusion.

The group N'sibi had been with had taken care of their selected group's slave driver and they were busily trying to break the shackles around the necks of the captives and set them free. N'sibi looked up and smiled at Raymond as we ran on by. Despite his wounds, Amana had launched into a great song or battle hymn as he ran. The joy of battle was clearly upon him and I doubted that he felt any pain from his wounds right then, although I knew he would feel them later on.

Two of our warriors lay dead from scimitar wounds as we approached the next group. This time, it was the captives themselves who had orchestrated their own victory. As we arrived upon the scene, we found two of the captives holding the slaver between them with the chain that linked them, wrapped around the slaver's neck, holding him tightly and unable to escape. The captives were taking a slow and painful revenge upon the slaver. Some were using his whip and cane over him, whilst another held the slaver's scimitar and was using it to slice small pieces of flesh off him in an effort not to kill him too quickly. One small, bloodied part of him lay directly in front of him. Presumably, the first to be separated from his body.

We kept running down the line, seeking to assist any of our forces where needed. For the most part, our warriors, especially those armed with scimitars and long knives, had succeeded in overwhelming the slavers as had those with nothing more than Mosi's little packets of eye-burning powder. The captives had been ready to use their chains to support their liberators and chain strangled and mutilated slavers lay on the ground. It was toward the rear of the line that the fight was at its fiercest.

The three remaining Arabs seated on horses had come together and were cutting a swathe through both the captives and our own men. A trail of wounded, dead and bloodied bodies lay behind and around them as the three Arabs battled one group of chained captives desperately attempting to bring them down.

Amana roared a blood curdling scream and ran full tilt at the leading Arab in the group, his scimitar whirling around his head. I did not like to see it but, instead of going the man, Amana suddenly changed the direction of his swing and brought it down across the front legs of the charging stallion. It screamed in pain, buckling and then tumbling forward, sending his rider flying through the air to be impaled upon the waiting sword of Raymond.

This incensed the two remaining horsemen and they both charged at Raymond as he struggled to release his sword from the dead Arab's body.

'Raymond! Lookout. Behind you,' I yelled as I began a sprint in the Arab's direction and initiating the mental process of visualising my intention, retaining the image and imagining the feeling of leaping high from the ground, kicking my foot forward and landing my heel under the chin of the rider, which is exactly what I did. The

Arab tumbled off the back of his horse where Amana fell on him with his scimitar, making short work of him.

My momentum had carried me over the top of the Arab's saddle only to land badly on my side, causing my knee to turn awkwardly and painfully. Immediately, I tried to get straight up and fell over again as my knee gave way under my weight. I was lying like a turtle on its back and the perfect target for the third Arab horseman to come bearing down on me, his scimitar lowered for the downward lunge into my defenceless body.

Amana had moved onto the next group of captives trying to subdue their tormentor; Raymond was too far away and the legs of the charging steed were only metres away from me. I could see the gleam of impending satisfaction in the eyes of the rider as he lined his scimitar up for the killing lunge. I honestly believed my time had come in that split second. The next instant, I realised my time was still mine as one of Ruth's knives suddenly appeared in the eye of the rider, sending him from his horse clutching his eye. Raymond was quickly on the Arab with his broadsword and sent him off to whatever paradise or hell awaited slavers in the Muslim world.

Ruth had caught up with us just in time, delayed by having to retrieve her knives from the earlier incident with Arab horsemen. She ran to my side, concern written all over her face and was quickly joined by Raymond. Ruth examined my knee, stating it was only badly sprained and there should be no lasting damage. All the same, it took the two of them to help get me to my feet and hold me there.

Raymond suddenly laughed and said, 'My friend that was one of the most spectacular demonstrations of the skills we learned from

Master Dari in the Buddha's Smile. I'll bet it will teach you not to show off so much again!'

'I'd still be dead if it weren't for Ruth, though,' I turned and kissed her on the cheek and whispered a quiet, 'Thank you,' in her ear. 'I'll be honest for a moment there, I thought I was a dead man.'

We were lucky that the Arab's horse was a docile one and had not galloped off in panic after losing its rider and was standing nearby with its head lowered, more intent on cropping the grass than escaping. Raymond grabbed its reins and with great difficulty and a certain amount of pain on my part, the two of them got me up into the saddle from where I suddenly realised, I had a very good view of everything that was happening around us.

# 18

Our skirmish with the last of the Arab riders must have been one of the final conflicts of the rescue mission. Only one small pocket of fighting remained and I could see a still battle-crazed Amana, covered in blood, wielding his scimitar like some whirling dervish against a small group of slavers who had rallied together to make a joint final stand. As he battled two of them at the same time, other slavers were being immobilised and slowly strangled in the chains that still bound the captives. At the same time, others were kicking, punching and stabbing at the slavers' defenceless bodies. It was brutal and bloody work.

Amana dispatched the last of his opposition with an intestinal spilling slash across the slaver's belly. As the slaver collapsed to the ground desperately trying to hold his intestines in, Amana drove his scimitar between the vertebrae of his neck and finished the job. Amana turned quickly and glanced around, looking for his next victim. Seeing no immediate options, he turned and ran to the rear of the column seeking yet more work for his blood drenched sword and arms. The battle craze was still upon him.

'It is almost over,' I said to Ruth and Raymond. I looked to the sky and the position of the sun and realised the whole raid had only taken about an hour. I wondered what the death toll would be. Certainly, all the slavers would be dead or dying. The captive slaves had had no mercy left in them after what they had endured and seen on their long march. In the distance, I could see a lone figure running through the savannah, an escaped slaver no doubt.

Hopefully, whatever message he might be able to deliver to his masters, should he survive the journey, would be a deterrent to any further slaving incursions by the Arabs and not an incitement for revenge.

'Ippolito,' said Ruth, 'We still have work to do tending the wounded. You will be able to do that in a sitting position. We will need to work together to save as many as we can.'

'You are right,' I replied, 'and I think out first patient is coming our way.'

Amana had returned from his sortie to the rear and was now staggering like a drunken man, the battle craze having lifted. He was covered in blood from numerous cuts and wounds. Three of his men ran to assist him and he let himself fall into their arms before losing consciousness from loss of blood.

'Do you have your needles and sutures?' I asked Ruth, who nodded.

'Get up here with me. We must get to Amana and quickly. Raymond, I can see pack horses and donkeys at the rear of the column. Get to them before they disappear and see if there are any hammers and chisels or whatever, to help break the chains and shackles around the necks of the captives.'

Ruth and I cantered off towards Amana, where he lay on the ground, his blood quietly spilling onto the savannah grass. When we arrived, we could see he was covered in so much blood it was impossible to see where the actual wounds were and there was no water nearby to wash it away.

'Who speaks Arabic?' I asked in Arabic to the group around us.

'I do,' came the reply in Arabic from one of our young men.

'Tell the men to come over here, get their pricks out and piss this blood off Amana so we can find his wounds,' I ordered, 'Quickly.'

At first, the men looked troubled and uncertain at this request. Pissing on a heroic chieftain, especially a wounded and debilitated one, was not on their list of acceptable behaviours.

'He is our chief,' said the young man trying to explain the men's reticence to do as I requested.

Ruth picked up on this and waved her scalpel telling the young man that if they did not do as I requested, she would slice the balls and penis off all of them. It worked.

Immediately, the men gathered round and, heedless of Ruth's presence, unveiled their hoses and released several streams of urine over Amana's unconscious form. It was far from a perfect wash but it did reveal the worst of the wounds.

'Oh, my dear God. We are going to have to work quickly to close so many wounds,' I said to Ruth.

Just at that moment N'sibi appeared. With a gasp of shock, she took the scene in while Ruth and I quickly threaded our sutures. N'sibi turned and disappeared into the savannah. She returned after several minutes with some root stock in her hands that she had obviously just pulled out of the ground. Ruth and I had just commenced our needlework on the first and worst of the wounds. N'sibi laid the root tubers on the ground and cut them all in half. As each severed end of the root began to ooze a white syrupy sap, she took them and ran the sap over the remaining wounds. Ruth and I kept working, the pain in my knee forgotten with the urgency of the situation. I briefly looked up at what N'sibi was doing and was pleasantly surprised to see that wherever she painted the white sap, the flow of the bleeding diminished. I presumed the sap had the same astringent properties that Master Kan Do had treated Ruth's haemorrhage with.

Ruth and I looked momentarily at each other before she smiled and said, 'If only I had had some of those roots at the battle of Gadragatta. Could have saved you a lot of pain.'

It was almost a joy to find myself once again in that special unity Ruth and I shared when treating the sick and wounded. Our hands flowed over Amana's wounds as one. As one pulled a suture taut, the other cut it. As one squeezed a bleeding artery, the other closed it up with a suture. All this with barely a word spoken between us. N'sibi watched on in silence as we repaired her father. She had a look of both absolute awe and serious concern for her father on her face.

Within an hour, Ruth and I had Amana all sown up with no further bleeding. He was still unconscious, but his breathing was normal, his pulse weak but regular and his skin colour was returning to normal.

And he stank of urine.

# 19

Due to the pain in my knee, the rest of the wounded and injured were brought to where Ruth and I had worked on Amana. Most were relatively simple cases of sewing up both deep and superficial wounds to the limbs but two had serious chest and abdominal wounds. There was nothing we could do for these poor wretches beyond keeping them comfortable. We had no poppy milk to give them, so we had to rely on Master Kan Do's needles to help palliate the dying men's pain. The needles helped to relieve some of their pain as evidenced by their faces no longer contorted in rictuses of pain.

The sun was low in the sky by the time Ruth and I had finished our work by which time Amana was fully awake and had been watching us working, with the same awed expression on his face N'sibi had worn earlier. All those who required a carer or assistance were accompanied by one of our group or by one of their fellow unharmed captives. Some water appeared from somewhere and all were being rehydrated by their carers. N'sibi used some of it to wash her father clean of the urine he had been soaked in, much to the relief of both.

It was just about then that a happily grinning Raymond rode back into our open-air makeshift camp and hospital, leading a string of two pack horses and four donkeys.

'Just wait till you see what I have here,' he chuckled.

He leapt down from his horse and went to the first animal in the line. He lifted what was obviously a very heavy saddle bag down to the ground where it spilled open, depositing shining golden Arabic dinars at our feet.

Ruth and I gasped in amazement, as did a few of our companions who knew the significance and value of the small, bright, round, yellow-metal objects.

'I suspect these are the slavers' ill-gotten gains,' Raymond informed us, 'There will be enough to get us home or to Salerno if that is where you choose to go.

'The other bags on the horses contain silver dinars. The bags and packs on the donkeys are mostly silks, other fabrics, some jewellery, and other small objects of possible value, like ivory figurines. I suspect it is all plunder from villages those bastards have raided for slaves.'

'There are other donkeys loaded with grains and dried fruit,' he added.

At this stage, after fighting most of the morning, injuring myself and then another half day of sewing up the wounded, I was too tired to think about Raymond's discovery. I looked at Ruth and made our sign for 'bed?' She quietly nodded and helped me limp off to a place we could have privacy, relative quiet and sleep.

We made our camp where we were for a week, to allow the wounded time to recover. Some of our party and others amongst the released captives who were uninjured or only slightly, were keen to return to their homelands and left in small groups. They were all provided with some of the booty, food and trade goods, that we had regained from the slavers.

When the time came for the rest of our troop to move on, I was surprised that none of the Bantu wished to ride on any of the horses and donkeys we had captured. Ruth, Raymond and I happily mounted three of the horses for ourselves, placed the remaining share of coins and goods on the donkeys and rigged a palliasse behind another to transport Amana after his wounds kept opening or tearing when he tried to walk. N'sibi walked beside her father the whole time.

The rest of the journey to the great lake, where our companions lived, took the best part of a month as we were slowed by our pack animals and the needs of those still recovering from their wounds but ambulant all the same. My knee had reduced in swelling and pain and was only noticeably uncomfortable to me when I had to put extra weight on it, such as getting down from my horse or carrying some load.

They were a lovely few weeks of travel. Ruth, Raymond and I led the way on our horses and shared views across the African landscape. Occasionally, we would hunt antelope for the cooking pots or widely scout the terrain for sources of potable water. For the most part, we spent our time leisurely ambling the horses and engaging in conversation. There was not a day went by when we were not surprised by some new or exotic feature of the African terrain or its varied and unusual wildlife.

My favourites were the elephants, while Ruth and Raymond were fascinated by what Amana had called the twiga, or jeeraffs. Ruth thought their ungainly gait was most amusing. Like India, Africa also had its share of animals and insects to avoid. There were the obvious large ones like lions, leopards, water buffalo, rhinoceroses, a huge, long legged but flightless bird and others. They were easily seen and avoided. Like India, it was the smaller creatures that we had to be careful about. I shivered with remembered horror when

I saw my first African scorpion, an image of one resting itself upon my penis coming instantly to mind. The insects were still a problem for the three of us and we had to keep constantly applying "Mosi's piss mix" as Raymond called it, to keep ourselves free from bites and the malaise that went with them.

Amana had been up and walking again for about a week when I noticed the smell of moisture in the air drifting on the occasional zephyrs of wind that blew our way. Part of me also felt the heat of the African sun did not seem as severe as it had at other times on our journey.

'Do you think it is getting cooler?' I asked the others riding with me.

We all agreed it was.

A little later we understood why. We had arrived at the Great Lake and it was so great, I thought it must have been a sea. I could not see a further shore and there were waves upon the surface, blown up by the winds out on the water. Most amazing of all, great parts of the Great Lake were pink in colour.

# 20

I later found out that the pink colour was not in fact the colour of the water but the colour of one of the most unusual looking birds I have ever seen. They came in all shades of pink and red and were known colloquially as the "flame feathered dancers". Amana informed me there were two types of the bird on the lake: the larger one, which stood four feet or more in height was known as heroe mweupe while the smaller one was named heroe mwekundu. Both had exceptionally long legs and long necks with a peculiar banana shaped pink bill and they clustered in what looked like millions out on the water.

After a week of rest, recovery and recuperation from the long trek, Ruth, Raymond and I felt it was time to plan the next stage of our long journey home. We needed Amana's advice and knowledge of the land ahead of us and the best way to negotiate our way through it.

'As I told you,' said Amana, 'I can take you to the headwaters of the Great River which in turn will take you to the Great Inland Sea. You can pass as simple fishermen, farmers or traders travelling the river. No one will look twice at you. You will be just another part of the normal river traffic.'

'But when you told us this, we did not have horses as an alternative,' replied Raymond.

'On horses, many people will see and notice you and look twice because they will assume you are wealthy and therefore worth robbing. Do you want that risk?'

Ruth very definitely did not want that risk and said so, saying she had had enough misadventure for more than three lifetimes.

And that is how it was decided. We would head north on the Great River.

Amana made a good-sized log canoe, about 20 feet long, available to us. He informed us the previous owner and his family had been killed by the slavers. Like the punt we had travelled down the Indus on, we attached a canopy at one end to keep the blistering sun off us as much as possible and to sleep under. We manufactured several sealed boxes to keep our food stores as unspoiled by heat and infestation as possible. Our stores were mostly grains, dried freshwater fish from the Great Lake and an assortment of dried fruits and vegetables.

Mosi presented us with a jar of her urine-laced insect deterrent which Amana emphasised we should smear ourselves with twice daily. Mosi also gave Ruth a stoppered jar and, with her hands, imitated rubbing her eyes and making expressions of pain. It was the red berry seed powder that burned the eyes. N'sibi gave us several of the blood staunching tubers should we need them in case of injuries or wounds. Amana advised that we should store them in a jar of only slightly moist soil to keep them fresh and efficacious. Various women presented Ruth with small pieces of jewellery which she accepted with feminine delight. Amana also made sure there was a portable but heavy sack of silver and golden dinars in the canoe as well.

'Use the silver dinars in the marketplaces and only the gold to pay for passage on a river vessel or a ship to go over the Great Inland Sea and never let anyone see more than one or two gold coins on your person. They will rob, cheat and kill you for them in the north,' he sternly advised.

N'sibi was not going to let Raymond go without some little reminder of herself for him and placed a beautifully wrought copper bracelet inlaid with coloured stones upon his wrist. Raymond was obviously touched by the gift, as was N'sibi by the sweet and chaste kiss of "thank you" he placed on her cheek.

The day finally came when we launched two canoes from the lakeside, Ruth, Raymond and I in one and Amana and two young warriors in the other. Many of the local villagers, both those who had been rescued and others who had escaped the slavers, came down to the lakeside and farewelled us in a shower of different coloured petals and flowers and a haunting song of, what I presumed to be, farewell. Never have I heard such rich voices in unison. No Byzantine or Latin church choir ever sounded as good.

We paddled for two days to the northern end of the great lake to a region which became marshy and difficult to navigate. Several times we became snagged on low lying logs and other hazards just below the surface. The region was riddled with water snakes that were highly venomous and aggressive, according to Amana. This meant being extra cautious when trying to free ourselves from any snags. No use getting free of an underwater log to die from a snake bite.

Eventually, the water cleared of obstacles and surface vegetation and we were able to tell we had exited the lake and were on a water course flowing north. It was not very wide and a canopy of trees completely overhung the water in places. From one of these canopies, a troupe of monkeys set up a frightful howling and shrieking as we approached and then as we passed underneath their treetops, we were bombarded with monkey faeces, urine and any other object they could launch at, or upon us. It was disgusting and one well aimed shot had made a dreadful mess in Ruth's hair.

After two days in which the river widened and the vegetation along the riverside thinned out, Amana and his two companions said their farewells, turned about and returned home. Amana's final advice to us was, if we came to any confluence of waterways to take the western alternative. He also advised us, if we decided to take passage on one of the many river boats travelling the Nile, to avoid the smaller run-down dhows and boats and try to book passage with one of the richer merchant traders along the river. He said they were safer as they often carried hired guards to protect the merchandise and crew from river pirates and the like.

We waved our farewells to Amana and his crew and paddled off into yet another unknown destination with unknown eventualities. One thing I did know, it was bloody hot, the sun burning us from above and its reflection off the water burning us from below. The heat was worsened by the effort of paddling. Raymond and Ruth both looked stressed by the heat as well.

'Do you think we should try and seek passage with a river trader as soon as we can?'

An emphatic and simultaneous 'Yes' was the reply.

# 21

Six days later, we got our wish when we arrived at the first village we had seen along our way. Using a patois of Arabic and the little bit of Swahili we had learned, we were able to negotiate covered passage – a tarpaulin canopy – with, of all things, a goat trader. The hull of the boat was choked with dozens of the plaintively bleating animals. They all seemed agitated and restless, crammed together the way they were.

Raymond pulled a golden dinar from his loin cloth, suggesting it was the only one and indicated the three of us. Then he pointed to the shaded area on the deck beneath the tarpaulin and indicated the three of us again. The captain trader never took his eyes from the golden dinar and he quickly granted us passage with payment, naturally, in advance.

We stowed our meagre items beneath the tarpaulin but made a pact with each other that at least one of us must always remain with our belongings. Whilst the captain did not appear to be a rogue, some members of the crew did.

'I'm glad the tarpaulin is upwind from the hull. All I can smell is goat shit and goat piss,' commented Raymond.

'Be glad the captain is not a pig trader,' I laughed at him.

A week later, after an uneventful river journey, the captain disembarked us at another river town with a wharf where several Nile boat traders were moored. We found passage with a trader in multiple commodities: spices, jewellery, fabrics, utensils of all kinds, animal hides and ivory. Again, we negotiated a tarpaulin canopy and set down the same rules about not leaving our belongings unguarded. Raymond withdrew a single silver dinar from his loincloth and offered it to the captain trader. The captain smiled but held up three fingers indicating he wanted two more silver dinars, one for each of us. We acquiesced and handed over the extra two dinars. It was still cheaper than what we had paid the goat trader.

Over the course of the next few weeks this was the pattern of our journey, leapfrogging between different river villages and towns with a variety of regional traders who worked up and down the river. For the most part, the cargoes they carried were inanimate, some pleasantly scented with the fragrances of different spices, perfumes or incense. Other merchandise included precious commodities such as ivory, gold, ebony wood, jewellery and the like. On two occasions we carried livestock, the first was a mating pair of cheetahs. Their offspring would no doubt be raised and trained to adorn some local magnate's court. Twenty caged monkeys of different varieties were aboard another trader. These were no better behaved than their counterparts we had encountered north of the Great Lake. If I were caged and locked up in a strange environment by another group of bipeds I'd throw my shit at them as well. I simply stayed out of range.

As we travelled north, the climate became less humid and more comfortable, but it was still extremely hot under the desert sun. There was no hope of a cooling swim thanks to the continuous presence of crocodiles either sunning themselves on the riverbank or submerged up to their eyeballs in the river. Accompanying them were the hippopotami who were just as disgusting as the monkeys in their faecal offensives. When feeling threatened, these beasts would deposit their waste upon the water and then use their great flat, fatty tails to slap the dirty matter in surprisingly great watery sprays that coated the side of our boat in a foul-smelling green patina that was difficult to remove.

At five locations we were required to disembark and proceed on foot to bypass fast flowing and unnavigable rapids, cataracts and waterfalls. Once past these obstacles, finding transport on the other side was easy. The further north we went, the more traffic on the river increased. At the same time the population of very dark-skinned Africans thinned and was replaced by the paler skinned Arabs who dominated and controlled these southernmost regions of what was now called the land of Egypt.

Despite the Arab dominion of this region, the captain of the trader we were sailing on warned us that this southern region was lawless and dominated by bands of Bedouin bandits and other robber cut-throat bands. He said some of these bands were as big as small armies and their leaders were considered warlords. He maintained we were quite safe as long as we stayed in the deep middle currents of the ever-widening river.

'Afterall,' quipped the captain, 'camels are food for crocodiles as well!'

I saw his humour and laughed with him at such an image.

A week later and another vessel Raymond and I were interested to learn from another passenger, that the emir Salah-al-din, whom we had met more than four years ago during one of the many truces at the time, was now the Sultan of Egypt.

All three of us were shocked to learn that, while we had been away, Salah-al-din had also retaken Jerusalem from control of the crusaders who were now much reduced and occupying only a handful of coastal cities and inland fortresses.

'All that effort. All those lives wasted and for what? Nothing!' said Raymond with considerable disappointment. I knew many of his friends and companions from the Knights of St. John were most likely dead and simply bleaching bones in the Palestinian desert.

'Apparently,' said the new passenger, 'It was because of the stupidity of that scheming coward, the new King of Jerusalem, Guy de Lusignan. Salah-al-Din outfoxed him in one simple battle. The Franks were lucky to have Sir Balian d'Ibelin to take charge and negotiate with Salah-al-Din for the safe evacuation of those refugees looking to leave Jerusalem once the city was besieged.'

Whilst this news was shocking and disturbing to the three of us, my attention was caught by a fast-moving galley heading south and coming directly toward us. My sixth sense suddenly kicked in and I called, 'Captain, there is something amiss with that galley coming at us.'

And there was.

# 22

The galley was equipped with a bronze headed ram and with the wind behind it was travelling at a ramming speed straight towards us. The presence of armed crew members, swinging grappling hooks at the bow and along the gunnels, made it evidently clear their intentions were hostile.

Our captain leapt to the helm and took the steer-board from the helmsman and immediately tried to swing his vessel to the shore in an evasive action. Raymond and I grabbed our weaponry. Ruth was always wearing her sheath of knives, but she ran to where our supplies were stashed and began rummaging amongst them in a desperate manner. The crew had collected what they could for weapons. Some had retrieved knives and scimitars, others held belaying batons, bale-hooks, short oars or whatever else came quickly to hand. I looked across the water to the other vessel and estimated we were outnumbered by at least two to one and every one of them was heavily armed.

The captain's evasive action had avoided our ship being rammed and damaged, but it brought the pirate vessel alongside us and penned us against the bank of the river. The grappling hooks flew across the water, biting into the wood of which ever part of the ship they struck and the pirates pulled our ships together. Raymond ran frantically up and down the deck using his mighty broadsword to sever as many of the grappling ropes as possible but it was not enough to prevent our two vessels coming together and allowing the pirates boarding opportunity. I held my stiletto ready for a throw or a close order encounter. I was also limbering up ready to use my body as a weapon. I was determined to be more careful this time and not wind up injured and drowning in the river.

It was then I saw Ruth. She had leapt up on to the now stabilised gunnel and was running along it. As she did so, she cast small clouds of Mosi's fiery berry seed powder in the direction of the raiders. The wind helped her, carrying the puffs of powder over those waiting behind the first wave of invaders. Within a few moments, Ruth had disabled over two thirds of the pirate crew reducing them to writhing eye rubbing wretches.

Raymond was quick on the uptake and yelled, 'Come on lads, get at them,' and waving his sword above his head, leapt onto the pirate galley. I quickly followed him, yelling encouragement to the crew to do the same which they very quickly did.  Ruth remained on board our vessel deftly picking off dangerous looking foes with her knives from a distance.

Initially, our invasion of the pirate ship was a blood bath as those nearest to us were unable to see and in eye burning pain. They were all quickly dispatched with swords, knives, bale hooks or whatever came to hand and tossed over the side - snacks for the now gathering and curious crocodiles. This evened the two sides up a great deal but the real fight was about to commence.

Raymond was swiping about him with his great broadsword like some crazed Grim Reaper. The pirates' scimitars were shorter than the broadsword and Raymond could cut and kill whilst being out of the reach of any opponent's deadly scimitar's tip. The only way the opposition could strike at him was from behind and I was watching his back.

Two scarred and ugly pirates came at me to try and take Raymond out. The first went down with a knife through the side of his neck, toppling against his comrade, giving me the time to slip my stiletto under his ribs and twist and turn the blade through lung and heart tissue. He died, gushing blood from his mouth and nose.

Just as I was pulling my blade free, another pirate charged me, giving me no time to retrieve the blade properly. I dropped it and let the pirate charge full tilt at me. Just as he was about to make contact, I shifted my stance and placed my foot in front of him tripping him up and sending him to the deck where one of our crew leapt on him and finished him off.

I was impressed to see our captain had entered the fray and was setting a good example of courage and skill for his crew by battling two pirates simultaneously. One of Ruth's knives quickly evened the fight and gave the captain the extra zeal he needed to feint and then lunge his blade through and all about the pirate's belly, spilling his intestines and tumbling him over the side to the waiting crocodiles.

I continued my rampage of flying feet and hands and sent several pirates screaming over the side of the boat. I suddenly saw what I really wanted and that was a six-foot bill hook stave that had been overlooked, as it was not a conventional weapon. I grabbed the stave and then commenced bashing heads, breaking noses, crushing larynxes, gouging eyes and smashing testicles. None of the blows were deadly but they were all disabling and rendered the victims ripe for members of our crew to fall upon and finish.

The fight continued for about half an hour, see sawing back and forth across the deck until finally, there were only six pirates left standing gathered in a pack around the mast. The six pirates were quickly surrounded by our crew. As one, they threw down their weapons and held their palms up and out in a gesture of defeat and surrender.

Members of the crew turned and looked to me for direction and orders about what to do. I turned and gestured toward the captain, deferring to him as the decision maker. The captain simply gestured with his thumb to the side of the boat. The crew needed no further encouragement and fell on the pirates as one, grappling with them or dragging them to the side of the boat and then over and into the gaping mouths of the crocodiles below.

Sometimes, I still hear the screams in my nightmares.

# 23

The butcher's bill of crew members was relatively light compared to what it might have been. Many had taken injuries but only three had been killed in the fracas. Raymond and I agreed it was a miracle, given the crew's lack of military training and prowess. Perhaps the same could have been said of the pirate captain and his crew.

Ruth and I spent the rest of the day sewing up the many superficial wounds of the crew and one or two serious ones under the analgesia of Master Kan Do's needles. The captain was beside himself with joy. He had not only survived a pirate attack from superior numbers, but also gained himself and the crew a prize captive – the galley. No doubt it had been stolen or lost in battle or traded for, somewhere along the line, but the captain and crew would be very much richer when they sold the vessel on in Cairo or Alexandria or any of the other major river ports along the length of the Nile.

The captain towed the prize, with the barest skeleton crew aboard, all the way to Alexandria as he could not get the price he hoped for in the larger, domestic ports along the length of the Nile. Alexandria was an international port and harbour and a centre of trade. It was a very wealthy Mediterranean entrepôt of the numerous cultures from around the inland sea and the African hinterland. Ruth delighted in some of costumes and jewellery that the wealthier women sported themselves in.

'It is a shame we will not have the time to sightsee and visit all there is to be seen. There is so much ancient history in this land,' commented Ruth as we strolled by the remnants of the Pharos, the ancient lighthouse, of Alexandria. It was a shame to see it in such a state of decay.

We were in the harbour district of Alexandria with a view to gaining passage on a suitable ship to take us across the Inland Sea to Italy and hopefully to a place named Salerno to find a female healer named Trano, Tratula or Trato, we were not sure. Hadar had not been able to be specific about her name but he was emphatic she taught at a university in Salerno and would complete our education in healing with her knowledge of women's health issues. Beyond that, we knew nothing else about her, which was only a little less than our combined knowledge of female biology, anatomy and reproductive problems.

The sailing season was coming to an end with the imminent demise of autumn and the upcoming onset of winter, along with the storm season. There were no captains willing to risk their ships, livelihoods and lives by putting out to sea and venturing across the Mediterranean. Except for one and he was keen to leave port as soon as possible.

'I sail on the tide, within the hour. If you are back here in time, I will accept you as passengers,' he said after seeing the golden dinar Ruth offered for the passage, 'And it will cost you one of those pretty yellow coins each.'

I spat on my hand, he on his and we shook hands. The deal was struck and we hurried away to collect our meagre belongings from the dockside inn we had spent the last week in. We arrived back with plenty of time in hand.

'You have a choice,' said the captain whose name was Enrico, 'You can sleep on deck where the air is fresh and clean or below deck with the crew, their smells, the rancid bilge water and the reek of the piss and shit from the livestock we carry on this trip. Of course,' he leered, 'the young lady is welcome to share the luxury of my own cabin at no extra cost.'

Raymond placed his hand upon the hilt of his sword at this perceived insult to Ruth's reputation. The captain and those members of the crew who were watching the exchange, got Raymond's message, 'This woman is out of bounds to all of you!'

'Please yourselves,' said the captain shrugging and then turned to continue preparing the ship to leave port.

We selected a spot in the bow of the ship. It was a small, covered area that was used to store coiled ropes of which there were not many and the space was easily refurbished into an accommodation that would snugly keep the three of us out of the wind and protected from sea spray and rain.

The Porpoise was an old trading vessel with a crew that had plenty of experience. The fact the crew had sailed for so many years under the one master, gave us an indication that Enrico was probably a very able captain and honest and fair in his treatment of the crew. Crews did not stay long on ships that had fools or rogues for captains. I forgave him his indiscretion toward Ruth.

For the first two or three days of the voyage, it seemed the three of us fell into a lethargy of fatigue and generalised body aches and pains. We had not had a rest since we left the Buddha's Smile and now, we were on board a ship at sea with no responsibilities and we could let ourselves just take it easy with naps, lazy reclining against what was ever available or just vacantly staring out to sea.

It was not long before Raymond and I felt the need to be more active and we recommenced our daily exercises and training routines on the ship's deck to keep ourselves in the best of physical form. It was not long before the crew took an interest in our exertions and combat training routines. Captain Enrico even joined them, sitting with the crew and discussing our activities and placing one or two bets with his members on the outcome of any training duel or exercise Raymond and I undertook together.

Neither Enrico, or any of the sailors, had ever seen anything like the oriental unarmed combat skills Raymond and I went through. Most of the crew sat in open mouthed amazement at the acrobatics, airborne kicking manoeuvres, body throws, hand chops and wrestling Raymond and I put on each day.

Ruth was not going to be left out and put on a display of knife throwing ability that amazed all, not just for its accuracy, but mostly that a woman could exhibit the skills of a deadly assassin.

Many of the crew, when free, approached Raymond and me for some tips and tuition on how to be more of an effective fighter. Together, Raymond and I showed them some simple tricks that might prevent harm should they wind up involved in some dockside brawl. They were all extremely grateful. Captain Enrico was too. You never knew when you might come under attack at sea and improving his crew's martial abilities was not to be sneered at.

All of this on a sun-drenched, brilliantly blue Mediterranean Sea, with the wind in our hair and The Porpoise bounding over the waves like its namesake, was too good to last.

# 24

The storm, when it came, was sudden, unseen at night and increased in ferocity with rapid intensity. Wind and rain lashed the deck while great walls of water threatened to crash over the side of the boat. The vessel was tossed up and down and from side to side in the turbulence, making the work of the crew to keep the ship as stabilised as possible, a hazardous and deadly occupation. From our position at the bow, we watched as two crew members were lost overboard as they were attempting to reef the sail. Others took their place with much more care and finally the sail was shortened and the ship gained some stability, less buffeted by the bullying winds.

Enrico stood heroically at the steer-board, his helmsman beside him, as together they wrestled the mighty oar to keep the ship head on into the huge waves. Any of the huge waves striking the ship's broadside would send us to the bottom of the sea.

'Do you think tying these ropes around our waists and securing the other end would be a good idea?' yelled Ruth above the screaming and wailing wind.

We agreed it was a good idea, which Raymond further refined by tying slip knots around our waists so we could quickly and easily release ourselves if need be. Those ropes saved our lives on more than one occasion as great washes of water swept the deck and rushed toward the bow where we were stationed. Any one of those deluges could have carried one or all of us away.

We did not sleep that night as we were too wet, cold, uncomfortable and, to be honest, too frightened. I have known fear in battle and conflict but could overcome it with determination to win. I could not beat the storm in any way, neither could Ruth or Raymond despite their own special talents and skills. We were helpless against an enemy too massive and powerful to defeat. That was why we were frightened. I held Ruth closely and tightly, reassuring her and telling her of my love for her. Raymond thoughtfully embraced Ruth gently from behind, adding to her sense of personal security and safety. I think the three of us felt more protected, huddled and cuddled up to each other in this way.

During the night there was a loud, slow, creaking noise that suddenly became a crashing explosion as the mast snapped and fell to the deck. That, in itself, was not the immediate problem. The spar to which the sail was attached was dragging in the water and turning the ship dangerously side on to the waves.

'Cut the sails away,' yelled Enrico to the crew, none of whom had safety ropes tied about them.

'Hold onto my rope,' said Raymond buckling his broadsword on, 'and don't forget to haul me back in if you have to.'

Raymond flashed us both a grin and ran across the water-washed deck to where the spar lay over the gunnel and was dragging its sail in the water. He mounted the spar as if it were a horse, wrapping his legs firmly around it and began hacking at the ropes holding the sail to the spar. The waves were jostling the boat up and down, making Raymond appear as if he were breaking in a horse as he rose and fell on the spar with each wave's peak and trough. Throughout his ride, he kept hacking at the sail and ropes slowly inching his way along the spar.

Ruth and I held our breaths throughout Raymond's ride, afraid his legs would lose their grip and he would be washed away. I kept a gentle tension on his safety rope and held it tightly in my hands. Periodically, huge waves washed over Raymond pushing him and the rigging under the water, but his legs held firm and he would reappear each time from underneath the waves to continue cutting and hacking free the spar and sail from each other.

After what seemed an eternity, Raymond finally reached the end of the spar and, with a few more blows and cuts from his sword, separated the sail from the spar, releasing the durable canvas to sink into the sea and free the ship to a course more chosen by Captain Enrico.

Raymond worked his way backwards on his bottom along the spar and back to the deck. Once he was safely on deck and standing, Enrico roared, 'Right, get that mast and spar over the side as well.'

The mast and spar were moving and rolling dangerously around the deck, further damaging the boat. It took all the available crew, along with Raymond and myself, to manoeuvre the great mass of timber to the side of the deck and then another huge effort to raise it and drop it over the side. The ship sat higher in the water as a consequence, the increased buoyancy making the ship more unstable.

The storm raged for two whole days and nights and none of us slept a wink during that time. The daytime was almost as dark as the night, thanks to the black cloud covering the sky. It was a permanent late twilight. At no time did we see the sun or have any idea where it might be in the sky. Thankfully, no more crew members were lost overboard, although seven had sustained injuries on the rolling, slippery deck. Captain Enrico showed remarkable endurance and never let the steer board leave his hands for the whole duration of the storm. I understood his crew's respect for him even more. It was he who saved us and the ship with his guidance, determination and courage.

Gradually, the winds abated, the swells subsided and the sky cleared into its beautiful Mediterranean blue. We had survived one of the most terrifying experiences of my life. Captain Enrico was quick to praise and thank the crew and, in particular, Raymond for his courage on the spar in the middle of the storm. The crew gave him a rousing cheer of thanks and appreciation for his courage.

There was, however, one big problem. The storm had driven us far away from our intended course and the captain had no firm idea of where we were. The second problem was we had no mast or sail, which meant no power to get underway.

We were adrift on a grey and unpredictable winter sea with little hope of another vessel coming to our rescue.

# 25

The first call of duty was to assess the damage to the ship and effect any immediate and urgent repairs that needed tending to. The falling mast and its consequent movement around the storm-tossed deck had damaged the hatches to the hold below, broken the capstan in two, leaving us without anchoring options, smashed several gaps in the bulwarks and two holes in the deck, and that was just above deck.

Below deck, the entire manifest of the captain's cargo was ruined, from the salt water and its barrage. Expensive fabrics were stained, ripped and wrinkled, food stuffs were spoiled or spoiling, metal objects were quickly rusting and saddest of all, the dozen sheep that were being brought back for inter-breeding purposes by a wealthy landowner, all had broken legs from being thrown around in the storm and had to be put down and thrown overboard, apart from the two we quickly cut up and salted to be kept for our own food store. Fortunately, the water butts that held our fresh and potable water were all intact and untainted by salt water. We would not die of dehydration, at least, not straight away.

The crew set to work repairing, as best as possible, the damage that had been done. Raymond, Ruth and I helped with this, much to the appreciation of the deleted and worn-out crew.

Once the worst and most pressing of the damage was repaired as best we could manage, the captain called a meeting of the crew and ourselves.

'As you know, when we left Alexandria, we were on a north-westerly heading making for Crete and then onto Italy. I fear that the easterly storm has blown us far to the west of our destination and further south than I care to be. The north coast of Africa is a devil's hole of Berber brigands and pirates. Let us hope we are not too near it.

'We cannot remain stuck here, dead in the water, as sooner or later we will all perish, dying from dehydration, starvation, illness or madness. If not that, then a pirate's sword will probably see us off.

'What I propose is that we use what spare timber we can muster from the ship and build as many small craft as we can, to row and tow The Porpoise northward to the closest European or island shore we can find. What say you to this plan?'

It was a plan and the only plan put forward, so naturally it was all hands saying, 'Aye, aye,' in response to the captain's proposal.

It was a good plan, as it took the edge of our current despondency over the state we were in, by giving us direction and tasks to do.

We began the task below deck which was now basically emptied of cargo. Shelving, hatches, doors, bulwarks, tables, bunks, barrels, decking and other larger wooden fixtures were stripped and removed. Above deck, the captain's cabin was entirely broken down into serviceable lengths of timber, as were the stores cupboards, the stairway and ladders.

Our biggest problem was that we had no ship's carpenter, along with a store of tools beyond the most basic ones for emergency repairs. I could not see that we were going to be able to build any sort of watertight sea going craft with our limited supply of timber and lack of specialist tools. Raymond had been most upset when he had to give up his sword as a makeshift wood plane.

I approached Captain Enrico with a proposal, 'We could make more narrow rafts to tow The Porpoise than we can make safe small watercraft. What does it really matter if we all get wet towing the boat compared to our other options?'

Enrico considered my proposal and said, 'I think you might be right in this thinking. The more doing the towing, the quicker and easier the job and the journey will be,' and he redirected his men to work on making rafts that could fit four or five paddlers as opposed to rowers.

Making rafts was easier than making boats and it was only two days before the crew had completed the task of building six rafts, each capable of supporting four paddlers which amounted to just about the entire crew, including ourselves, leaving just Enrico and the helmsman aboard to steer The Porpoise.

There was enough timber left over to shape 24 paddles, all slightly different shapes and depth, but they would do the job. The next day we lowered our rafts into the water, tethered their towing lines to the bow of the ship before climbing down to sit gingerly on the wooden planks without falling in. The captain and helmsmen lowered our paddles to us once we were safely seated.

Slowly we dipped our paddles and moved forward in the water until all the towing ropes stood taut out of the water.

'As one and on my call,' bellowed the mate from the leading raft, 'Try to keep an even and steady stroke at the same time so we all bite the water together.'

It was clumsy at first, paddlers missed their beat, some fell in the water and others lost their paddles getting tangled with those in front or behind. The helmsman solved the timing problem by placing a barrel upon the prow of The Porpoise and commencing a steady beat on it with a belaying baton. It worked very well in maintaining a rhythm that all paddlers could work to and slowly The Porpoise began its long and arduous journey north.

We were a tired and exhausted group of men and one woman who climbed back aboard that evening as the sun was setting. The captain was pleased with our efforts and assured us it would get easier as we got used to the repetitive paddling and we would travel further each day.

Although the capstan was broken in two, we found we could raise and lower the great round stone we used for an anchor if twelve or more men raised and lowered it manually with a rope. This allowed for security at night and prevented us drifting onto any unseen shoals or rocks in the dark.

# 26

For 13 days we clambered down the side of The Porpoise and boarded our rafts and then paddled from sunup to sundown with only three or four short breaks. The captain was correct in that it did get easier and we guessed we were travelling further and faster each day, particularly as the helmsman picked up the tempo of his barrel beating. It was constantly cold and wet work and when it rained, it felt miserable, but no one complained and we all kept paddling. Mercifully, there were no more storms or severely inclement weather.

It was mid-morning on the 14th day that we heard the captain yell, 'Land Ho,' as he pointed away to the north-west. He was higher up than we were at sea level and we could not see the land, but we altered direction and struck off to the north-west. An hour later, we were able to make out an island with a small mountain arising from its centre. As we got closer, we were able to discern that most of the island was surrounded by rocks and reefs. We paddled around the island and eventually found a small and sheltered bay into which we could tow the damaged Porpoise and run it up onto the beach.

'Do you suppose anyone lives on this rock?' queried Raymond.

'I saw no signs of habitation as we came towards the island, nor as we paddled around it. No smoke from cooking fires to be seen, no people to be seen. You would think the sight of so many rafts towing a stricken ship would have attracted some attention,' I replied.

'Perhaps they are waiting to see what we do and are watching us whilst hiding at the same time,' commented Ruth.

Just then Captain Enrico called us all together and the two dozen of us mustered around him.

'Firstly, my thanks and appreciation to you all for the amazing job you have done over the last two weeks. Well done men ...er... and lady,' he stammered, which made us all laugh.

'I suspect that we are going to be marooned on this rock for a while, at least until the recommencement of the sailing season in a few months. That means we are going to have to make the best of this situation as we can. Whilst we have a supply of water in the butts it will only be enough, with rationing, for three weeks so our first priority must be to find a source of water. I want three teams of two men each to scour the island for water starting right now. I call for volunteers please.'

There was no shortage of volunteers willing to search for water. I suspected that many were equally keen to explore the unfamiliar environment as well. Who knew what treasures might be found? The captain chose his three teams and they quickly dispersed in three different directions.

'The rest of you, I want to break into groups and to scavenge the surrounds for any materials we can use to build shelters or repair our poor old Porpoise.'

I looked over at the 'poor old Porpoise' canted on its side on the beach and thought the captain's remark somewhat hopeful. I had not seen any trees anywhere, tall or straight enough, to even approximate a mast, and besides, Raymond had sent the sail to the bottom of the sea.

I had an idea.

'Captain, if I may,' I offered, 'I think rather than try to repair The Porpoise you might have more luck rebirthing her as a rowing galley,' and went on to explain about the trees and the sail.

'A good idea,' replied the captain with delight, 'And it will take only half the time to make the modifications. Take your friends aboard and start working out the preliminary plans. I will join you soon.'

Ruth, Raymond, and I headed off down the beach to where the wounded and stripped vessel lay. We clambered aboard and did our best to move around on the sloped deck and make our way below decks.

I saw all that needed to be done almost straight away.

'We can remove these bulkheads to open the space up. We can use the timber from the rafts to make the rowing benches and oars and then all we need to do is cut some holes in the sides as ports for the oars. It will not be very fast or fine looking in the water, but it should do the job,' I explained to the others.

'Barring any further storms,' Raymond reminded us, 'I think we will still have to wait until the sailing season. The old Porpoise would not be able to take another beating from sea and storm without breaking apart.'

When Captain Enrico came on board, we detailed the plans and the caveat about waiting until the sailing season was open. He was pleased with the redesign concept and complimented me on my foresight and planning.

'We will begin tomorrow,' he said with enthusiasm, 'I am putting you in charge of organising the work crews. You cannot have all the men as I still need to send out fishing and foraging parties. If you have the time, you can put your mind to some signalling device or method.'

We spent that evening and night under makeshift lean-tos around four small fires and slept on the sand. I was concerned that my sudden appointment as work supervisor for the revamping of The Porpoise might raise some animosity amongst members of the crew, but they all seemed to accept the decision as just another aspect of their captain's wisdom and experience. No one grumbled or made any objection.

If there had been any misgivings, they were dispelled the next day as I threw myself into working just as hard as any other member of the team. By the end of the day, we had removed the three bulkheads from below deck and brought all the rafts aboard to make the benches and oars with.

# 27

The captain kept everybody busy which was good for morale and kept any trouble down to a minimum as everybody pulled together. The captain even had the foresight to rotate the teams so that everyone got a chance to change their tasks and avoid monotony. I was the only one who remained at one task, that of "ship rebuilder" which I did not mind as the project was very much my idea, but I would not have minded a day or two off to go fishing.

Each night, we would return to the campsite to find new modifications; huts replaced lean-tos, tables and benches for eating appeared, clothes lines were erected, bark guttering collected and ran rainwater to the butts – the only fresh water on the island was on the other side of it. We collected enough rainwater to meet our needs, but it was reassuring to know that if we had to, we could make the journey to the other side of the island for emergency supplies.

Ruth and I were returning one night to the campsite to see most of those present grinning at the pair of us with some, as yet, secret knowledge. Captain Enrico invited the pair of us to join him for a short walk. He led us along a path we had trodden to a clearing where stood a newly erected hut. The captain led us inside where we found that a bed had been manufactured from otherwise unserviceable timber with crossed ropes for suspension and layers of broad palm leaves for a mattress, tucked into a sheet that appeared from somewhere.

'The men built it for the pair of you,' he smiled and then raised his voice for those outside to hear, 'They say you have been keeping them all awake at night!' and suddenly from outside we heard the guffaws of bawdy seaman having a good belly laugh.

Ruth and I were both red-faced with embarrassment when we stepped outside to thank everyone.

Just as our campsite became more civilised, so did The Porpoise and, like the Phoenix, change and rise again she did. The crew voted to keep her name despite all the changes we had made to its structure, both externally and internally. The basic modifications I had originally recommended had been completed and we took a couple of test runs only to find other problems, mostly leaks from timbers that had warped. This problem was solved when one of the crew discovered that the thick syrupy sap from one of trees hardened into a serviceable waterproof resin. When mixed with the fibrous and stringy bark of another tree it made a serviceable caulking mixture.

The changes and modifications to both campsite and ship took a month to complete. Captain Enrico complimented the men and me on the quality of our work. I was pleased at long last to be able to go fishing and enjoy long walks with Ruth while we foraged for fruit and other edibles. There were plenty of edible tubers to be dug up, herbs to be gathered and fruit to be plucked. Combined with fresh fish and shellfish, our diet was healthy and nutritious.

'The only thing missing,' said Raymond smacking his lips after one tasty meal, 'are several glasses of good wine to go with the meal.'

It may not have been wine and it was rather rough and burned the throat, but the crew did manage to distil a crude liquor using the skins and cores of a variety of fruits. Almost predictably, a fight broke out between two of the crew the night the brew was first sampled. Enrico, as captain, did not want his crew fighting and injuring each other, nor did he wish to take away one of the few rewards the crew could enjoy at the end of their day. As a compromise, he commandeered the still and rationed the crew to two cups of an evening – an amount of the strong liquor that had a euphorically pleasant but not inflammatory effect.

Without the daily regime of boat and "village building" boredom became an issue. Fishing and foraging for food along with its preparation and cooking was about all we had to occupy ourselves. Raymond and I recommenced our morning regime of exercises and, before too long, found we had a band of followers we were training in self-defence and disablement of an attacker. Enrico actively encouraged all his men to join in and took delight in both being dropped on his bum or doing the same to an opponent. The training ground was a level playing field where rank and seniority held no sway, only martial prowess mattered. By the end of our stay on the island, the men were fitter, stronger and capable of defending themselves if needed.

It proved to be a mild winter on the island. The storm that had disabled The Porpoise was the first and the worst of the season and the only rainfall thereafter was simply sufficient to keep our water butts full. The weather was kind to us. Gradually, the days became weeks and the weeks saw the months of the winter storm season go by.

It was while we were all breaking our fast one morning in early spring that Enrico announced it was time to prepare to leave the island. He laid out a plan whereby half of the crew would work at catching and drying or salting fish and others at collecting and preparing fruit and tubers for drying. The rest of the crew were taken aboard to man the oars and build the necessary strength to maintain pulling an oar for hours on end. Enrico took them through the commands and actions for manoeuvring The Porpoise on the water. Enrico rotated all the crew through this training and another month later we were ready to depart our little island home.

The sun was bright, the sky was clear and the sea a flat and opalescent blue as we launched The Porpoise off the beach and in a northerly direction. We still had no idea just where in the Mediterranean we were.

Hopefully, we would bump into southern Europe sooner or later.

# 28

It was not southern Europe we bumped into. It was the southern coast of Sicily and it was not a good place to be. It was probably the absence of a mast and sail which gave us a low profile in the water that saved us from detection and attack by any number of regional threats. Muslim corsairs and European pirates operated with immunity, capturing vessels and enslaving crews and passengers or holding the odd wealthy one for ransom. Muslims, Berbers, Sicilians, Lombards and Normans all fought with each other for control of the island while the Holy Roman Emperor Henry IV watched events on the island from mainland Italy planning his own invasion.

Enrico, who was Calabrian by birth, had grown up in these waters and recognised our location from the familiar coastline and headland we were approaching.

'We are near the southernmost tip of Sicily, Cape Passero,' he informed us, 'From here we can run a course straight to the north of the island and then row up the coast of Italy to Salerno. Our other alternative is to row entirely around the island, increasing the risk of attack from any number of possible sources and taking three to four times as long.'

'Well, let us take the shorter route,' said Raymond.

'It is not quite that simple,' replied Enrico, 'This is the most populous side of the island and sees the most traffic at sea. We have been lucky to remain unseen so far, but I do not expect that luck to hold. Secondly, at the northern end of the strait, it narrows between the tip of Italy's boot and the eastern side of the island, causing strong currents and a notorious whirlpool which sucks ships down to the depths of the strait. It will take strong arms at the steer board and at all the oars to get past the turbulence that draws vessels into the whirlpool.'

'We seem to be plagued by one problem after another,' said Ruth sounding exasperated at yet another turn of events appearing to go against us.

'That's it,' I exclaimed with a sudden jolt of inspiration, 'Why not be plagued? In fact, let us make this whole ship a plague ship!'

Enrico liked the idea and laughed with some merriment at my proposal. The others looked at me with some confusion.

Noticing their looks Enrico enlightened them with, 'No captain or ship's crew would come anywhere near a plague ship for fear of bringing the disease on board their own ship and having it sweep through the crew. There is a small cove not far from the Cape where we can drop anchor and plan this little deception.'

We rounded the cape and to our relief found the nearby cove empty of any shipping or habitation. We dropped anchor and began to plan.

'The majority of ships at sea carry different flags to signal other ships. Any ship flying a yellow flag or yellow and black flag is letting other shipping know they have plague or illness aboard and other shipping should stay away,' Enrico informed us.

'Unfortunately, my flags disappeared when we had to strip the ship after the storm and we have no yellow flags. Any suggestions?' he asked.

'Guido has a yellow blouse and he is a big man. Would that serve as one flag?' suggested Ruth.

'Better, it will serve as two if we carefully unstitch it and use the front and the back of the blouse as two flags. Good suggestion,' said Enrico.

Guido was willing to part with his blouse in exchange for one of the captain's, despite its very tight fit on his bulky frame. That was the first problem solved.

'There is always a dreadful smell of illness and corruption that surrounds any diseased vessel. Some say a plague ship is smelled at sea even before it is seen,' Enrico informed us, 'I hate to say this, but we must cease pissing and shitting over the side and collect our waste in some butts and toss our rubbish and food scraps in it as well. A couple of days fermenting in the sun should make a foul enough smelling concoction. We will just have to put up with that discomfort if we are to succeed.'

The crew were informed of this new toileting directive, which was received with collective moans of disgust, a few jokes at the expense of some notorious farters on board and a general consensus that the job had to be done.

'We cannot afford to be seen to be travelling well,' began Enrico, 'I will reduce the number of men at the oars to half and we will appear to only proceed at a slow and laboured pace.'

This news was greeted with cheers and applause by the crew as it meant a considerable reduction in the work required of them.

'This is all very well,' said Ruth, 'but all of us are tanned and healthy looking. No one looks sick. We will need to make at least six men look very unwell and have them on deck so they can be seen to be sick. I think my colleagues and I can come up with something to fool a not too close inspection.'

'And a dead body or two, or rather dummies, to be seen thrown over the side,' added Raymond enthusiastically.

'Nice touch,' I commented.

Finding six volunteers for cosmetic sick duties was easy as the role required no work beyond standing or laying around on deck looking sick and dying.

'I think some dried vomit stains down the side of the ship would add a final splash of convincing colour,' concluded Raymond.

# 29

We spent two days holed up in the cove by Cape Passero preparing our ruse while lookouts on the headland kept an eye out for any shipping coming our way. Guido's yellow blouse was soon flying from the bow and the stern, after careful unstitching by Ruth. The barrels were filling with all the refuse that twenty-four men and one woman could generate. The cook prepared a glutinous and tenaciously sticky porridge of left-over scraps that clung to the side of the vessel and dried in place. The crew had some fun making the dummies we would pretend were corpses to be thrown overboard. They made a special effort to make them look as life-like, or should I say death-like, as possible.

Ruth and I had a slightly more complicated task. Making six healthy looking men appear as if they were at death's door. Our first task was to create a deathly pale pallor to their skin. We solved this problem by making a thin paste from the crushed and powdered, sun-bleached shells that lay upon the beach of the cove. We simply painted the paste over all the exposed skin of each sailor and let it dry. On close inspection the makeup dried with lots of tiny cracks, but these would not be seen from a distance. The men were told to keep their conversation to a minimum and to be conscious of keeping their facial muscles still. It was not quite the light duties job the crewmen had expected.

Around the mouths of two of the crewmen we painted some red juices we extracted from a plant with dark red leaves. The men looked as though they had vomited blood or were bleeding orally.

121

On the necks of two more crewmen, we managed to apply the shells of some mussels that looked like big purple buboes, the hallmark of the plague. The whole process turned out to be quite a lot of creative fun for all involved and did a lot to raise morale before we undertook the critical and dangerous run to and through, the Straits of Messina to Italy proper. As we would all mostly remain below decks and out of sight, the only people I did not envy were those who had to remain on deck with the reeking barrels exuding their sickening and miasmic odour of decay and corruption of the flesh and everything else a human can make waste of. It really helped the overall effect that the captain and helmsman both looked as nauseated and sickened as those we had made up to look sick and unwell.

As the sun rose on the third day of our stay in the cove, we hoisted the anchor, ran out a half dozen oars and began a slow passage north along the east coast of Sicily. Below deck, there was almost a party atmosphere as we took it in leisurely turns at the oars or simply sat back in idle conversations. Much to the encouragement and cheers of those present, Ruth took to the oars and did her very best to compete with the men. She did not shame herself in effort. She did, however, miss a stroke through the water and went flying back off her bench, landing on her back with legs in the air and everything she kept private, up for inspection. I admit I laughed but did not gawk as much as the rest of the crew present.

We kept a slow and almost leisurely pace at the oars as we crept along the eastern coast of Sicily not wanting anyone on land or sea to suspect we were moving too fast for a plague ship. Keeping the coast close to our portside also meant we only had one side of the ship to keep a look out for hostile shipping.

The first day at sea saw two vessels approach The Porpoise. The first was clearly a Barbary corsair that drew in close enough to have a good inspection of our decks. Captain Enrico put on a fine performance of trying to wave them away and pointing at the yellow flags to indicate we had plague on board. His performance did not deter the corsairs from their inspection and they continued to shadow us closely, obviously trying to make up their minds whether to board our vessel or not.

'Toss a dummy overboard,' suggested one of the crew below to the men on deck.

From the deck of the corsair, they would have seen one of the deck crew wander over to where the two dummies were located, hidden behind the ship's bulwark. The corsairs would have seen the crewman lean over, examining something and then call another crew member over to him. Next, they would have observed the two appearing to struggle as they hefted a dead body up onto the ship's bulwark and then tip it over the side. This was all the convincing the corsairs needed to shift their sails and veer away to find safer prey.

The second vessel looked to be one of Norman design, probably one of the powerful de Hauteville dynasty's possessions. Captain Enrico did not need to perform any "warning off" antics and we hung onto our last dummy. The Normans got close enough to see the two yellow flags, front and rear, before speedily altering course and turning well away from us. That night we anchored in a small creek well hidden by tall rushes and overhanging foliage.

At our inhibited pace we were six days rowing up the eastern coast to the awaiting Strait of Messina. Each day saw vessels approach us and then suddenly turn away after seeing the yellow flags. Such was their fear of contagion that none approached us to offer assistance or take any messages onto our destination port. Enrico was obviously pleased with the success of my ruse and made a point of expressing his thanks to me in front of the crew who quietly expressed their thanks and approval as well.

'The leisure cruise, however, is coming to an end,' continued the captain after his little speech, 'Tomorrow we face the straits and may God protect us, guide us and save our souls.'

A shiver ran down my spine.

# 30

The Strait of Messina was going to be a nightmare ride of approximately 17 nautical miles between the northeast tip of Sicily and the tip of the Italian boot, Calabria. At its narrowest, the strait was one and a half nautical miles wide which, in itself, was not a problem. The problem was, the relatively narrow straight was at the confluence of the Tyrrhenian Sea to the north and the Ionian Sea to the south. The problems for sailors lay in the alternating currents that ran through the strait, the primary currents between the two seas alternating every six hours and further complicated by the random alternating currents arising along both coastlines.

Such ongoing changes in water direction was conducive to the formation of suddenly occurring counter-currents, complicated wave patterns, upwellings, choppy seas and, more forbiddingly, the formation of whirlpools. Added to all this, the winds were constantly unpredictable and fog and rain could roll in at any time.

Captain Enrico spoke to the crew at first light.

'We have three hours before the current will be running with us. We are going to have to rely on speed to take us through the strait, so it will be all hands on the oars while the helmsman and I hold the deck. Some of you will have to sit two to a bench and oar. We will make our run keeping as close to the east coast of Sicily as we can and you will all row like the hounds of hell are after us for the time it takes.'

'Ruth, you are to be water girl and ensure the men are kept adequately hydrated. There will not be any time for eating until we have passed on through to the Tyrrhenian Sea. In the meantime, make sure you fill your bellies and get everything that is not tied down, tied down.'

Three hours later we were underway and moving at what the Romans would have called ramming speed as the Ionian current carried us speedily up the coast aided by our own efforts at the oars. We were still flying our yellow flags but any other pretences of being a plague ship were abandoned as we battled to stay at our benches and in control of our oars in the increasingly turbulent sea. Conditions weren't as bad as the storm that disabled The Porpoise but we were buffeted around and a number of loosed oars caused bruising injuries to some of the crew. At least there was no blinding rain and sleet. Ruth bravely kept her balance and delivered cup and pitcher to any man calling for water.

I was becoming concerned by an increasing lean The Porpoise was taking to the port-side when the captain's voice came bellowing from above, 'Two strong hands on deck, NOW!'

'That's you two young men,' said Guido, indicating Raymond and myself.

We left our benches and scurried up the ladder to the deck where the captain indicated the helmsman who was struggling to hold the vessel on course. We were perilously close to the rocks of north-eastern Sicily's shore. Raymond and I grabbed the remaining length of the steer-board, adding our youthful strength to the helmsman's efforts to turn the vessel from the threatening shore.

'Steer-board crew! Back water,' yelled the captain to the crew below. In a rather clumsy and unco-ordinated attempt, the oars on our right side reversed their pulling and the ship began to turn away from the rocks. Once clear, the captain ordered all speed ahead again and the pulling of the oars changed direction once again.

The helmsman's platform afforded a good view of the sea around us as Raymond and I assisted the helmsman in guiding The Porpoise over the tempest. The water all around our vessel was boiling with a turbulence I had never seen before; waves suddenly rose up and crashed into each other from opposite directions, patches of swirling white water simply appeared and chased each other around, forming small whirlpools that we could feel pulling on the steer-board.

The next thing I knew, Captain Enrico was beside me and pulling on the last length of steer-board with all his might.

'Pull like all fuck and keep us out of that white water over there,' he urgently snapped at us before yelling to the men below, 'More speed. More speed. Row. Row, you dogs of the sea!'

I cast a quick glance at the white water and realised it was turning in a fast anti-clockwise swirl and was as wide as The Porpoise was long. As we drew nearer to the edge of the watery merry-go-round, I felt the ship beginning to tilt sideways. Water rushed over the gunnels, almost sweeping the four of us off the steering platform. From below deck, we heard the cursing and bellows of pain as men were rolled from their benches and oars crashed violently into bodies.

'Hold, hold, hold,' yelled Enrico as the four of us struggled with all our might to keep the steer-board hard to our chests and The Porpoise away from being swallowed into the vortex. It seemed like an eternity of burning agony in my arms and shoulders as our momentum kept us to the periphery of the whirlpool. Our tilt increased its angle and we heard more chaos and bedlam arising from below. One side of the ship had its oars in the air while the other side's oars were beneath the water.

'Hang on boys. Pull, pull. That's it. Keep it up. We are almost through it,' roared the captain.

It seemed that the ship momentarily increased its speed and then we suddenly found we were past the vortex and moving rapidly towards calmer water. The current was carrying us away, which was just as well as many of the oars down below were either broken or had shifted from their row locks and lay across the deck of the hold.

From down below, I heard Ruth's plaintive voice calling out, 'I'm going to need some help down here.'

# 31

'Get down there and check it out you two,' said Enrico, 'We can control things from up here now.'

Raymond and I headed to the hatch and down the ladder into what looked like an absolute disaster had occurred. I doubt there was not a single uninjured sailor and that included Ruth, whose left eye was swelling nicely from a blow by the end of an oar. Guido took temporary charge of the situation, organising the least injured half of the crew to salvage what oars they could and get back to rowing on the benches.

'Let us get as far away from this watery hell hole as we can,' he growled at the make-shift rowing crew.

Ruth and I organised a rough triage system and found there were several serious injuries amongst the crew mostly caused by whiplashing oars breaking bones and, in one case, a head. The pinkish brain fluid seeping from both ears told us the victim would not survive. Fortunately, he never regained consciousness and passed peacefully a few hours later.

Ruth, Raymond and I got to work at setting the host of broken bones. Ruth provided pain relief during the settings with her needles, while Raymond pulled on the limbs as I felt for the two ends and approximated them together. Keeping the limbs immobilised was going to be a problem as we had no readymade splints to hand, right then.

Despite the damage and destruction to bodies and boat, the crew gave a rousing cheer to Captain Enrico when he came down the ladder to check on the crew.

'Well,' he said, 'looking at you banged up lot makes me think it will be a very slow voyage from here on in,' to which he received a mixture of groans and laughter from his men.

'I just wanted to say, thank you men for a job well done.'

'Thank you for hanging on in there when you were up there,' said one sailor pointing to the deck, 'otherwise I reckon we be down there,' and pointed to his feet with the other hand, which brought a few laughs.

Ruth and I moved onto suturing the dozen or so wounds that needed some attention, while Raymond found a ship's saw and set about cutting splints from one of the rowing benches and some of the broken oars. By day's end, we had everyone either sewn up or splinted and put back together again, so to speak.

With all the damage to the ship and only half the crew capable of pulling their weight, we limped The Porpoise over the Tyrrhenian Sea to a small-town harbour called Scilla on the west coast of Italy. There, we put our ship in for repairs.

It was as we were standing on the mole of the harbour that the captain came up to us.

'Your destination is not that far away from here,' he said, 'Salerno lies on the coast about 180 miles away to the north. The coastal road over there is your best and straightest route.' He pointed in the direction. 'If I were you, I would attach myself to some group travelling that way, as these are very troubled times in this land

and you would be sitting ducks for cut-throats, deserters, robbers and slavers.'

'One moment please Captain, while we retrieve our belongings,' I said as I motioned for the others to join me.

'Enrico is a fine man and an excellent sea captain,' I told the others, 'I think we should part with some of our golden dinars to help him with the ship's repair and care of the crew.'

The matter was quickly settled between the three of us and later we left a very grateful and smiling captain more certain and reassured of his future, standing on the mole. As we walked our way to the centre of the town to find some accommodation, members of the crew waved us farewell from the deck.

We found a local hostelry where we chose to stay for the night. The food was good, as was the wine, and the beds clean and comfortable. After the meal and the ordeal that we had survived, we were all very tired. Ruth and I had some ideas of our own, so we made sure Raymond had the luxury of a bed and room of his own.

The next morning, as we broke our fast over hot bread and cheese and well-watered local wine, we discussed what we thought might be the best plan for travelling north.

'Scilla does not appear to be a major port in any way. The Porpoise is the only vessel tied to the mole. We could be weeks waiting on a ship to take us north to Salerno and I am keen to get there as soon as possible,' offered Ruth, 'I vote for travelling overland, either with a group or somehow disguised.'

'I was talking to the publican. The danger appears to be the number of renegade and mercenary bands of soldiers terrorising the countryside and the villages. The official armies of the Holy Roman

Emperor: Lombards, Normans, Byzantines and others, are seeking to fight each other over lands and territory and would probably ignore three poor and harmless looking travellers,' volunteered Raymond. 'Purchasing horses for the journey is not a bright idea for the same reasons that Amana advised against it. Too many people want to steal them. We would be targeted by the first rogues we encountered.'

'I think travelling in disguise is a clever idea. I worry about Ruth's vulnerability and the fact that she might be an easy target for assault by some of these villains and mercenaries,' I said not wanting to go into any further details that might be upsetting for Ruth.

'We can repeat our plague ruse to make me, or all of us, look sick,' said Ruth.

I heard the town church bell calling the faithful to prayer and services.

'I think I have an idea,' I said, 'But first, let us go to church.'

The others looked at me as if I was mad and had gone way off the track. We went to the local church all the same. It was a new experience for Ruth and I said nothing about what was turning over in my mind.

# 32

The mass was a long one as it turned out to be a feast day for one of the many saints of the Latin Church. When it was over, we waited while the congregation left the church and then approached the priest.

Holding several silver dinars in my open hand, I asked directly and honestly, 'Father, we are in need of travelling quickly and in a disguise that will not attract attention or violence. I am hoping we may purchase two old monk's habits and one sister's habit along with three crucifixes.'

The priest regarded the coins in my hand and simply gestured us to follow him to the small vestry to the side of the church. He indicated a large chest, which we opened, to find full of old habits. Many were patched and had tears, but all were serviceable if not presentable in an assembly of God. There were no sisters' habits.

'I'll travel as a monk,' said Ruth, 'That's not a problem.'

I handed over the six silver dinars which the priest happily placed in a purse under his surplice. He then offered to bless us and our journey, which we accepted. As an added surprise, he gave us three wooden crucifixes, blessing them as well.

We exited the church with our bundles of monks' habits and went back to the inn.

'Now,' I said back in the room Ruth and I shared, 'all we need to do is purchase a donkey and a cart and a load of hay.'

'I begin to see your plan,' said Raymond with a smile.

Finding a villager, a farmer or a merchant with a donkey and cart for sale proved to take longer than expected, despite the offering of many silver dinars to various owners. However, by the time evening came around, we were the proud owners of an old donkey and a rickety two wheeled cart with a tray.

Ruth named the donkey Cicero.

The next day, we bought a load of hay from a farmer and started our journey north. A little way past the village, we pulled into a small coppice by the side of the road and changed into our monks' habits and donned our crucifixes. Raymond drove the cart while I sat in the tray with Ruth and applied her "make down". I painted Ruth's face, neck, arms, hands and feet in lots of tiny red dots with dye bought from a tailor-dressmaker in Scalli. Along with some suspicious looking stains down the front of her habit, she looked like a victim of Scarlet Fever – a sure-fire deterrent to anyone looking to get too close to her. Officially, Raymond and I were two brothers taking one of our beloved sisters back to her hometown to see her family before she died.

Cicero clopped along at a steady pace up the dusty road that made its way beside the flat coastal plains. The old donkey would have struggled if we had to negotiate any hilly or rugged terrain. Raymond was content to take charge of the cart while Ruth and I lay in the back upon our bed of hay and chatted the days away. We decided to avoid staying in the towns and villages we passed through, simply stopping to buy and replenish provisions from time to time. At night, the three of us slept warm and snug under the hay in the back of the cart.

'And what do we have here?' came a rough voice as the sun was rising. At the same time the side of a sword swept away the hay that covered us.

I looked up, blinking the sleep from my eyes and saw six or seven variously clad men with weapons drawn, standing around the back of our cart.

'With respect, Sir. We are humble monks returning a dying sister to her home and family before she dies,' I said gently drawing back the cowl of Ruth's habit to reveal the rash of red spots on her face and neck. Ruth put a pained and unwell expression on her face. It was enough.

'It's the spotted fever,' said one of the mercenaries, drawing back and away from the cart. Within a moment the whole party had retreated several paces from the cart. They had all lowered their weapons as they did so.

'Leave them, Captain,' urged another of the soldiers.

The captain looked undecided. Scratched his head and looked us over once again. Ruth mimed a small gagging dry reach. I comforted her, pretending concern and care. It was enough to make our little show finally convincing.

'What is there to steal anyway?' offered another, 'I'm not taking any chances.' He turned and made his way back to his horse. The captain and the others followed, mounted and swiftly galloped away.

'That was a close call,' said Raymond once the mercenaries were far away from us.

'I think from now on we should pull well off the road at night. I do not think having a cooking fire is a good idea, either,' said Ruth, 'We won't be able to fool everyone we meet and not all may care about catching a disease if they are desperate and hungry enough.'

'It is a nuisance. I don't fancy cold food any more than you two, but you are right, Ruth,' I replied.

The extra precautions slowed us down somewhat, as in some places we had to travel across fields to find a coppice or rocky outcrop to provide cover and protection for us overnight.

We were fortunate in that we had no further encounters with wandering bands of soldiery. We saw several of them in the distance of the coastal plain and were able to take evasive action each time they appeared to be coming our way.

Our journey from Scalli to Salerno took the best part of three weeks and it was with a sense of sweet relief that we breasted a low coastal headland to look down onto the coastal town and harbour of our goal.

'Now all we have to do is find this Trano, Troto or Trotula or whatever her name is and see if we can undertake further study with her,' said Ruth with a degree of excitement, 'I am looking forward to learning about my body and those of other women. It was, after all, how and why I wound up with you two.'

'I like the idea of learning about women's bodies too,' said Raymond with a grin.

# 33

Salerno was situated on a peaceful looking bay that faced the Tyrrhenian Sea. Gentle rolling hills tumbled down to a narrow coastal strip, dotted with houses, businesses and small farms and orchards. A small dock and mole catered to vessels plying the Mediterranean trade routes. The city wall was comparable to any of the other warring city states on the Italian peninsula at the time. The city skyline was dominated by two buildings: the royal palace, known as the Castel Terracena and a magnificent cathedral dedicated to St Matthew, naturally named il Duomo di San Matteo. A third, less magnificent building, also arose above the domestic skyline, which we quickly learned was to be our destination and home for the next year and more: La Schola Medica Salernitana – the medical school of Salerno. Next door to the medical school was the hospital.

'I know you two are keen to barrel right on in there and start your studies right away but I think you need to consider just how you are going to be received with your request,' said Raymond, realistically putting a damping over the enthusiasm and excitement Ruth and I were experiencing. 'Let us find a comfortable inn, with some good hot food, passable wine and there we can make some plans to get you two enrolled. You would only be redirected to a monastery dressed the way you are and besides, Ruth's face is still a mess of spots.'

He was right. We pointed Cicero to the end of town near some warehouses where we found a suitably deserted alley way and were able to quickly change into our usual travelling clothes. We left

137

the monks' habits lying on a doorstep where they would be found and probably put to use somehow. Two crucifixes joined them, Raymond keeping his as he had lost the Cathar cross given to him by his mother when he left Occitan for the Crusades.

There was no shortage of accommodation to choose from in Salerno. The town was in a scenic location, situated on a bay surrounded by green rolling hills and was a popular holiday destination.

'How do you suppose we are to go about enrolling ourselves at La Schola Medica?' asked Ruth as she sat scrubbing the red spots from her skin in a room of one of the local inns.

'May I suggest we spend some time in simply observing the schola. Seeing who, and what kind of people, come and go. Perhaps, find some helpful person, a student probably, who will tell us what we need to know about studying at the academy,' offered Raymond.

'I agree,' I said and later that morning we sat on a bench unobtrusively observing the comings and goings of the different schola personnel and students.

'The students dress as everyday people, in everyday clothes, but even so, their clothes are clean and well presented. You can tell the tutors and professors by their capes and coloured caps,' observed Ruth, 'We need to improve our standard of dress. We have become too used to being adventurers and travellers and we look it. We do not look like prospective physicians in the clothes we have.'

'Have you noticed all the women coming and going?' said Raymond.

'Raymond. Keep your mind on the job,' chipped Ruth.

'No. The universities of London, Paris and other places in Europe do not welcome women as students or instructors. Women are denied education. There are women coming and going here who are both.'

'That is not what I notice,' I said, 'Have you noticed that there are Christian, Muslim, and Jewish people coming and going as well? This place seems to be an academic melting pot where all may study. Men and women from all religions and regions. What a marvellous and enlightened place.'

'I have seen enough,' said Ruth, 'We must buy some suitable clothes. How much money have we got left, Ippolito?'

I felt the weight of the heavy purse with its golden dinars beneath my tunic, 'Plenty,' I replied, quietly jingling the coins in their purse for her to hear.

Two hours later, we had purchased some new, inexpensive outfits that would blend in with the student fashions of the Schola. As he was not going to be a student, Raymond was content with a new pair of shoes, some blue hose and a red tunic.

'It has just occurred to me,' said Raymond, 'While you two are studying, what am I meant to do?'

'Why, be our manservant, of course,' laughed Ruth, 'Carry those bags, clean that room. That sort of thing.'

Raymond looked discomforted by this relegation.

'Do not worry. It is only in public,' I said reassuringly.

'There is not enough time left in the day,' said Ruth, 'We will go back to the Schola tomorrow and try our luck at finding someone to help us. Perhaps we can think of something tonight.'

That evening, as we finished off some cold chicken, salad and flat bread in the bar of the inn we were staying in, I said, 'I'm for a bold approach, but a polite and respectful one all the same. I say we find out who the head or principal of the Schola is and directly approach them with our proposition.'

'Might I suggest, a small display of wealth would improve your chances?' said Raymond. 'Hide most of your coins back here but place enough of them in your purse to give it a slight bulge as it hangs at your waist. Do you still have the ring your father gave you?'

I nodded that I did. The ring, with the de Medici crest and two small ruby insets, was wrapped in a small secret cloth with my belongings.

'Wear it. It will lend you a touch of aristocracy. And that, my friend, opens doors.'

Whether it was our clothes, my ring, the purse or our earnest and polite manner, I do not know but the next morning when we approached one of the cape and cap wearing professors with our request to enter la Schola as students, he indicated a building next to the hospital and said, 'Be there tomorrow shortly after Tierce. You can meet the members of the Almo Collegio Salernitano then. The panel will interview you and make the decision of your admission, or not, to la Schola.'

With that he bid us good day and wished us well on the morrow.

# 34

The next morning, Ruth and I presented ourselves at the academic residence pointed out to us the day before and were ushered in by the same professor we had spoken with. He introduced himself this time as Professori Giovanni Afflacio and we introduced ourselves by name only, not wanting to give too much away at this stage. Professor Afflacio led us through the foyer to a chamber off to the side of the building. Inside, seated around one side of a long table, were four men and one older woman, all dressed in academic capes and caps. Two empty chairs faced the panel from the other side. Another stood vacant with the panel.

'Firstly,' said Professor Afflacio, 'allow me to introduce the members of this panel. Seated in the middle,' he indicated the woman, 'is the chair of the Medica faculty, Professor Medicus Trota de Ruggerio.'

I sensed Ruth's excitement at this introduction. We had reached our goal and found the woman Hadar had charged us with seeking out, despite the many adventures and setbacks we had experienced on our way. Trota was a small, slender woman with a head of black shoulder-length hair. I suspected she had used some dye in her hair, as the light coming from the window behind her gave it some dark blue and purple highlights. She smiled warmly at the both of us and bade us sit with a gesture of her hand.

We did so before Professor Alfacio continued with his introductions. The other male professorial members of the panel were Ruggiero di Fugaldo, professor of surgery, Nicolo Salernitano, professor of anatomy, Saladino d'Ascoli, professor of pharmacia, and Giovanni Plateario, professor of therapies and treatments.

'May I present Master Ippolito de Medici and Ruth di Jerusalem. Both are seeking to become physicians through entry into our school,' finished Professor Alfacio before taking his seat with the panel.

Professor Trota opened the proceedings. 'Tell us why and how it is you two have come to be here.'

Ruth and I looked at each other, neither of us exactly sure where to begin, but begin we did. Three hours later, I had shown the panel my great scar for inspection and we finished with the story of Ruth's red spots and supposed scarlet fever. Our examiners had sat in silence with only a few questions the whole time it took for us to recount the how and why of our arrival at the Schola.

'And you say,' asked Trota seeking clarification, 'that your previous masters, Hadar and Kan Do, have deemed you knowledgeable and competent in all other areas of medicine, with the exception of women's health and for that, this Hadar, has sent you to learn from me. I am flattered that my reputation has spread so far afield. I have never heard of some of these places you say you have been.

'However, we only have your word on what you say you have been taught and have learned. You could both be young charlatans and quacks, for all my colleagues and I know. I have no way of knowing if you are safe to practice the honourable art and science of medicine.

'At this stage I would ask you both to step outside the room while my colleagues and I discuss your case,' she finished.

Ruth and I arose from our chairs, bowed our heads in respect and left the room closing the door behind us.

'I feel sick,' said Ruth sounding despondent, 'I don't think that went well at all. That professor of anatomy…'

'Salernitano,' I said.

'Him,' said Ruth with plain distaste, 'He seemed more interested in my anatomy than what I had to say.'

'I agree. He reminded me of someone else we once knew,' I said lacking some tact and sensitivity.

'He could not be that bad,' said Ruth with a shiver recalling Benedict, the priest who had raped her years ago.

We sat twiddling our thumbs, while our dreams and futures were decided by the lone woman and six men behind the closed door. Finally, it opened, and we were beckoned back inside.

'You have presented us with an interesting dilemma,' began professor Trato, 'Our curriculum studiorum here at Salerno normally consists of three years of logic before commencing five years of medical studies, followed by a year of practice under an experienced physician. We have no way of knowing at what level of expertise and knowledge your previous masters have imparted to you and whether that knowledge and those skills are acceptable and compatible with the ethical practice of our school's values and philosophy.

'Normally, we would not consider such a case as yours, but we have decided to make an exception in your circumstances. You will each be separately given opportunity to demonstrate your skills and knowledge before a panel of examiners made up of representatives of this board.

'The subjects you will be examined in will be human anatomy, illnesses of the human body, herbology and mineralogy, treatment of disease, prevention of disease and the theory and practice of human surgery. The last will be without red hot embers,' she said, the latter with a smile directed at Ruth. 'With the exception of a demonstration of practical surgery, all examinations will be oral in nature.'

'When do you propose to conduct these examinations?' I asked feeling anxious about the prospect.

'Would one week from today in this building be acceptable to you both?' replied Trota.

Ruth and I both nodded our agreement.

'Well with that, I think we can consider this meeting over. I look forward to seeing you next week,' Trota smiled at both of us. I liked the way she seemed to want to reassure us.

Ruth and I rose from our chairs, bowed to the panel of learned professors and left the room to go back to the inn where Raymond was no doubt worrying and wondering where we were after being away so long.

'I don't think I am going to like these examinations,' commented Ruth as we left the grounds of the Schola.'

'My stomach is churning already,' I replied truthfully.

# 35

'We have a week to prepare for the examinations,' stated a worried sounding Ruth, 'But how are we meant to prepare when we have no books to study or no one to ask us questions and assess us?'

We were sitting in our room back at the inn having just finished telling Raymond about the morning's interview.

'I suppose we shall have to try and assess each other. Not only answering questions but coming up with questions for each other, should help prompt our memories of everything we have learned in the last few years,' I replied trying to assuage Ruth's anxieties.

'You know, I learned a few things along the way as well,' said Raymond, 'Perhaps I might even be able to ask you both some tricky questions.'

Raymond was grinning as he said this and I was not sure if he was having a jest with us or not.

'Let us approach this from a timeline perspective,' I suggested.

'What do you mean by that?' asked Ruth.

'Well, instead of flying into a panic and trying to remember everything at once, why don't we retrace our memories of where we were and what we were doing and what we were learning at the time. Do you remember that first day, after we met, when I showed you the Liber Herbalis?'

'Yes. We looked at the amaranth flower.'

'Which is useful for?'

'Lessening a woman's moon flow and the pain of it.'

'What other herbs did we look up in the book that day?'

'Peppermint and passionflower,' replied Ruth eagerly before going into their therapeutic properties.

Thus, it was that our "study" over the next week became a game of recollections and their associations with medical lore and practice. Raymond was able to take part by prompting us with his memory of incidents as well. It was a new learning experience as each piece of medical knowledge gained its own associated memory hook that enabled us to remember pertinent information about the relevant medical fact or practice. Occasionally, we got side tracked remembering humorous incidents. Sharing a few laughs along the way broke the monotony of the study.

There were a few times during our revision when I sorely missed Hadar's knowledge and expertise and I'm sure Ruth did too. Not knowing if he still lived or not, I tried to imagine him as the kindly and caring man he always was, but was now looking out for and helping, Ruth and I from above. I told Ruth of my imagining and she took it on board, saying it would give her confidence in the examinations thinking that Hadar was just behind her and watching over her.

'Maybe, with a few helpful prompts whispered in our ears,' I joked.

'Enough wishful thinking,' interjected Raymond, 'What were you discussing the day we arrived in Shiraz?'

With Raymond prompting other memories and other discussions, Ruth and I continued our revision of all we had learned of medicine over the rest of the week. Raymond was helpful in other ways; organising meals, insisting on a break with a brisk walk twice a day, organising our laundry, and, once or twice, surprised us with his own knowledge of medicine with "bits and pieces" he said he picked up riding behind, or beside, Hadar, Ruth and me, while we talked.

As the day of our examinations drew closer, both Ruth and I found ourselves having restless and sleep disturbed nights. We both experienced plagues of self-doubt, repetitive questioning of ourselves, annoyance at not being able to remember the name of something or its use or purpose, and, for me at least, the fear of looking a fool in front of the examiners.

Finally, the day of our examination came. Raymond had ensured we both had clean and freshly pressed clothes to wear and ordered a breakfast large enough to feed a horde of hungry students.

'Energy and inspiration for the mind and body,' he said as he placed another boiled egg on my plate, 'In fact I am that nervous myself, I think I should have another one as well.'

This latter comment made us laugh and helped relieve some of the tension and anxiety we were all feeling that morning.

The time arrived and Ruth and I set off for the Schola Medica holding hands, both in love and affection but also in reassurance and a hopeful optimism that the day would turn out well. Raymond stayed behind at the inn having wished and hugged us both, 'Good luck' before we left.

As we walked through the grounds of the Schola to the academic residence, my feelings of anxiety grew. I could feel that Ruth's palms were moist with perspiration or were they my own that were so wet?

We rapped the lion's head knocker of the front door of the residence to have it opened by a young man who, by his dress, was clearly a student of the Schola.

'How may I help you?' said the young man looking us both over with a rather supercilious expression on his face.

'We are Master Ippolito de Medici and Mistress Ruth de Jerusalem. We are expected by the Academic Board this morning for an entrance examination,' I replied.

'Yes. So I believe,' he said, again with that supercilious air, 'If you will follow me.'

He never introduced himself but led us down another corridor to a door where he stopped and bade Ruth knock and then enter. With a "Wish me Good luck" look in her eyes, Ruth did as she was directed and disappeared behind the door.

'This way, please,' said my host, as he led me to another door further down the corridor and bade me do the same as Ruth had at the previous door.

I took a deep breath to reassure myself and did as requested.

# 36

Inside the examination room, I was greeted by professors d'Ascoli, Alfacio and Salernitano, sitting along one side of a table. Professor Alfacio bade me sit in the single chair opposite.

'This will be a long day for all of us,' began professor Alfacio, 'This morning you will be examined by the three of us, focusing primarily, but not solely, upon anatomy, diseases and conditions of the human body and pharmaceutical intervention. There will be a short break for lunch after which you will be examined by our colleagues in the next room as your colleague will be examined in here. You and your colleague must remain separate and are to have no conversation with each other until the examinations are over. Do you have any questions?'

I had none.

'So,' began professor Alfacio, 'Let us commence.'

And begin they did. After three hours of question after question, requests for further information and details, and answering the question, 'Why do you say that?' so many times, I felt absolutely wrung out and was wondering where I could find the mental energy to face a further three hours of such interrogation after a short lunch break.

I wondered how Ruth had fared and if she felt as exhausted as I did. I wanted so much to talk to her about the questions I had been asked. It was difficult knowing she was just in the next room taking her lunch while a solitary supervisor watched over her and went with her to the privy. I was not very pleased to see that my supervisor was the same supercilious-looking student who had admitted us earlier. I did not show my displeasure at his company but I ate my simple lunch in silence.

The afternoon proved to be just as taxing and exhausting as the morning, although I felt the examiners less demanding in their manner of interrogation. Perhaps it was the female presence of Trota on the panel that lessened the intimidating process of being under academic scrutiny.

Eventually, my "trial by academia" came to an end. My examiners, like those of the morning, remained totally non-committal as to how I had fared in the examination and gave no clues away in what they said, their facial gestures, or general demeanour.

'Ippolito de Medici,' began Trota somewhat thoughtfully, 'both you and your companion, Ruth of Jerusalem, have given this panel much to consider regarding your application for admission to the Schola. As all members of the panel have other duties that require their attention, we can only reconvene and meet with you and your colleague in three days' time, Friday after tierce, to give you the result of our deliberations and advise you of the success, or not, of your efforts today. Do you have any questions?'

I had none and was politely shown the door. Ruth was waiting outside in the corridor. If I felt drained and exhausted, Ruth certainly looked it.

'Come, let's hurry back to the inn where we can talk,' I said.

'Talk!' said Ruth with exasperation, 'A jug of red wine first would be a better idea. I don't think I have ever felt so mentally exhausted and drained in my entire life.'

'Agreed. On all points,' I said, which made us both laugh.

Some hours later, back at the inn, after a liberal amount of therapeutic alcohol, we were much more relaxed.

'The worst thing,' said Ruth, 'was in the afternoon. That creepy anatomy professor, Nicolo Salernitano, kept looking at my breasts again. I don't think he looked me in the eye once. Not even when he was asking me questions.'

'A shame you could not have kicked him in the balls under the table,' offered Raymond.

'I wanted to,' admitted Ruth with a sly grin.

'Well, I for one am ready for some sleep. What will be, will be and we will find out on Friday. No point in fretting about it all now,' I said as I rose from the bench of the inn and headed upstairs to our room.

Friday came around very slowly, but come it did, and found Ruth and I seeking to enter the academic residence once again. The same arrogant student opened the door and, without saying a word, guided us to yet another room within the residence we had not been in before. Seated within the room on one side of a table were professors Trota, Fugaldo and Plateario. Trota welcomed us both and bade us sit in the chairs provided opposite the panel.

'Firstly,' began Trota, 'I want to congratulate the pair of you on the excellence of your responses and demonstrated understanding of scientific and medical principles. Whilst your own medical training has been unorthodox and drawn from more than one school of thinking, it is very plain that you have had teachers of extraordinary ability and knowledge. We could not fault your understanding and knowledge of human anatomy, pharmacology of herbs and minerals and the conditions and treatment of human illness. In fact, some of the knowledge you have gained in your studies is of interest to some of our faculty members as areas of further study and investigation. It is not often that an acolyte can show a master the way.'

I could sense that Ruth, like me, was feeling much more relaxed with this evaluation.

'There are, however, some shortcomings in your knowledge base which I am sure you are aware of, as it is why you came here on your previous master's instruction. I speak, of course, of women's health and its own particular features and modes of treatment.

'The second area in which we feel further studies are required is in surgical treatments and techniques. This should not surprise or worry you as it is very much a new field of medicinal endeavour in which Professor di Fugaldo is the foremost authority in Europe.

'Ippolito de Medici and Ruth of Jerusalem, I and the faculty are happy to offer you both places at the Schola Medica. Your previous studies will be recognised and you will be granted credits of successful completion in all subjects with the exception of women's health and surgical procedures and techniques. An accelerated program of learning will be offered to you both so, by the end of next year you will be qualified and licensed by the Schola to practice medicine in Italia.'

Ruth was barely concealing what would have been squeals of joy and delight.

# 37

Ruth and I were to spend the next six months as constant companions of Professori di Fugaldo, accompanying him to tutorials, lecture halls, demonstration labs and the surgical theatres of the local hospitals. We attended introductory classes to surgical techniques, intermediate surgical approaches and advanced surgical procedures, along with other students who had achieved these and previous levels of competency. Professor di Fugaldo maintained that whilst this serendipitous approach to learning surgery was unusual and initially confusing for the two of us, he felt confident that it would all eventually click and come together in a holistic understanding to the science and skills of surgery.

A typical day for Ruth and myself might mean attending and observing the amputation of a leg at the hospital in the morning, followed by a cataract removal before lunch, while the afternoon might be spent treating a host of minor lesions and conditions from lancing boils, excising rotten teeth, suturing wounds and other treatments on patients attending the Schola's free clinic.

This arrangement of attending classes across different levels of the curriculum made it initially difficult to form friendships with other students as we were never in one group, or year level, long enough to socialise or join in study groups with them, as Professor di Fugaldo would summon Ruth and myself to join him at his next teaching or demonstration engagement, rather than allowing us to enjoy some time with our colleagues. Professor di Fugaldo had been correct in his hypothesis that his ad hoc approach to teaching the two of us surgical skills and techniques would eventually click and come together. Within three months we were assessed as competent in minor procedures and were tasked with regular independent practice at the free clinic.

'I do not want to see or smell another boil, carbuncle, abscess, rotten tooth or infected toenail ever again,' complained Ruth on our way home after a long session in the clinic.

'I spoke to Professor di Fugaldo about the next stage of our education and he told me he expected to advance us to an intermediate level of competency within a matter of weeks. We will be doing much more invasive procedures for which I am hoping Master Kan Do's needles may surprise the good professor with their effectiveness in pain management. I have to admit, I have hated watching some of those poor wretches undergoing major surgery without any pain management. That poor devil with the crushed leg, whose heart burst during the amputation last week, was very upsetting.'

'You would think that with so much Muslim and Eastern influence of ideas and knowledge, they would be making greater use of the poppy,' observed Ruth.

'Perhaps the doctoris are uncertain about just how much poppy to use. We both know "a little helps a lot, but a lot can only kill",' I said quoting Hadar.

'Even if it does "help sweeten the bitter end",' she replied, throwing another quote from Hadar back at me. The quickness of her retort made me chortle.

Raymond, by virtue of having served as a squire with the Knights of St John's Hospitallers, had found a position as an assistant in the apothecarium of the Schola and as such, his knowledge of herbs and their therapeutic usage, was rapidly expanding. His smiling and jovial presence at the Schola was a pleasant diversion to the seriousness of the studies Ruth and I were undertaking and the three of us often met for lunch.

True to his word, Professor di Fugaldo advanced Ruth and I to more complicated and life-threatening surgery, mostly amputations, bone setting, excisions of deep lesions and tumours, trepanning of head injuries, cataract couching and removal and general surgical repair and correction. Both Ruth and I found this work challenging and exciting at the same time. It also gave us the opportunity to work with each other again. Ruth and I found we still had the capacity to think ahead and anticipate each other during operations, working as if we were one body with one mind and four hands. Professor di Fugaldo noticed how our work complimented each other and stated it was very unusual.

'You will learn that many surgeons can be prima donnas in the operating suite and do not like working with other surgeons who might diminish their own performance. When I watch the both of you, I see two surgeons who complement and enhance each other's work,' he commented to us one evening.

He was even more impressed with Master Kan Do's needles. Before every amputation, Ruth or I would place a series of needles along the meridians that would be affected most by the amputation. The needles did not eliminate the pain of amputation but lessened it and Ruth and I did not lose a single patient to shock as was common with many major amputations.

'I wish we could access some of those astringent herbs and tubers we have seen in other places here in Salerno,' said Ruth wishfully after one of her patients died of blood loss post operatively.

'Perhaps we should ask Raymond about this. His knowledge of herbs has become quite extensive and there may be some local herb that has similar effects in reducing blood loss,' I ofered.

Raymond did not let us down.

'Rosa Canina is what you need,' said a confident sounding Raymond, 'The common "Dog Rose". There is a bed of them in the gardens of the Schola. You know those pretty, pink, little flowers that grow near the fountain. I can make a tincture that can be taken internally, as well as applied externally. I'm surprised your professor has not thought of using it operatively or post-operatively.'

'More likely, no one else suggested it to him. These professors are very protective of their knowledge particularly around each other. You might call it a type of professional rivalry.'

'It is kind of funny,' commented Raymond, 'They are trying to save lives and help people, but their jealousies and rivalries undermine each other and their patient's wellbeing. I'll bet if you mention the Rosa Canina treatment to your Professor di Fugaldo he will try and take all the credit for it.'

I did raise the Rosa Canina with Professor di Fugaldo.

Raymond was correct.

# 38

Ruth and I finished our surgical training and education with an academic accolade from the faculty for excellence in teamwork during surgery. I suspect this was Professor di Fugaldo's way of thanking me, or paying back, the debt he owed me for the breakthrough in post-operative bleeding that the Dog Rose had provided to him and other members of the surgical profession in southern Italy. The Schola Medica Salernitania's reputation had been extended yet again.

Raymond was beside himself with satisfaction that it was, in reality, thanks to him, that this surgical breakthrough in post-operative complications had occurred. He was also very drunk, thanks to Ruth and me showing him our thanks as the real agent of our academic accolade.

'You know … I shink I like thish aposhecary bishnish,' he slurred and dribbled all over the place, 'Do you shink … we could all work together shumday?'

It was not a bad idea and one I stowed away for later when Raymond was sober. Ruth and I would have to help him up the stairs later that evening.

Ruth was particularly excited about moving onto women's health especially as it was with Professor Trota. As head of the Schola Medica, Trota had been quietly observing our progress under Professor di Fugaldo and had taken an interest in our progress, particularly Ruth's, with whom she felt an obvious regard, given what the professor had learned of our past during our initial interview. I could not help but feel there was something maternal in the way

Trota regarded Ruth and, given what I knew of Ruth's past life in the "Rocking Horse" brothel, I was glad that a mother figure was taking an interest in her well-being.

Trota had some controversial ideas on women's health that rocked a few of the established patriarchal views of women held by her colleagues and, more significantly, the Holy Latin church. Her most controversial opinion was that women should be able to choose when to become pregnant and her early lectures were on contraception. She naturally spoke of the withdrawal method prior to male ejaculation but stressed that men could not always be trusted, or able, in the middle of pathological thrusting to suddenly withdraw and deposit their semen on the sheets. Trota also displayed, for our education, a range of contraceptive devices from condoms, made of sheep's intestines, sewn silken penile envelopes, to douche devices for flushing unwanted semen from what the professor referred to as 'the holy font of procreation'.

One of Trota's biggest battles was against, not just her colleagues, but also the church, yet again. Trota maintained that the use of small doses of poppy during the birthing process, not only eased the pain of childbirth, but enabled a much more relaxed and less complicated event for mother and child. The Holy Latin church would have none of this, as women were meant to bring forth children in pain and suffering, according to Genesis and the Bible as a consequence of Eve's transgression in the Garden of Eden.

During the early days of our schooling in obstetrics, we were witness to numerous normal and sometimes complicated births. We both learned how to turn an infant in the womb, so it was facing the right way, how to remove the umbilical cord from around an infant's neck so it was not strangled at birth, how to massage the womb to ensure the complete expulsion of the placenta, clearing breathing passages on a newborn – the list went on.

I had to admit, the birth of a new human being was one of the most moving experiences one could go through. I never had completely dry eyes when observing the arrival of a new little person into this world.

It was when Ruth and I attended our first caesarian section, under Trota's orchestration, that I realised the sense in Ruth and I undertaking surgical studies prior to women's health studies. Trota conducted the operation with Ruth and me assisting. The exhausted mother-to-be had been in labour for almost 48 hours but was resting comfortably between contractions in a low dose poppy induced stupor. Too high a dose of the poppy could affect the newborn's health.

'Utter poppycock,' was Trota's view of this church directive.

Being the only male in the delivery suite, I was given the onerous task of keeping both sides of the lower abdominal muscles separated far enough apart for Trota and Ruth to open the womb. My arms were shaking from the effort of keeping the two sides apart – the abdominal muscles were very strong and wanted to return to their natural position and shape. Finally, with a great sucking sound, Trota lifted the tiny blue form from the womb and held it upside down to initiate the respiratory reflex. There was no intake of air and no wail of shock or surprise. Trota gently slapped the little boy's bottom in the hope of initiating breathing. Still no response.

The infant was turning a darker blue when Ruth grabbed the little boy and placed her mouth over its mouth and nose and then drew a great breath in drawing the contents of the young lungs into her mouth. She turned and at once spat a mouthful of womb fluids out onto the floor. The child coughed and made some distressed choking and gurgling sounds. Ruth repeated the procedure to which the baby began to give a strong and hearty wail of protest.

Later, after the new mother had been sewn back up and the newborn was feeding contentedly at its mother's breast, Trota asked Ruth where she had learned the technique to clear the infant's lungs and airways.

Ruth laughed and then with a grin replied, 'From a village witch and a baby goat.'

Ruth noted the surprise on mine and Trota's faces and then continued, 'It was in Africa. I was with Mosi and N'sibi attending a nanny goat giving birth. The kid was not breathing and Mosi simply picked it up and sucked the muck from its lungs like I just did.'

# 39

Our studies in women's health issues continued apace: basic gynaecology, obstetrics, breast management, skin disease and other conditions pertinent to women. Trota had written a manual entitled Passionibus Mulierum Curandorum (The Diseases of Women). The text was 63 chapters long and Trota expected we knew it from front to back and back to front again. Surprisingly, the text also supplied general medical advice on treating snake bites, curing bad breath, lightening freckles, general facial cosmetics and the manufacture of different coloured hair dyes. The latter were not of much interest to me but Ruth found much of it intriguing and, in later years, I would notice Ruth putting much of this knowledge to use upon her own person.

We completed our studies and another round of examinations ahead of time, with Ruth being awarded an accolade, not just for her newborn resuscitation techniques but also for some simple tricks with Kan Do's needles, which she quietly shared with Trota. We still had the year of our surgical internship in front of us. It was the Schola Medica's policy that all graduates spend a year working in the faculty hospital with professorial supervision before being fully licensed and accredited to practice medicine in Italy.

'You know,' said Ruth, 'One day I hope you and I can open a hospital for the poor.'

'I like that idea,' I replied. In fact, I liked it a lot.

So it was that Ruth and I began the practice of medicine and saw the realisation of our own personal dreams. It was bittersweet for both of us as there was no Hadar to witness our achievement and share in our satisfaction.

It was also very timely. War was coming to Salerno.

The war arrived suddenly and somewhat unexpectedly. One day, Salerno was at peace with the world, the next day, the city was surrounded by soldiery and siege engines and the harbour was blockaded by ships and galleys all beholding and belonging to the Holy Roman Emperor Henry VI. Henry wanted the kingdom of Sicily, which at that time included southern Italy. The town of Salerno was ruled by powerful Norman families.

The emperor had been besieging Naples to the north unsuccessfully and suddenly changed tactics and moved his forces with remarkable rapidity to try and take Salerno instead. The lack of any warning meant Salerno was not adequately provisioned as there hadn't been time to bring in extra food from the outlying farms and villages. Water would not be a problem as the town was served with plenty of freshwater wells.

The town had a garrison of 60 Norman soldiers and the council and elders organised a militia as best they could with some old soldiers and mercenaries coming out of retirement to take charge in field positions. We were fortunate in that the walls of Salerno had been heightened and reinforced within the last 50 years by the previous overlords, the Lombards. Raymond was all for joining the volunteers on the walls but Ruth and I dissuaded him, saying he would be needed in the hospital when the fighting began and the wounded started arriving at our doors.

The Imperial forces were only two days in setting up the bulk of their siege operations. Overnight, a tent city had sprung up, out of range from the city walls, as the weaponry of war: mangonels, trebuchets, battering rams and siege towers were assembled and positioned. On the morning of the third day, three riders from the Imperial camp approached the city walls of Salerno. One of the riders with a booming voice bellowed out the obligatory demand or option of surrender or face a siege and a sack. The defenders on the walls knew to expect the demand as part of accepted military protocol and had their answer ready. A hail of rubbish, refuse, rocks and rubble rained down on the embassy as they turned their horses and swiftly galloped away.

Retaliation from the Imperial forces was swift. Barely had the riders arrived back at their own lines, then the first bombardment from the siege engines began. Great counterweights were released flinging stone laden slings, launching their rounded rubble high into the air and toward the city walls. The emperor's artillery crews would naturally take a while finding their range as their first enfilade saw most of their stones fall short of the walls. Several of the stones overshot the wall and landed in the city.

Our work in the hospital began quickly as a result of the overshoots. The first through the hospital entrance was a father carrying his unconscious son. The boy was bleeding profusely from a head wound and a probable skull fracture.

'Raymond,' I called across the triage room, 'we are going to need as much of your Dog Rose brew as you can give us.'

'Already taken care of,' replied Raymond, indicating a row of flasks on a cupboard shelf, 'I started brewing it up when the tents went up outside the walls.'

Our team in the triage/operating suite consisted of six qualified surgeons: Trota, Ruth and me, Professors di Fugaldo, Salernitani and Alfasco. All were aided and supported by a team of students acting as porters, restrainers, nurses, messengers, cleaners or whatever else was required of them.

I liberally soaked the young boy's head in the Dog Rose lotion which reduced the bleeding and was able to palpate his skull where I suspected a fracture to be. There was one and it was, mercifully, small. I placed a small wick under the scalp to drain any excess fluid leaking from the brain and bound his head up, before giving him back to his father with strict instructions of resting in bed and to return to the clinic in a week.

Others had been making their way into the hospital while I was working on the boy. I looked over to where Ruth was working and saw she was extracting a large and long wooden splinter from the leg of a young woman. The splinter had obviously penetrated a major vessel and blood was pumping everywhere from the hole in her thigh. Raymond did not wait to be told and sloshed his brew into the wound, giving Ruth the chance to clamp and close the artery before closing the leg up.

I smiled encouragement at her and then laughed to myself. Her hair was dripping with blood, bright splashes were splattered across her face and her hands were drenched and yet she still looked beautiful.

# 40

Most of the first patients into the hospital were townsfolk who had been hit by falling timbers or masonry. Anyone hit by any of the stones the emperor was sending over the wall, would not be coming in. Their remains would be splattered across whatever place they had been in when the stone struck.

We could hear the occasional crashes of stones in the city as they demolished buildings, plazas, churches, statues and people. Each crash would bring more of the injured to the hospital, which we treated as effectively as we could before sending most of them back home. There simply were not enough beds to accommodate all the wounded civilians. I wondered how chaotic it would get when the artillery found their range and the poor soldiers and militia on the walls got their first poundings.

I did not have to wait long. I heard the poor wretch before he was placed before me on a stretcher. The lower half of his leg, shin and calf were pulverised to a bloody mess of flesh, blood and bone. It was going to have to come off.

'Raymond, I need poppy juice. Lots of it,' I called.

Within a moment, he was beside me holding the vial of the precious fluid and was supporting the poor victim's head as he gently poured the juice into his mouth.

'You will be alright, my friend,' he said in a most reassuring and caring manner to the young man who was about to lose his leg.

'Raymond. Would you get me those two leather straps on the hook by the door please?'

By the time he got back with the straps, our young soldier was starting to succumb to the numbing effects of the poppy.

'Raymond, get Bruno over here to help. All the other students are busy assisting the professors. You both will have to help me. In a moment I am going to cut through the flesh of his lower thigh about an inch above the knee. I will cut to the bone but leave enough skin and flesh at the back to form a padded flap for the stump.'

Bruno joined us at the table.

'How can I help?' he asked.

'Raymond, take hold of his legs and keep them still and steady. Bruno, I want you to use your weight to restrain his body as much as possible.'

I saw the fear in the young man's eyes and his lips moving in silent prayer. Once he had finished, I slipped a leather pad between his teeth. Using a scalpel, I slit the side of his breeches and tied a tourniquet as tight as I could around his upper thigh.

Bruno and Raymond took up their positions and I took up the narrow scythe- shaped blade deftly, quickly drawing it in a circular motion around the circumference of the thigh and deep into the flesh until I felt it touch bone. The young man bucked and screamed and then mercifully passed out.

Once the flesh was freed from the bone, I directed Raymond to place the two leather straps into the flesh on either side of it and pull the flesh back up the leg as far as he could. This exposed about an inch and a half of proud bone, to which I took the bone saw and, in less than six cuts had sawn through it, dropping it on the floor with all the other bloodied bodily detritus. Raymond released the straps and the large fleshy pad of muscle slid back down the bone giving it a good layer of padded protection. It also bled profusely.

'Brazier,' I called and within a moment, a young student wearing thick gloves, came up with a brazier full of red-hot coals and pokers of various shapes and sizes. I grabbed one and plunged its redly glowing end into the bleeding vessels of the severed leg. The young man bucked again, even though he was still unconscious. The smoke and the smell of burning flesh permeated the room. I loathe the smell and was trying not to gag on it but I managed to cauterise all the bleeds and he was ready to be sewn up.

Using the flap of skin and the layer of flesh from beneath it, I folded it back over the exposed raw flesh of the thigh and sutured them both together, placing drainage wicks every couple of inches. I then poured spirits of wine over the wound. The young man was still unconscious, very pale, breathing shallowly but still alive. He was moved to a recovery room where other medical students would monitor his recovery and try to manage the pain he would have to go through.

The whole procedure from first cut to last wick had been less than 10 minutes. Professor di Fugaldo would have told me I needed to be quicker as the shock of prolonged surgery of this nature often kills before blood loss or infection.

'You know,' said Raymond, holding the leather straps and looking rather pale, 'some of these straps attached to the sides of the operating tables would eliminate the need to hold patients down. You could simply strap them to the table.'

It was a promising idea and I told him so.

More soldiers were brought in from the walls, many of whom bore sword and weapons wounds. Most were from crossbow bolts, but a few were from sword wounds indicating that the emperor's forces had succeeded in mounting or breaching the walls and fighting was being pursued along the battlements of the city.

I began extracting a crossbow bolt from the neck of another soldier who was miraculously still alive. The bolt, having missed all the large vessels in the neck and his spinal column, came away easily and there was a minimal amount of blood requiring only a suture or two to close the wound. As soon as I had finished, he sat up, swung his legs off the table, thanked me and then hurried back out the door to the fighting. I admired his courage and determination.

# 41

I had been on my feet performing operations and treatments for over six hours when the stone came crashing through the ceiling of the operating suite with devastating effect. Fully one half of the room was rubble, dust, dead and broken bodies. Ruth, Raymond and I and the professors, were lucky the stone had crashed into the triage area of the room and not the operating area.

'You, you, you and you,' ordered Professor di Fugaldo, indicating four students 'Get the living out of that mess. The rest of us must continue our work. Everyone else back to your patients.'

'Spoken like the true healer he is,' said Trota with admiration as she passed by me.

I was exhausted and I could see that Ruth was pale with fatigue as well but still the wounded kept coming, albeit through the back door, as the front had been demolished and was just a pile of rubble now.

Raymond brought me a skin of water and I drank thirstily before handing it back. I was also starving but there was no time for a meal break. There was no point in complaining as we were all in the same boat, so I got on with my work like everyone else in the hospital.

Later in the day, I noticed the crashing sounds of bombardment had faded away. Raymond noticed it as well.

'Perhaps they have run out of stones,' he said hopefully.

Shortly after, the sounds of hand-to-hand fighting in the streets carried to us in the hospital. The bombardment of the walls had ceased because they had been breached and the emperor's soldiers were in the city.

The sack of Salerno had begun.

We kept operating. I was secretly hoping the enemy would view the hospital as some sort of asylum of safety for all and that the emperor's troops would leave us alone. It was not to be. Battle brings a raging blood lust in some men whilst others have their blood up just trying to survive, when everything boils down to kill or be killed. Such was the nature of the angry men, with their swords drawn, who came bursting into the operating room cutting down anyone who stood in their way.

One of them, presumably their squad leader, yelled at us in a guttural language that none of us recognised or understood.

Professor di Fugaldo looked up from the table he was operating at, turned to the squad leader and said indignantly, 'How dare you come in here like this. This is a hospital. Get out of here.'

They were his last words. The squad leader ran the professor through with his sword. This was too much for Raymond and he, at once, launched himself at the leader, striking him bare-handed under the chin and snapping his head back with such force, he broke the man's neck causing him to slump dead, briefly jerking to the floor.

Raymond turned to face the next oncomer and lashed out with a kick to the side of his knee that dropped him to the ground. By this time, I was beside Raymond and together we faced six armed and dangerous men. I was sizing one of them up for a head kick when a scalpel appeared in his eye socket, courtesy of Ruth.

'That was my only knife,' she called out.

I turned and faced another soldier and, like Raymond, I brought him down with a kick to the side of his knee and finished him off with a heel to the throat. Raymond had managed to disable another with a wicked two finger jab to the eyes which had left one eye hanging out of its socket.

Only three of the enemy remained and they were looking like they were having second thoughts about attacking us when a commanding voice came over the ruckus, 'Halten, schwein. Halten.'

The three soldiers turned and faced a tall and ornately, heavily armoured and helmeted officer. The officer snapped further orders at the soldiers in their guttural language. The soldiers turned and left the building without any comment. Raymond and I stood and looked at each other, then over at Ruth to check she was unharmed, which she was. The other professors, students and wounded stood or lay around wondering what was to happen next.

'That was a splendid display of fighting skills by you two young men. I have never seen the like of it before,' he paused, 'Although I have to admit I think I have seen one of you before.'

His Latin was perfect, with no trace of the guttural German he had been speaking a moment before. There was something familiar about the officer; the way he stood laconically leaning on his sword, a hand lazily scratching his ear and the voice and manner of speaking was familiar, but I could not recognise it in those brief moments, despite it gnawing at my memory.

The officer turned to all present and said, 'Please, good doctors continue with your work. No further harm shall come to any of you, providing, that is, you agree to treat my own wounded men, as well as your own.'

It was Trota as the senior professor who spoke up.

'We are physicians and surgeons who have taken the serious Hippocratic oath to preserve life at all costs. It is a sacred oath to us. We cannot refuse any needing treatment or help. Bring your wounded but also command those soldiers you trust, to keep the peace and maintain good order in here. This is a hospital, in case you had not noticed.'

'Well said, gracious lady,' replied the officer, 'I will ensure the right men are stationed here and you and your colleagues can continue your work for whom ever should need it. Is that agreeable to you and your colleagues?'

Trota simply bowed her head in affirmation, turned back to her table and proceeded to continue staunching the blood flowing from an open wound in a young man's side.

'You,' he said pointing at me, 'I would speak to outside.'

'And you sir, I would willingly oblige if I could see your face,' I replied, overcoming my surprise at being singled out by this powerful officer.

'You were never backward in coming forward young de Medici. It is what I liked and remember most about you,' said the officer as he pulled the helm from his head to reveal his face.

'Rudolphus!' I blurted with surprise and stunned recognition.

# 42

'Frei Herr Rudolphus actually,' corrected Rudolphus, 'The emperor made me a free lord in appreciation of certain services I rendered to the crown, if you know what I mean.' He tipped the side of his nose in a conspiratorial fashion.

I did indeed know what he meant. Years ago, Rudolphus and I had found an ancient document that brought into question the integrity of the letters of St Paul and the Holy Gospels. Rudolphus had been in the employ of my father and was supposedly going to deliver the document to him for a decision on what to do with such a damning narrative.

'There is a lot I need to tell you, young de Medici but right now is not the time. I have men who need to be curbed and brought under control. I don't want them destroying the city completely. I will return,' and with that he turned on his heels and went to join his men.

I turned back to get on with what had been an interrupted surgery, only to find that my patient had died in the interim. He was portered away and, before a new injured man could be brought before me, Raymond approached me.

'How in the hell do you come to be on a first name basis with one of the emperor's high commanders?'

'It is a shocking story, Raymond, one I promise to tell both you and Ruth, but not right now.'

The garrison of Salerno wisely chose to surrender soon after this episode. They were hopelessly outnumbered and were now being overrun. The decision induced the emperor's clemency upon Salerno and he called off the sack, much to the disappointment of his troops who were looking forward to the standard three days of rape and pillage.

We continued operating on through the afternoon and well into the evening, before I closed up a wound on the last of the injured waiting to be seen. Only a handful of Imperial soldiers were brought to us, mostly with minor wounds. The only difficulty I encountered was in understanding each other's language. I spoke Italian, Greek, Latin, Hebrew, Arabic, some Persian and some northern Hindi but no German.

Fortunately, Rudolphus returned and acted as an interpreter for all of us, as well as reassuring and settling his men, thanking our doctors and staff, and assisting where he could. It was hard to think of him as an enemy in this light. It was even harder to think that way, after he had a dozen flagons of good red wine brought in and distributed to all present who had worked so hard that day.

'There is little point in our catching up with each other tonight, Ippolito. I can see that you and all your colleagues are just about dead on your feet from fatigue. I shall come to the hospital tomorrow around noon, after the emperor's morning council. Will you be here?'

'I shall,' I replied. There was much I was keen to know.

As it turned out there was much more. So much, I wished he had never told me.

Rudolphus arrived as he said he would at midday. I grabbed a wedge of cheese and flat bread from the kitchen, along with a skin of well-watered wine and we retired to a bench in the gardens of the Schola. There were only distant and sporadic sounds of unrest and disturbance coming from within the city.

'So, what news of my father and my family?' I asked cheerfully, expecting it all to be good.

Rudolphus looked clearly uncomfortable with what he was about to say.

'Firstly, as far as I know, Cherubino, your youngest brother, is away at sea learning to captain one of your father's trading vessels. The last I heard, he is very much a reliable first mate and will soon have his first command.'

This pleased me greatly as Cherubino had always loved ships and the sea. As a child he could name every type of ship and its country of origin that was moored to the great mole of the Acre harbour, where we lived next door to our father's warehouses and emporia.

'I am glad for Cherubino. The sea is in his blood, like the white shock of hair on his forehead,' I said, 'What of Gaetano?'

'I am sorry Ippolito, but he is dead,' came Rudolphus' quiet reply.

'How? Why?' I said, shocked and stunned by the news.

'You know how he and his friends were always feuding with the Genoese and the Venetian gangs.'

'Yes,'

'Well, the Genoese killed one of his friends and lacerated Gaetano's right arm and hand so badly, he would never carry a weapon in that hand again. Once he was recovered, he swore he would get revenge on all the Genoese. As it happened, Gaetano and two of his friends were caught in the act of urinating and defecating in the water cisterns of the Genoese quarter. An automatic death sentence lay over the three of them for attempting to bring illness to the Genoese quarter of the city. As they were caught red handed, all three were "broken on the wheel" and their broken bones and bodies hoisted up on poles for the birds and climbing animals to finish off.'

I shivered with horror at this news. To be broken on the wheel was one of most painful ways to die and being left on the wheel high above the town to rot and be eaten by carrion birds and animals, one of the most degrading.

'The bodies were visible from your father's house and a constant reminder to Bartolo of his grief and pain. It was his undoing in many ways. Your father became vaguer and forgetful and became heavily dependent on the bottle to help him forget his pain. Unfortunately, it too, killed him. He was well into his cups and fell down the stairs one night and broke his neck. Letters were sent to Jerusalem to tell you of all this, but you must have left for Hind by then and they obviously never reached you.'

The shock of learning that my brother and my father were dead brought a welling of tears to my eyes. I wiped them away.

'What of Baldo, my eldest brother?' I asked.

'He is still alive and very much a problem.'

# 43

Despite feeling overwhelmed with grief for my father and my brother, Gaetano, I needed to know what my brother Baldo was up to. He had always been a bully at home when I was growing up, picking on me as the smallest and youngest of the family. He was a sly, lying, low and cunning fox.

'As your father became more morose and isolating himself from the world in his sorrow, Baldo stepped up and took control of the shipping and trade business. Upon your father's death, he sold off most of the extraordinary valuable stock, the golden peacocks, the water clocks, all the ivory statuettes, the gems and the like to different members of the nobility and aristocracy. He has since gone on to sell off all the stock of perishables and less valuable items. Ippolito, your father's warehouses and emporia are now empty and I am sorry to tell you that your family home has been put up for sale, although with all the uncertainty of the war at the moment, I doubt any one has made an offer.

'Needless to say, Baldo has pocketed an awful lot of money. Enough to make him a very rich man in this world as your father had succeeded in being. Baldo has also disappeared. Before I left Acre, he had not been seen in many months. I am sorry to say this Ippolito, but I fear he has taken what would have been your share, and Cherubino's, of the inheritance from your father with him, along with everything else.'

My grief turned to bitter anger against my eldest brother in an instant.

'Ruth and I had hoped we might build and set up a hospital for the poor one day with that money,' I said with rising distress in my voice.

It was not the loss of the money that angered me, it was the destruction of a dream I had shared with Ruth that was really making my blood boil. Rudolphus gave me time to calm down and get my feelings under control. He had always known when to give me time and now was one of the moments where, torn between grief and anger, I could have exploded in a fit of blind fury.

Eventually, I calmed down by getting my breathing under control and using some of the relaxation techniques I had learned from the monks of the Buddha's Smile.

'So, tell me,' I finally said, 'How is it that you come to be a Free Lord of the Holy Roman Emperor Henry VI?'

'When I first arrived back in Acre your father and brother were still alive. Bartolo did not want the letter from Nero's imperial secretary going to the Pope as he said it would only be destroyed under the disguise of heresy. Instead, he bade me to cross the Alps and offer it to the emperor, which I did. The emperor was interested but not in monetary terms. He was prepared to offer a title for it. Of course, this meant my return to Acre to consult with Bartolo and, many months later, I arrived to find all that I have just related to you had passed and I was now the sole possessor of the letter.

'I decided to return to Germany and accept the emperor's offer of a title and land. Thus, my title, "Frei Herr", Free Lord. The emperor has the letter and tells me he has plans for its revelation should his current campaign in Italy fail. He has yet to conquer

Sicily and I do not think the Norman rulers there will be quite the pushover Salerno has been.'

'So, instead of being the third son destined for a career in the church, you are now a landed lord and confidant of The Holy Roman Emperor?' I commented with some surprise.

'And I owe it to your father and you. You were the one who found the letter hidden in the codex after all.'

'I had forgotten about that. So much has happened since we parted ways,' I replied.

'I can see that. You are no longer the stripling youth I took on a relic hunt. You are quite the man and quite the warrior. Where did you learn to fight in the manner I saw you doing in the hospital?'

'Monks, but not Christian ones,' I answered enigmatically.

'Ippolito. I know you may think of me as bit of a scoundrel and a rogue, but I do have a sense of honour. If there is anything I can do to help you, either here and now in Salerno, or in tracking down your brother Baldo, I am willing to help. I owe it to your father's memory and all he did for me.'

I was taken aback by the genuine nature of this offer and thanked Rudolphus for it.

'I will need to discuss all of this with my friends and colleagues before I make any decision. How long do you expect to be here in Salerno?'

'Just between you and me, the emperor has a bad case of haemorrhoids at the moment and cannot sit upon a horse. We will be here at least another week while his doctors reduce the swellings.'

'I will talk with my friends tonight. If you come back tomorrow, I will give you an answer,' I said before smiling and adding, 'And thank you again Mein Frei Herr.'

That night, over dinner in our room, despite being desperately tired from all day surgery, I outlined everything Rudolphus had told me. Raymond and Ruth were sympathetic and upset for me over my dual bereavement, but also angered by Baldo's duplicity and theft.

'I don't care about the money,' I said, 'Ruth is all I will ever need but we have both shared a dream of opening a hospital for the poor and my inheritance would have been a good start to such a project. It is the loss of a dream that is making me so upset.'

'Well, the answer is simple,' said Raymond, 'We track this brother of yours down and get the money back. By fair means or foul.'

He said the last with a smile upon his face.

# 44

Rudolphus joined the three of us the next evening, after we had spent yet another day of tending the wounded, removing the dead, changing dressings and reviewing treatments.

'My family originally came from Pisa, when Baldo was in his early teens and before I was born. Do you suppose he might have gone there?' I asked the others.

'It is a possibility. It is the place he probably thinks of as home, the same way you see Acre as your original home,' replied Rudolphus, 'Wherever he has gone, he would have had one big problem, though.'

'What kind of problem would that be?' piped in Ruth.

'Transporting the large amount of money he has stolen. There is only one way he could have safely transferred his wealth from Outremer to Europe. The Templars. They have a banking network that covers the Mediterranean, most of Europe and what is left of Outremer. If Baldo transferred the money via the Templars, then there is a chance we may be able to find out where he has gone.

'There are senior Templars at the emperor's court and two of them are here in Salerno. I am sure that one of them may have some knowledge on this matter. The problem will be getting them to divulge what is considered private and confidential client information. Give me a couple of days to work on this and I will get back to you.'

Rudolphus was good to his word and, two days later, arrived at the hospital in the early evening. Raymond and I were in the infirmary, Ruth was having a well-earned rest.

'He is in Florence,' he said before any one of us could ask.

181

'How did you find out?' asked Raymond.

'Let us say, "I called in an old favour",' he replied with a wry smile, 'But that is not all. My source informed me that Baldo is also moving in some very unsavoury circles with known Florentine criminals and thugs. He and his cronies are suspected of several murders in the city, kidnapping and holding people to ransom and extorting money on the threat of menace. Just another upstanding Florentine.'

'After all his bullying, I always thought he was a low life, but he was my father's first son and he could do no wrong in his eyes,' I said with a degree of bitterness.

'What I am saying, Ippolito, is that you will not simply be able to walk up to your brother and demand your share of the inheritance, let alone Cherubino's portion. I do not think that you and your colleague, Raymond, even with your amazing fighting skills, would be enough to take on Baldo and his gang of thugs.'

Rudolphus was unaware of Ruth's deadly talents at this stage.

'As I told you the other day, I am indebted to your father and yourself. It is on this account that I wish to help you in this matter. I am, after all, a free lord and I am not bound to stay at the emperor's pleasure. If you decide to pursue your brother, I offer you my services in the quest. I admit I never trusted the little shit, anyway. I'm sure it was he who stole a ruby handled blade from my kit many years ago, but I could not say so to your father.'

'So that was where it came from,' I said, 'He did indeed steal it. He said he had taken it off a Venetian in a fight.'

'That settles it then. If he still has it, I might find a dark little hole of his to stick it in!' Rudolphus chuckled to himself over this.

'I'd like to see that,' said Raymond, 'I'm beginning to dislike this brother of yours more and more, Ippolito.'

'You did not have to grow up with him,' I replied, then continued, 'Rudolphus, I am happy that you wish to help us in this matter. My heartfelt thanks to you for it.'

'We cannot do much sitting here in Salerno,' said Rudolphus, 'The best thing will be to make for Florence as soon, and as fast, as possible.'

'How do you propose we do that?' asked Ruth walking into the room.

'We can easily slip away when the emperor moves his army on to take Sicily in the next few days. We four will not be a match for Baldo's gang of thugs, so I will bring an additional six of my most trusted men with me to make a more even match of things. You will need to be ready to leave at short notice. I will bring spare horses for the three of you. Just be packed and ready to go when my men and I arrive.'

That seemed to settle the matter for the time being and Rudolphus returned to the emperor's camp.

'We need to talk with Trota and tell her of our plans and the reasons for them,' said Ruth, 'It is not a good time for it as I am afraid, she is greatly mourning the death of her friend and colleague, Professor di Fugaldo. I heard from one of the students that she cancelled one of her classes this morning. The student said she had tears in her eyes when she told them.'

Despite her grief, Trota was very understanding of our predicament, applauded our dream of a hospital for the poor in Jerusalem and stated she would very much miss two talented young doctors in her Schola. She even thanked Raymond for his contributions. She reassured us we would be able to practice medicine anywhere in the Mediterranean with the certificates of graduation in medicine she issued us with.

Four days later, all was chaos around the wreckage of Salerno as the emperor's men broke camp, dismantled siege engines, loaded horses, donkeys and carts, formed up into marching ranks and prepared to head south on the next leg of the emperor's campaign into Italy and Sicily. While all this was going on around the city, six soldiers and an officer rode into the courtyard of the Schola leading three spare horses.

# 45

The three of us had been ready for Rudolphus' arrival as soon as we noticed all the sudden activity going on in and around the city. We had already said goodbye to all of those we had come to like and care for in the year and a half we had been in Salerno. Trota gave each of us a hug farewell and wished us the best for the future and for our future hospital.

I helped Ruth up into the saddle of her horse, a dappled palfrey mare.

'I selected the mare just for you,' said Rudolphus, 'She is gentle and tractable but can run like the wind if needed.'

Raymond and I mounted our steeds to find them spirited but obedient to the bit. At least my horse showed no inclination to bite me as so many other beasts I had ridden tried to do. Raymond had scored that "lucky horse".

Once we were mounted, Rudolphus turned to us all and said, 'Men, allow me to introduce Mistress Ruth of Jerusalem, Master Ippolito of Acre and Master Raymond of Toulouse. Do not under-estimate them because of their age and sex. They are warriors all, and physicians. So, let us have some manners and respect on this mission.'

He then turned to the three of us and introduced his men, 'This ugly sod is Gunter,' said Rudolphus immediately forgetting his manners and respect, 'He is my sergeant and master swordsman.'

A large man, with one of the most pocked faces I have ever seen, nodded his head and touched his brow to each of us. Ugly or not, I liked his face. It was honest.

'Next to him with the crossbow across his back is Aldo and, by his side, is fellow marksman with the crossbow, Rico.'

Rico rested his crossbow across his lap. Both nodded their acknowledgement.

'They are both Genoese mercenaries who happen to like my company,' he laughed and then continued, 'Behind them, the tall fellow with the axe at his waist is Bjorn, followed behind by two other swordsmen, Wilhelm and Hermann.'

Each of the soldiers nodded their heads in turn, when introduced.

Rudolphus gave the command to head off and we turned to the entrance of the Schola at a slow walking gait.

'No faster than this until we are well clear of the area,' said Rudolphus.

And so, we ambled our way through the departing army as if we had nothing to hide and our six companions from the emperor's ranks were simply going about their normal business.

An hour later, Rudolphus suggested we could pick up the pace and we moved across the countryside at a comfortable canter. Our armed party at 10 in number was big enough to deter any villains considering an ambush and, aside from one or two officious individuals at some town gates and entrances, our journey was uneventful. It gave us the ease to get to know our new colleagues and them us.

I was curious as to why two Italians, the Genoese crossbowmen, Aldo and Rico were riding with the emperor's largely Germanic army when it was invading Italy.

'The emperor wars with the pope, not with Italy, nor with Genoa,' replied Rico, 'There are plenty of Genoese mercenaries in armies all over Europe. Our fame with the crossbow puts us in high demand and pays us well. Rudolphus is offering to pay us more, so we are now selling our skills to him. Business is business after all,' he smiled as he said this as though it was the most natural thing in the world.

Wilhelm and Gunter had a similar mercantile outlook when it came to selling their sword arms to the highest bidder.

'It is the way of this world, particularly here in Italy where we have so many city states all competing and warring with each other. Money, power and greed are powerful motivators amongst the magnates and let's not forget, the spiritual purity of the papacy,' said Gunter which made Wilhelm chortle in wry amusement and agreement.

It seemed loyalty was not a highly prized commodity in Italy at this time.

Gunter, on the other hand, was loyal, but only to Rudolphus. Neither Gunter or Rudolphus would give away any of the details of why this should be so, but the fiercely pock-faced veteran was not only Rudolphus' second in command when on campaign but also Rudolphus' castellan, or as Gunter called it, "Rudolphus' Burgmann" and was in charge of running Rudolphus' castle and surrounding lands when not campaigning.

He always rode beside Rudolphus, or just behind him, and one eye was always watching out for his benefactor. Rico had a theory that Rudolphus had somehow rescued Gunter from the gallows and that Gunter had pledged himself to Rudolphus as his lord, in appreciation of having his life saved.

The "tall fellow with the axe", Bjorn, was perhaps the most enigmatic of the party. For most of the journey, he was taciturnly silent as though talking to any of us was beneath his dignity. It was Ruth who broke his ice.

Bjorn was practicing his axe throwing against some trees around one of our campsites one morning and was just about to retrieve his axe from the trunk of a tree when a knife unexpectedly embedded itself in the base of the handle of the axe, only inches from Bjorn's outstretched hand. It startled him to an extent that he stumbled back a step in surprise, tripped and wound up on his backside. Looking momentarily indignant, he cast his eyes about until they fell on Ruth standing further away from the tree than he had been. She was looking straight at him with a mischievous smile on her face and nonchalantly tossing one of her knives up and down in the air. Slowly, a smile broke the face of the stony warrior and then he started laughing in booming guffaws.

He got up off the ground and, leaving the knife stuck in the handle of the axe stuck in the tree, walked over to Ruth, smiled and bowed to her. The two began an instant conversation, of sorts, from which Ruth was able to learn that Bjorn was from a northern land, known as Sweden, and had travelled south to the German lands as a mercenary to the highest bidder. The reason he was so taciturn, he said, was because we spoke too quickly in languages that were unfamiliar to him.

# 46

We had all seen Ruth's display, putting her knife in Bjorn's axe and that evening, before it got dark, Rudolphus made a request.

'Mistress Ruth, that was a fine throw of your knife this morning. Is it possible you have some other demonstration of your skills you might show us?'

Ruth looked at Raymond and me and we understood each other perfectly – the circus show. Years earlier, the three of us had put together a show as part of a travelling circus in India. Thus, it was that we went through our routine with Ruth hitting targets thrown into the air, splitting fruit placed on our heads and, as a finale, bringing down a pigeon which went into the stew. Our comrades appreciated the skill of the show and applauded energetically. Bjorn made some comment about a Valkyrie, whatever that was.

'So, Ippolito and Raymond, how do you account for yourselves when you have the protection of a warrior goddess like Ruth to look after you?' said Rudolphus hoping to bait Raymond and me into a demonstration of the fighting skills he had seen us display in the hospital.

Raymond was up for the challenge, which meant I was too. He was tossing an apple in the air and said, 'Whoever can take this apple from Ippy and me, can have it. No weapons, just the two of us against the six of you,' and with that he placed the apple on the ground between the two of us as we stood back-to-back.

Aldo and Rico decided to be the first to try their luck. It was only a moment before two separate kicks to the side of their knees from

Raymond and I dropped them both and almost simultaneously. They were tenacious and got up again to have another go, only to go down again, get up again and then go down again before deciding they had had enough of the game. Wilhelm and Hermann were bigger than Aldo and Rico and had had time to watch our moves. There was nothing graceful about their approach as they both charged at Raymond and me like wild bulls. Raymond side-stepped Wilhelm's attack, tripping him with one foot and sending him sliding face first onto the forest floor. Hermann managed to grab the front of my tunic as I rolled backwards and used my legs to flip him up and over the top of me to land with such a thump on his back that it left him winded and gasping to catch his breath. The apple remained untouched between Raymond and myself.

Gunter and Bjorn were the largest and most powerful of the six.

'I think we might have to change tactics here,' said Raymond softly.

'High kicks?' I suggested just as quietly.

Raymond nodded and then snapped, 'Now,' as we charged at the two giants, launching ourselves into the air, visualising where we would place our mid-air kicks and landing our heels as planned: Raymond's on Gunter's chin and mine on Bjorn's forehead. Both were felled and dazed but arose unharmed after a few moments and signalled the apple was ours.

Rudolphus and the others applauded us before Rudolphus added, 'And they are not afraid to use this unarmed combat against those bearing arms as I swear I am witness to.'

The events of that morning and evening placed the three of us in a new light with the soldiers. I felt we were no longer regarded as the weak link in the chain but were valued and respected fighters and members of the mercenary band. Rudolphus indicated this approval to us saying, 'You have shown these men each of you are worthy of their respect as warriors and have engendered their comradeship. I feel more confident that we will be able to stay together as a group until this matter with Baldo is resolved. Well done to the three of you.'

The journey continued uneventfully with the weather favouring us kindly and trouble keeping well away.

'We should start thinking about what we intend to do when we reach Florence,' I said to Rudolphus as we rode beside a creek that bubbled and gurgled away.

'I suspect, locating your loathsome brother in Florence will not be difficult. Any recent newcomer will have been noticed, particularly if they have been splashing money around, buying property and furnishings. Knowing your brother's tastes, I think a visit to any of Florence's brothels or taverns will provide us with at least a rough idea of where to find him. The big problem will be, how do we get your inheritance back from him? We do not know where the money is. Is it in a bank or with the Templars for safe keeping or does he keep it tied up in commodities, the way your father did? I have a feeling that your brother would like to keep it close by and we may be lucky enough to find out he has it under lock, key and guard, wherever he is living.'

'Much as I despise him for what he has done to Cherubino and myself, he is still my brother, well, half-brother actually, and I would not see him killed for what he has done. Maimed a little, yes hurt.

Definitely, begging for mercy, probably destitute, yes, but not dead. I would not like to be known as a fratricide.'

'You don't have to kill the bastard. One of my lads will do that for you,' offered Rudolphus.

'I would prefer that we somehow trick or swindle him into releasing the money to us but without him knowing who it was that robbed him. It would plague him for years and years, particularly if he had to endure being poor as well,' I replied.

'Mmmh, you like to make things difficult for yourself, Ippolito,' commented Rudolphus, 'Much simpler to force our way in, bash a few heads together, grab the money and get the hell out of Florence as quickly as possible.'

# 47

We crested the hills surrounding the city of Florence and looked down on a hive of building activity. All over the city, we could see buildings going up, typified by towers that seemed to characterise the skyline of the city. I later learned these towers were used for military purposes associated with the rivalries of the supposedly noble families and clans. Each tower controlled a section of the city. The old city walls were still intact within the boundaries of the larger modern city. A ring of new outer walls and defences to encompass the recent residential expansion were nearing completion. What appeared to be a cathedral was also under construction, along with smaller churches and other public buildings and amenities. Florence appeared to be a wealthy city and one that was booming economically. Most definitely, the perfect patch for a conniving thief like my brother.

And it was. It was a city riven by factionalism: noble house against noble house, nobles versus the merchants and craft guilds, rich guilds against poor guilds, ubiquitous class struggles, those who supported either the pope or the Holy Roman emperor – the Guelphs versus the Ghibellines and the gang warfare of the youths and apprentices. It was, in so many ways, a city of murder and mayhem. Yet, despite all this division, the city was thriving and it was on the sheep's back that it was doing so. Wool and cloth were the chief industries and exports and they were making the city rich.

Unusually, Florence was not the territory or property of any individual prince, duke, count or other magnate. It was governed as a commune. The governing body was made up of both religious and secular members of the community with three major groups: consorts of nobles, the merchants and the military knights and horse soldiers. Like the rest of the city, the governing body was also riven with rivalries and feuds and murder was often the quickest resolution to any dissent or access to civil promotion. If murder did not resolve an issue, then a quick civil war in the streets of Florence between noble families was the next step.

I could not help but feel it was going to be a city of troubles and it began the moment we tried to enter the city gates.

'Hold up there,' ordered the city guard as he and his companion crossed their halberds in front of us, effectively barring our way into the city. 'State your names and purpose for entering Florence.'

'We are mercenaries,' replied a quick-thinking Rudolphus, 'As should be obvious by our attire and weaponry,' he added taking a little dig at the guard, 'And like any mercenaries, we are seeking employment with one of Florence's noble lords. Do you know of any lord seeking a small band of warriors such as ourselves? As for our names…'

'Don't bother,' said the guard, 'You and your fellows are just a few of the many like yourselves in the city. Behave yourselves and you will stay out of the city keep.'

The crowd behind us was growing restless so the guards uncrossed their halberds and allowed us into the city. The mercenary disguise was a good one as it allowed us to enquire more freely without attracting suspicion about what our real motives were.

'There's any number of wealthy families in Florence who would pay well for skilled swordsmen,' said a very helpful barkeep in the first inn we visited. 'You could try the Gherardini, the Porcelli or the Guidi families. They have been losers recently and are probably looking to reman their forces.'

'I'm not sure I want to tie my fortunes to losers,' said Rudolphus, 'Who are the young lions in town? Those who look like getting ahead and don't like to lose a fight, by fair means or foul.' He said the last with a conspiratorial grin at the barkeep.

'Well, if you are not too fussy about the morals of your lord and the type of work you might be asked to do, there are the Bardis, the Fifanti and there is a new man in town making a name for himself, Baldo de Medici.'

'Baldo and de Medici!' exclaimed Rudolphus, 'I like both those names. What say you men?' he said, turning to us seated at the benches.

'As good as any', 'It's a start', 'As long as he pays well', came some typical gruff replies.

'Where can we find this lord de Medici?' asked Rudolphus.

'He is no lord, leastwise, not yet. More like a bandit if you ask me,' replied the barkeep spitting on the rush covered floor.

'All the better. As I said, where can he be found?'

'The old Casa di Amidei by the Ponte Vecchio over the Arno River. Look for the warehouses and find the tallest tower next to them. That is the Casa di Medici, as it is known now. You will find him there.'

'My thanks, good friend,' said Rudolphus, tossing the man a silver florin before turning to us and saying, 'Drink up lads. There may be a bit of work in the offering.'

With that, we drank up and exited the tavern, leaving the barkeep grinning at his good fortune. We left our horses stabled at the inn along with payment for accommodation.

Once out in the street, Rudolphus turned to me and said, 'I believe we have just accomplished stage one of our plan. Let us make our way to the Ponte Vecchio and see if we can locate the tallest tower in the neighbourhood.'

We casually made our way through the city in twos and threes, not wanting to attract attention to ourselves. We strolled along the via Arno until we arrived at an old bridge that somehow remained standing. Alongside the bridge were several warehouses and behind them, the tall red brick tower of La Casa di Medici.

# 48

La Casa di Medici was more a compound than a house. The entire property, except where it met the River Arno at its wharf, was surrounded by an eight-foot-high red brick wall, similar to most of the powerful family estates and compounds within and around the city. Within the boundaries of the wall were warehouses and outbuildings and the actual casa with its defensive tower built in the middle of the estate. The battlements of the tower and its embrasures offered excellent defensive coverage of all approaches to it on land and river, for those who might have to defend the property.

Baldo had not just acquired a new home, he had acquired a fortification and, as we observed, numerous men to man it. Added to this were the deep throated barks we could hear coming from the guard dogs. He was obviously protecting something and protecting it very thoroughly.

'Shite,' said Gunter, 'How do we get in there?'

'Don't forget the goal and get back out again,' added Rudolphus, 'This will take more planning than I expected.'

'How many men do you think he has in there?' I asked.

'At least a dozen, possibly more,' replied Rudolphus., 'I'll wager there is someone always on watch from that tower, night and day.'

'In that case let us keep walking. We don't want to arouse any suspicions,' suggested Gunter.

We walked on past the compound. Not far behind us, Ruth, Raymond and Bjorn pretended to take a casual interest in the compound as they too strolled by. The others in our group were not far behind them.

We returned to the inn and met in the room Rudolphus shared with Gunter.

'That was a depressing tour,' said Raymond, 'How are we to get into that fortress?'

'Our only real chance will be if one or more of us are in Baldo's employment. It would give us the cover and the freedom to reconnoitre la casa: learn what is kept where, what their routines are, opportunities for sabotage and the like,' offered Gunter.

'A good idea, but who to do it?' replied Rudolphus, 'Gunter, Wilhelm and Hermann would be turned away as soon as they heard their guttural German. Florence is for the papacy not a German emperor. Bjorn is not fluent enough in Italian. Baldo has met me before and would readily recognise me. Even though it is more than five years since he has seen a stripling Ippolito, you are still easily recognisable, as I saw in the Schola hospital the day we invaded. That only leaves Aldo and Rico as our possible alternatives. How do you both feel about going inside la casa undercover?'

Aldo and Rico grinned at each other before Rico said, 'Us Genoese have no great love for Florentines, nor they us, but they do love our crossbows and the way we use them. But how do you know they will seek to employ us?'

'That,' said Rudolphus, 'will be taken care of tonight.'

Later that night, Rudolphus, Gunter, Raymond and I stood in the shadows, not far from the casa's front gate, silently observing and waiting. Half an hour later, three of Baldo's men emerged from the front gate in what looked like good spirits, obviously anticipating a night of drinking and carousing. We broke up into twos and followed them from a distance.

Four hours later, the three were practically falling out of an inn into the street. One was wanting to go to a local brothel and the arms of his "Sweet Rosina". They staggered back and forth along the street with their arms over each other's shoulders, singing a song about a shepherdess and a handsome ram. They never saw us coming.

Three solid blows across the back of their heads with the flats of our blades laid them out on the boulevard that ran beside the Arno River. We quickly bound and gagged them and then deposited them in the bottom of a vacant flat-bottomed barge tied up nearby. We released the barge from its mooring and watched the river's current take the three of them down to the sea. It was kinder than just dumping them in the river to drown.

'Good work men,' commended Rudolphus, 'I should think the lord Baldo will be seeking to employ suitable replacements for his errant men on the morrow.'

It was as Rudolphus predicted. Rico and Aldo returned from their midday excursion to la Casa di Medici mid-afternoon to retrieve their belongings before returning for duty at the casa.

'Di Medici keeps 20 men as his personal and house guards and there are servants about the place that could be a problem as well,' reported Aldo, 'And there are six great hounds that he keeps guarding the grounds at night. We get one evening a week off duty and two florins a week in pay. And that is about all I can tell you at this stage.'

'You forgot,' said Rico to his companion, 'Baldo wants us working primarily in the tower, where we can most usefully put our crossbows to work if needed.'

'And from where you can send messages to us as well,' interjected Rudolphus, 'Simply tie a note to one of your bolts and fire it at the trunk of the elm tree that stands not far from the gates. One of us will be near the tree after sunset to retrieve any messages you send.'

'Good idea,' said Rico cinching the saddle of his horse and then mounting.

Aldo joined him on his mount and together they both cantered from the inn's stables back to La Casa di Medici. We wished them luck.

# 49

Every day for the next week, a different one of us would make the journey around sunset to the tree, in the hope of finding some kind of communication from our two spies. When it was my turn to take the walk, I spied Rico in the tower but did not wave or acknowledge his presence in any way. I heard no bolt thumping into the tree and casually inspected the trunk as I walked by in the remaining twilight. There was no bolt and no note.

The next day, there was a note. Hermann brought it back. It simply read, 'Heavy door and locks on underground crypt.'

'Do you suppose that is where Baldo is keeping his wealth?' asked Ruth after Rudolphus had read the note to us back at the inn.

'Every chance of it,' replied Rudolphus.

Later that evening, as Ruth and I were lying back in the warm afterglow of our lovemaking, she said, 'You know I have been thinking. Trying to take Baldo's casa by force and with less than half their number of men is going to leave us with casualties, which I do not really care for.'

'And I thought you were thinking of me,' I jested, 'What are you suggesting?'

'We find some way of disabling Baldo's men before we storm the casa.'

'Such as?'

'There must be apothecaries in Florence. I'm sure we can find some interesting ingredients to incapacitate his men. The problem will be in getting all the guardsmen to take it around the same time and alerting Rico and Aldo not to take it.'

'Do not forget the dogs. From the sound of their barking, they are not only large but savage as well.'

'Let's investigate the apothecaries tomorrow to see what is available. We have not really done any sightseeing in Florence beyond hanging around the inn. It will be good to look around.'

There were apothecaries in Florence, in fact a whole street of them with a guildhall representing their interests on the commune council. The herbs and ingredients we were looking for were hard to find as those that Ruth and I were familiar with, were not common in central Italy.

As fate would have it, it was in the apothecary of an old Jew, by the name of Hiram, that we found the first of the ingredients we were seeking.

'Make sure you wear gloves at all times when handling any part of this plant,' cautioned Hiram.

Ruth and I knew this about the purple flowered wolfbane we had just purchased but did not seek to tell Hiram how we knew.

Instead, Ruth offered, 'My father has been killing the wolves in the hills around here for years. We always wear gloves and a mask when preparing the wolf-brew.'

'A wise precaution,' commented Hiram sagely.

After we left the apothecary Ruth led the way to a butcher where we purchased an entire rump of horsemeat.

Upon our return to the inn, we got the landlord's permission to light a small fire in the courtyard over which we placed a pot of water into which we poured the entire contents of wolfbane and let it boil and simmer down several times. In the meantime, I was cutting the rump into two-inch cubes. When the contents of the pot had cooled, I placed the cubes of meat in the wolfbane solution to let it seep into the meat. We covered the pot and left it in the shade at the back of the stables.

'That should take care of the dogs, providing they eat the bait a couple of hours before we storm the casa,' said Ruth with satisfaction.

Rudolphus was pleased with this solution to one of the many logistical problems he was currently worrying over.

'If only we could do the same to the meals the guards are eating,' said Rudolphus wishfully.

'I don't wish to poison the guards the way I am the dogs,' replied Ruth, 'but the problem is accessing their food so we can adulterate it with something to send them to sleep or render them unconscious.'

We were interrupted by a disturbance coming from outside. Curious, I put my head out the window and looked down into the courtyard where a delivery of wine casks was underway. The innkeeper was remonstrating with the delivery driver over a broken barrel and a puddle of red wine spreading itself out over the courtyard. It gave me an idea.

I pulled my head back inside and said, 'We do not have to put the drug in their food. What if we managed to get it into their drink somehow.'

'Go on,' said Rudolphus.

'Let us suppose a barrel of red wine happened to fall from a cart outside the gates of the casa just on sunset and the driver just kept going. What do you think would happen?'

'Why the guardsmen would gather it up and have a bit of a party in their barracks or, at least, those without any duties to perform would. It might be that they take it to the mess hall and share it over a meal. Whatever, a barrel of free red wine will not remain untapped for long amongst Baldo's retinue of guards. They will drink themselves unconscious one way or another,' answered Rudolphus.

The next day, Ruth and I visited Hiram again. I was not sure if he was curious about what we bought or the quantities of them, but his only comment was, 'Well someone should sleep well tonight,' as he took our coins.

Ruth and I made our way back to the inn and began steeping the herbs in skins of red wine that we re-stoppered and left in the shade next to the dog's bait.

'We will have to let it cure for a week,' Ruth told an impatient Rudolphus.

A week later, we transferred the contents of the skins to a medium-sized half empty barrel of cheap red wine we bought off the inn keeper. He agreed to let us use his cart as we wished to deliver the wine "to a friend".

That evening, we all met in Rudolphus' room and planned our attack.

# 50

The next evening, just after sunset, the two guards at the gate of the casa observed what they assumed to be an obviously drunken carter singing a loud and slurred love song that was out of key and out of time.

> *'Oh, my darling Ricalda*
> *You are far, far above me*
> *But tonight, you shall be mine*
> *Oh, my darling Ricalda*
> *Kiss my lips and not the wine*
> *Kiss my lips and not the wine'*

As he passed the gate, the driver veered his cart as if drunkenly and, with a little help from myself lying unseen flat on the tray, a barrel toppled from the back of the tray. As fortune would have it, the barrel rolled itself to rest up against the gate post. Raymond continued his braying and pretended not to notice the loss of a barrel from the back of his cart. The guards certainly noticed it as they were out the gate and rolling the barrel back inside the compound before anyone else noticed it. I could only hope that either Rico or Aldo, whichever was in the tower, would understand that 'Ricalda' was a feminisation of their combined names and the message in Raymond's tuneless song was 'Don't drink the wine.'

Raymond steered the cart around the next corner and we travelled alongside the west wall of the compound. I pulled on a pair of thick gloves and took the lid from the pot of wolfbane baited meat. Every few yards, I would hurl one of the chunks over the wall.

At one point in our progress, I thought I heard dogs fighting over something, hopefully, a chunk of meat. Once the pot was empty, I told Raymond to steer for home.

Back at the inn, the others were all armed and in readiness for the assault on the casa. Ruth had obviously put her foot down, demanding to come along as she had her belt of knife sheaves strapped across the top of her tunic not under it. Gunter, Wilhelm, and Hermann were quietly honing their swords to a razor sharpness, as was Bjorn his axe.

'How did it go?' asked Rudolphus.

'Mission accomplished,' I replied, 'In about two hours, I expect all the dogs to be dead or paralysed and most of the men snoring in their cups. The only uncertainty is whether, after Raymond's performance, Rico or Aldo got the message.'

'They are bound to,' said a grinning Raymond, 'I sang beautifully!'

'You probably made them puke with that "Kiss my lips not the wine",' I retorted jokingly, 'Where did you come up with that?'

'As we rode, the muse came upon me and I let it forth to the world,' he replied theatrically as if an actor on a village stage.

'Letting forth, more like a fart,' I said, which got a good round of laughs.

We still had the best part of two hours to kill before we rode the short distance to the casa.

'There are still some issues we need to sort before we assault the place,' said Rudolphus gaining our attention. 'I suspect the dogs will not be a problem. They do not think, they eat, shit, bite, bark and sleep. Hopefully, they will all have been removed from the picture. The guards and other household men are a different story. as not all will have been at liberty to enjoy the wine that was on offer. Baldo and his senior men will probably drink their own better-quality wine, rather than the wine his men have commandeered for themselves.

'The key to capturing the compound will be speed. We must ride in there and take out all who oppose us. Let us hope Rico and Aldo are in position in the tower to help eliminate those on the ground outside the casa.

'Ippolito, Ruth, myself and Bjorn with his axe, must be the thunderbolt that strikes the house and captures Baldo as quickly as possible. I know the sly dog and he will have made plans and established escape routes for an eventuality such as we are about to bring upon him. The rest of you will have to deal with those who are unaffected by the drugged wine, either in the grounds, the out-buildings or the casa. Are there any questions?'

'We are relying on Rico and Aldo to provide covering fire from above to protect us,' said Gunter, 'What if they did not understand or receive Raymond's alert and are lying drunk and drugged somewhere in the grounds or the buildings?'

'We deal with it the best we can. The key is for us to capture Baldo. Once he is in our control, we can get him to order his men to lay down their arms to us and then proceed to recover the money as planned.'

'Rudolphus, Ruth and Bjorn. I do not wish for my brother to come to any fatal harm during this raid,' I interjected, 'I simply request that you all leave the final reckoning between my brother and me, to just the two of us so I may have satisfaction for myself and my brother Cherubino, for his treachery against us.'

'Granted,' said Rudolphus.

'Understand,' said Bjorn.

'Are you sure?' questioned Ruth.

'Yes,' was my emphatic answer.

Two hours later, we were armed and mounted in the courtyard and ready to leave for Baldo's casa. The innkeeper stood by the back door, taking the spectacle in with an airy boredom as if such occurrences were common in Florence. Which they were. Rudolphus waved his hand in the air and we clattered out of the cobblestone yard. Once out into the street, we quickened our pace to a slow canter and made directly for our destination.

# 51

We clattered to a halt by the front gate to find it deserted of any guardsmen.

'A good sign,' commented Rudolphus.

The gate however was barred with a chain and lock.

'Bjorn. The back of your axe head if you please,' said Rudolphus, indicating the lock and chain.

Bjorn dismounted and pulled the hefty war axe from the belt around his waist. Reversing the heavy blade, he drew the weapon above his head and brought the back of the blade down upon the chain and shattering it into pieces across the ground. He quickly checked his blade with his thumb, satisfied that it was still sharp and intact, he casually kicked the gates open for us to enter.

'You noisy bastards would wake the dead,' came Aldo's voice from up in the tower.

'They know something is up. Baldo has withdrawn all his remaining men into the house,' called Rico, 'Wait for us. We are coming down.'

Within moments the two grinning Genoese were beside us, their crossbows loaded and primed.

'You will sing me another song one day won't you darling Raymond?' said Aldo sweetly and in obvious jest.

'No time for foolery,' ordered Rudolphus spurring his horse, 'To the house.'

We spurred our horses down the driveway, the Genoese running behind us. Just as we pulled up in the forecourt, Wilhelm let out a pained grunt, 'I'm hit in the leg,'

The sound of other crossbow bolts hitting the ground around us gave Rudolphus second thoughts.

'Retreat back to the garden,' he cried as he turned his horse around for us to follow.

Back in the garden and out of sight, Rudolphus said, 'I should have expected that. Bloody stupid of me. Wilhelm, how is the leg?'

'Arrgh! Ruth is …removing the bolt …as I speak.'

'Rico. Aldo. Is there another entrance?'

'Several,' replied Rico, 'But I'll bet they are all guarded. But there may be a way in through the kitchen pantry. Leave the horses and follow me.'

We quickly tied the horses to some nearby trees in the garden and followed Rico through the shadows to the rear of the house, where he pointed to a deliveries hatch for receiving pantry stores and goods. It was secured with another lock and chain. Rudolphus did not have to ask, Bjorn simply stepped up with his axe and in three blows had smashed the wooden hatch door into splinters. It was dark down below but, thankfully, silent of any voices or movement.

A ladder led down into the pantry which we quickly descended, apart from Wilhelm who Rudolphus bade stand guard as he was wounded in the leg.

'Protect our rear in case they come this way and keep the hatch open in case we have to make a retreat through here,' he ordered Wilhelm.

Gunter led the way through the pantry into the kitchen, where we surprised a couple of kitchen staff. One grabbed a meat cleaver, the other was already holding a carving knife. They both ran at us screaming blue murder and alerting others in the building. Gunter put his sword neatly through the cleaver bearing man's solar plexus but not before he had thrown his weapon directly at Gunter. Gunter saw the move and managed to duck his head in time. Sadly, the cleaver continued its path directly into the forehead of Rico who was coming immediately behind Gunter. He dropped dead instantly.

It took two of Ruth's knives to finish the foe with the carving knife. The first, a miss, high on his shoulder, the second, a kill, straight in the larynx.

'Don't stop,' yelled Rudolphus from behind, 'Keep going.'

Just as we emerged from the kitchen into a room at the bottom of a stairwell, six swordsmen emerged from a corridor opposite and came straight at us. Bjorn was the first to take them on, wading straight into them with his heavy axe swinging broadly and mightily. Behind him came Hermann, Gunter, Rudolphus, Raymond and myself. Ruth and Aldo moved up onto the stairwell from where they could aim their bolts and knives without risking injury to our men.

Bjorn's first mighty swing took the guts from the two leading men in the pack. Sword thrusts from those behind Bjorn quickly took out another two of the enemy. The other two quickly turned and fled the way they came, leaving their comrades writhing on the floor either trying to hold their intestines in or gasping to take one last breath. Aldo got a shot off at one of the fleeing soldiers, taking him in the kidney. He staggered, almost fell, but stumbled on after his colleague and escaped with him. He would die slowly and later on.

'Ruth. Aldo. Hold the stairs,' called Rudolphus as we pursued the two escapees down the hallway.

Suddenly, we burst into what was obviously the dining room. At least a dozen swordsmen awaited us. Behind them stood Baldo, issuing commands and goading his men to attack.

'So, the fox is still in his lair. I would have thought a piece of chicken shit like you would have bolted by now,' sneered Rudolphus at Baldo.

'Rudolphus! You weasly rat. I might have guessed. Come to steal more de Medici goods and money, have we?'

'More like reclaim stolen de Medici goods and money,' I interjected.

'And who might you be?' he said, sneering down his nose at me.

'Someone keen to beat his older brother back into his place,' I replied somewhat enigmatically.

Baldo looked confused for a moment then a grin slowly crept across his face.

'Why if it isn't the little mouse, Ippolito. I had assumed you dead in some Arabian desert, your bones bleaching under a hot sun.'

'As you can see, my bones are standing here wrapped in my own flesh and ready to take their revenge for the theft of my inheritance and that of Cherubino.'

'I somehow doubt that. Look around you, little brother. I see six of you. There are 18 of us. Three to one. Not particularly good odds. Why not lay down your arms now and I might consider extending some clemency to my youngest brother.'

'Up your arse, brother.'

'Kill them all,' shouted a red faced Baldo.

# 52

I thought it had been a mistake by Rudolphus to leave our airborne weaponry with Ruth and Aldo, back at the staircase. Baldo had all his men with him, none would be upstairs and those that had been downstairs were all congregated in the dining room.

'RUUUUUUTH,' I yelled at the top of my voice as if it were a war cry and then I charged at my first adversary.

Our swords met with a resounding clang that sent jarring sensations through my hands and down my arms. I ignored the pain, stepped back, quickly crouched and then leapt forward swinging my sword with all my might at knee level. My opponent's sword swept above my head as my sword separated both his shins from their knees and he toppled forward falling on his face exposing his neck for the coup de grace.

Having finished him off, I turned and saw Ruth and Aldo run into the room as I turned and faced my next adversary. Unfortunately, with the first clash of our swords, mine broke just above the handle. A vicious smile formed on my adversary's face as he drew his sword back to thrust it through my body. I turned and twisted and felt the blade slip by my ribs opening the skin but not penetrating to any depth. He came at me again only this time much more quickly. He was not going to give me a second chance.

Again, I leapt backwards and commenced rolling just as he thrust at me. I kept rolling backwards as he kept thrusting and missing. The furniture saved me as I suddenly realised, I had rolled under the dining table. My foe blindly and foolishly thrust his sword under the table hoping to score a strike somehow. Instead, I was able to grab his sword wrist in both hands and twisted it so painfully, he dropped his blade. I let his wrist go and grabbed the blade before rolling out from under the other side of the table. I jumped up onto the table and then leapt across it to run my adversary's sword through the side of his neck.

Out of the side of my eye, I could see Ruth and Aldo holding their weapons and poised to shoot or throw but there was so much chaos in the room they could not risk an attempt for fear of hitting one of our own men. I realised why Rudolphus had deployed them where and when he had.

Bjorn was cornered by three swordsmen but was holding them at bay with wild strokes of his axe. His face was covered in blood. Whether it was his or someone else's I had no idea. Either way, I could see he was in trouble and one of the swordsmen would run him through sooner or later. They all had their backs to me and it was a simple matter of making a long and wide sweeping slash across the back of their legs to hamstring all three in one stroke and leave them on their backs for Bjorn to finish with his axe. Bjorn laughed with battle joy, nodded his appreciation and then did the job on the legless men at his feet.

Rudolphus and Raymond were working as a team and three dead guards lay around their feet as they stood back-to-back and took on all comers. I turned, ready to jump back into the fray when I saw Hermann suddenly stumble backwards clutching his side, blood gushing from between his fingers. His opponent stepped forward and thrust his sword down Hermann's agonised and gaping mouth, twisting and turning it as he did. Hermann's body arched in pain before slumping back down into the stillness of death.

I was enraged and flew at Hermann's assailant. I should have done it silently, as it would have been done quickly, instead I bellowed my rage, which alerted Hermann's killer to my intent. Instinctively, he turned with sword arm pulled back ready to unleash a powerful stroke that would have taken my head off had it connected with my neck. I threw my sword arm up, hoping my sword would hold back the power of the upcoming stroke, when the front of his face burst open as a crossbow bolt emerged from where his nose had been displaced and he dropped dead in front of me. I quickly threw Aldo a grateful salute, turned and looked for my next assailant.

I was trying to get myself close to Baldo and drive him down to the point where he would call his men to drop their arms and cease combat, but I could not see him in the melee, so I kept thrashing at those foes about me. My arms were starting to ache from the effort of wielding my sword over and over and some mental fatigue must have been creeping in as I almost launched a slash at Gunter as he moved too close to my side at one point and I thought him an enemy. We both turned and faced each other about to strike, when we realised the grisly mistake we were about to make. He held his hand up in a gesture of peace before the red fog of war cleared from my vision and I apologetically blurted, 'Oh shit! That was close. Sorry.'

He grinned and then turned around to look for another adversary, as I did.

I did not like killing my last enemy that day. He was not a man; he was little more than a teenager obviously recruited from the domestic staff. But he was brave and had courage, which surprised me at first. He threw his whole weight at me in a desperate attempt to take me off my feet. The clumsy attempt saw us both fall to the floor losing our swords and then engaging in a brutal wrestling match. He clawed at my eyes, I bit into his wrist, his knee made painful contact with my testicles, my forehead broke his front teeth, he used his broken teeth to tear my earlobe, I finally got my hands around his neck.

I still have nightmares about looking into the eyes of and choking the life out of, someone who was so much younger than me.

I rolled off his dead body and looked around. The fighting had ceased. All Baldo's men were dead or dying, along with those of our own.

Baldo was nowhere to be seen. With dreadful panic, I realised that neither was Ruth.

# 53

Aldo lay dead on the black and white tiled floor. There was a red and very wet line across his throat that was slowly seeping onto the tiles.

'We've got to find them,' I said, my panic rising even further, 'They can't have got far.'

'Gunter, Bjorn,' ordered Rudolphus, 'Check upstairs. Ipp and Raymond with me.'

We exited the dining room and dashed to the front entrance and out onto the forecourt from which led two paths. One to the front gate and the other to the estate wharf on the River Arno.

'Which way?' said Raymond urgently.

'Silence,' ordered Rudolphus as he cupped an ear and turned his head between the two paths.

'This way,' he said indicating the path to the wharf.

We raced along the gravel path towards the wharves by the river. The moonlight was glittering brightly upon the water, revealing the silhouette of a small goods barge departing from the side of the wharf.

I felt the wood of the wharf beneath my feet and put on a burst of speed before leaping from the side and landing on the barge fortunately on a bale of fabrics to soften my crash landing. I heard a thump against the side of the barge and a splash followed by another splash. Raymond and Rudolphus had not been able to make the long jump and had wound up in the water.

Baldo had been poling the barge away from the wharf but threw the pole to the side and drew his sword when I landed on the barge. Ruth lay huddled in the foetal position at his feet. Baldo had quickly and brutally beaten and kicked her into submission. Her mouth and nose were bleeding heavily, and her face was already swelling. I went to draw my sword only to find it was not there at my waist, nor was my sword belt. They must have been lost in the mad dash to the wharf or in my leap to the barge.

'You are tenacious, little brother. Is it revenge or love that motivates you?' he sneered before violently launching his boot into Ruth's side. Ruth grimaced and a pitiful whimper of pain escaped her bloodied lips.

'Revenge now, brother, after that heroic little effort, you gutless pig,'

'I suggest you simply jump overboard, right now,' he said as he lowered his sword to rest the point against Ruth's neck. He gave it a little twist causing a bright little bead of blood to well on Ruth's neck.

'You bastard,' I said as I edged backwards and away from him.

'Only protecting my interests in the smartest possible way,' he replied as I continued backing my way to the side of the barge. It was the side Baldo had thrown the barge pole. As I turned and pretended I was about to mount the side of the barge to jump off, I deftly grabbed the end of the pole from where it lay and turning with as mighty a swing as I could manage, brought the pole smashing into his left shoulder.

The blow was unexpected and faster than he was prepared for and knocked him away from Ruth, allowing me the opportunity to use the pole as a lance and lunge the end of it at him. Despite the blow to his left side, he was quick and managed to turn and twist out of the way of the pole and battered it down with his sword. I withdrew it and then lunged again, not so much to harm him but to keep him and his sword the distance of the pole away from me until I could come up with some other plan. Sooner or later, he would slip by the pole and slip that sword into me or Ruth.

I moved back and away from him, hoping to mount one of the bales and gain the advantage of height and lure him away from Ruth. It was not to be. I could not look down to find a foothold to climb up on and watch my brother at the same time. And so, we began a macabre dance around the vacant deck of the barge. My pole was too long and too heavy to use as a stave, otherwise I would have had Baldo's measure earlier.

At one point in our duel, he got close enough to me to slash my tunic before I brought my pole around and crashed it again into his left shoulder. The momentary look of excruciation on his face told me I had done some damage with this blow. He still had his sword arm in good form but a damaged left side would affect his balance and performance. The next blow I managed to place to his left side took him in the upper arm and I clearly heard the bone snap and Baldo's gasp of pain. His left arm was now hanging limply by his side. Ignoring his pain, he kept coming at me.

His pain had clearly enraged him and seemed to invigorate his efforts to dispose of me as I found myself being pushed back again by the speed of his swordplay. By this stage there were a number of large cuts and slices taken from the barge pole. It was weakening and when Baldo brought a particularly heavy blow a yard from my grip, he sliced enough of the pole for it to suddenly snap in two leaving me with a yard long length of wood in my hand. I jumped back and hurled the stump directly at Baldo taking him in the face and stalling his attack, but only for a moment.

He advanced slowly on me, his weapon raised and ready to lunge and pierce as I slowly backed away. Walking backwards, I tripped and fell back over a coil of rope landing on my back on the deck beside the bulwark. Baldo was quickly standing over me with his sword pointed down at my throat.

'And now little brother, prepare to die,' he said.

Suddenly, a shocked look came over his face and he unintentionally jerked forward, launching himself over the side of the bulwark and into the river. The last thing I saw of him was one of Ruth's knives sticking out of his arse.

# 54

Ruth was on her hands and knees, just past my feet and had struck her blow from behind and below thus saving my life. She crawled her way up beside me and into my arms. We could hear Baldo's thrashing about in the water and his gurgled calls for help but I knew, with only one good arm and a knife up his backside, he would not stay on the surface much longer. We did not move ourselves to look. The struggling noises ceased shortly after.

'Thank you, my love,' I finally said.

'I would not have you wearing the mark of Cain and besides, after he had beaten me, it was I who owed him the payment of revenge.'

I could hear voices calling out from afar and realised we were adrift and floating down the River Arno. I knew the voices would be those of Rudolphus and Raymond.

I managed to get myself up and found the wharf anchor and threw it overboard ending our drift out to sea and giving the others time to follow us down the river side.

Rudolphus and Raymond were still wet from their dip in the river. Raymond, holding his side from where he had crashed into the side of the barge. We hailed an early morning passing barge poler and, after raising the wharf anchor, he towed us back to the casa's wharf. Rudolphus thanked him with enough coins from his purse to ensure his silence on the matter before he continued on his way. We almost released the barge to find its own way to the sea but realised we might still have a use for it and left it tied up to the wharf.

As we slowly staggered along the wharf path to the casa, I was a bit saddened to see the number of dead hounds lying around the grounds. They were big and black and had not been visible last night. I felt sorry for them as, in a way, they were the innocents in this family feud.

We were greeted at the front of the house by the other survivors of our group: Bjorn, Gunter and Wilhelm, his leg wound now neatly bound. Aldo, Rico and Hermann, although cold and pale, had been washed clean of obvious blood and neatly laid out on the couches of the front entrance foyer.

'We found two servants hiding upstairs and sent them on their way grateful for their lives and health,' reported Gunter, 'Otherwise, the house and grounds are ours to search. I do not think we need to worry about the authorities as no dead are lying in the streets and the commotion was all in the house and probably went unheard by those outside the grounds.'

'We will have to do something about all the dead. They will start to stink before long,' volunteered Raymond.

'The river. Like their master,' replied a grim sounding Ruth. It was the obvious practical solution and the one most commonly used in Florence.

'Thank you, Gunter,' said Rudolphus, 'Have you explored or investigated any further?'

'Only upstairs after we found the servants. The casa is free of any human threats, although I cannot speak for the warehouses and outbuildings.'

'What about the underground crypt with the heavy door and locks that Aldo's note mentioned?'

'No sign, but we have not investigated every inch of this place yet.'

'Then, let's start looking.'

We were two hours finding the false wall that slid to the side at the back of the pantry revealing the heavy door with its chains and locks.

'This looks like the real thing,' observed Raymond, 'I wonder how Rico or Aldo learned of it, hidden the way it is.'

'Probably from other guards. They do gossip you know,' I replied before calling out to Bjorn to bring his axe.

The six of us mustered in the pantry as Bjorn wielded the back of his axe, breaking chains and locks in a handful of blows. Casually, he kicked the door in.

The room was not filled with gold and jewels of every type, like something out of a middle eastern fairy tale. Instead, there were seven chests all chained and locked. These were easily broken by Bjorn's axe to reveal layer upon layer of small gold ingots in two of the chests, silver ingots in another two chests with another two chests filled with coins of various denominations and countries of origin. The last and smallest chest contained the deeds and titles to both my father's house and his warehouse properties in Acre.

'There is a king's ransom here,' observed Ruth, 'Ippolito, you are rich. We can build a hospital. A big one and the absolute best one with all the best practitioners and equipment. We can open a college and train the greatest physicians in the world. We can -'

'Slow down Ruth,' I said, 'Half is Cherubino's, wherever he is and we have some debts to pay our friends here, plus we must not forget to pay for graves and headstones for our dead friends. Good ones too. I liked those cheeky Genoese.'

'May I suggest,' said Rudolph, 'that we commence dividing it up tomorrow? None of us slept last night. We have barely eaten all day and I could suck a skin dry of wine in a second. I vote we grab some coins from the coin chests and find the nearest good tavern, have a grand meal and just enough wine to celebrate with and discuss how we are going to manage this wealth.'

We all agreed to this and put the false wall back in place, closed the front door and proceeded to the nearest tavern where we availed ourselves of a private room where we would not be overheard and ordered the best meals and wine of the house.

I opened the proceedings with, 'First, the hoard must be divided in half. One half for me, one half for Cherubino. My half is to be divided three ways between Ruth, Raymond and myself. From each half we take an equal amount, enough to pay the gravediggers and stone masons for Rico, Aldo and Hermann. Agreed?'

'Agreed,' was the common response.

'Rudolphus. As principal organiser and captain of our little band I propose a cut of 10 percent, taken equally from each half and for Wilhelm, Gunter and Bjorn, five percent taken equally from each half. You have seen the wealth that is in the casa. Are you happy with this division of the spoils?'

Wilhelm, Gunter and Bjorn were more than happy and as Rudolphus said, he was already rich enough not to have to worry either way.

'Rudolphus,' said Gunter, 'I think I can retire now. I'm getting too old to be picking up after you. Please accept my resignation as your Bergmann,'

'Happy to accept,' smiled Rudolphus raising a toast to us all.

# 55

We slept the night in the casa and all of us awoke, not necessarily sore headed, but certainly a bit dry and thirsty after our evening of celebration. Naturally, everyone was keen to start dividing the spoils. Dividing the ingots of gold and silver was easily done but the two chests full of different coins posed a problem of what coins were of equal value. Fortunately, Rudolphus, being the most travelled amongst us, had a good idea of the exchange value the coins had on the money market and assured us he was dividing the coins up according to their commonly accepted market price. The doling out of rewards into equal portions took all morning.

After a brief lunch, we decided to investigate the warehouses and out-buildings in the casa's grounds. Disappointingly, all were devoid of anything of value. I found this a little bit sad when I thought about the rows of warehouses and emporia my father had filled with his business and trading in Acre. I only hoped that Baldo had got a good price for the wealth of goods my father had owned.

Gunter and Bjorn were keen to depart with their share and get over the Alps before the winter set in and made the mountains impassable. With warm and friendly thumps and punches on shoulders and across backs, we said our farewells the next morning in the tradition of all soldiers parting ways.

'Ippolito, there is one aspect of this business we have not resolved. As Baldo's brother and only known locatable heir, this casa should also come to you.'

'I do not fancy hanging around Florence waiting for this to sell. In all truth, I want to return to Jerusalem as soon as possible. It has been over five years since we left.'

'I feel the same,' said Ruth.

'Me too,' agreed Raymond.

'We will need to do some business with the Templars,' Rudolphus informed us. 'Firstly, we must arrange the transfer of your money to Acre. We can no longer use the Templars in Jerusalem since it has fallen to Salah al Din. Secondly, for a 10 percent commission I believe we can prevail upon the Templars to sell the casa for you and then transfer the money to you in Acre.'

Fortune was truly smiling on me that afternoon. Rudolphus and I entered a very unassuming building in one of the older parts of Florence. We were introduced to a Sir Antony and took seats in his office. After discussing my monetary security with the Templar, he scratched his chin in a thoughtful way and asked if he and some of his colleagues might have a look at the casa with a view to purchasing it themselves. The old building they were in was no longer meeting the growing needs of the order.

Ruth and Raymond were surprised when Rudolphus and I returned with six Templar knights and proceeded to take them on a tour of the casa, the tower, the walls, the wharf and the warehouses and outbuildings. It was the river access to a private wharf and then the warehouses that sold the property for us. As Rudolphus told me later, the Templars would find the compound very handy for the trafficking and hiding of some of their more clandestine activities.

There was no need for haggling and bartering over a price. The Templars had the money, wanted the compound and were keen to transact the business as quickly as possible and made a very generous initial offer which, on Rudolphus' nod, I accepted and shook hands on the deal with Sir Antony. We returned to their premises where various papers were drawn up, inspected and reviewed favourably by Rudolphus and signed in several places by myself and Sir Antony then by others present as witnesses to the transaction.

'One thing,' Sir Antony said before we departed, 'you will make sure all those dead dogs are removed before you leave?'

'Not a problem,' I replied grateful that the dead human bodies had been removed and dumped in the river before the inspection.

Rudolphus and I strolled back to the casa at a leisurely pace feeling very pleased at how matters had resolved themselves.

'You and your companions have enough money on you to purchase sea passage back to Acre and should think about departing for the coast before the sailing season comes to an end in a few weeks,' said Rudolphus.

'I was thinking the same,' I replied, 'Now that this business is all tied up, do you think the quickest way to the coast might be on a small river barge that is tied to a wharf at the casa?'

'I certainly do and trust you will not mind taking me along with you to the coast at the port of Arno. It is there we will have to part company.

The next morning, we stowed our belongings on the barge and, after replacing the barge pole with a spare from the outbuildings, we poled the little boat out into the middle of the River Arno to let the current carry us to the sea.

It was a very peaceful and relaxing voyage. Our days were spent enjoying a warm autumn sun and taking in the varied colours of leaves getting ready to fall. Shepherds were bringing their flocks down from the hills, the last of the crops were being harvested in the fields and roofs rethatched and repaired before the winter storms arrived.

Two weeks later, we arrived at the outskirts of the coastal port of Arno and made our way to the wharves where the last of the ships, preparing to sail before the season ended, were making their final preparations.

Again, fortune smiled on us and Ruth, Raymond and I were able to secure a cabin berth on a ship bound for Constantinople and then Acre. Rudolphus had similar success with a berth on a ship bound for Marseilles from where he would travel overland to his "Frei Berg" in northern Frankia.

Suddenly, it was time to say our goodbyes.

'I can't thank you enough for all you have done for me and my friends,' I said to Rudolphus.

'As I said earlier on, I did this for your father and all he did for me. It is just another case of what goes around, comes around. Keep that in mind when you establish your hospital and you will do well, Ippolito.'

With that, he turned and walked up the gangplank to his ship without looking back. We walked along the wharf to our vessel and did the same.

# 56

The Mermaid was a Danish trading cog: fat bellied, high sided and slow in the water. She had a covered deck with cabin spaces at the stern of the ship and a single mast with a large square sail. Her captain was named Svein Trollface, which was definitely an eponymous appellation as he was probably one of the ugliest men I had ever met. His head was large, in fact, almost bulbous above his eyebrows. His nose must have been broken a dozen times as it was pushed almost flat against his face which forced him to breathe through his mouth, resulting in a whistling, wheezing sound. His skin was heavily pocked and what teeth he had, ranged in colour from green through brown to black. Consequently, his breath, which came through his mouth, was like death with its nauseating smell of corruption.

His body had not missed deformity either. He had a minor hunched back with one shoulder clearly higher than the other, but both shoulders topped heavily muscled arms. His spine was crooked, which placed his right hip higher than his left and forced him to walk with a rolling, bobbing, up and down gait. Despite all this deformity, what was really upsetting him was a boil on his buttocks that would not heal and kept reappearing, only to burst and suppurate before beginning all over again. The result was, the captain could not sit down as it was too painful to do so and hadn't for months.

'We can cut it out,' I offered, showing him our medical licences from the Schola, 'and there will be no charge for what is an emergency, related to the comfort of an important person. You need proper rest, Captain and sitting is a part of getting proper rest.'

Svein was used to his ugliness being on display to everyone and had no qualms about baring his backside over a barrel on a well-lit deck. It was another aspect of his projected lack of glamour and ugliness in front of the crew. In fact, he invited the crew to watch the excision, just to prove he was man enough to take the pain without complaint.

Well, almost.

When the appointed time came for the procedure, the captain called the crew together and made the following speech, 'You bastards know I am a pain in your arse but you have no idea of the pain in mine. These two young physicians tell me they can cut that cruel, bloody gruel out of my arse without any undue pain or agony. If it should be that I scream in agony, you have my permission to throw the three of them overboard.'

Ruth and I were not expecting this condition upon our performance as surgeons. No surgery was without pain, but some approaches could ameliorate it. Ruth still had the needles Master Kan Do had given her. It was time to put them to work again.

Ruth removed the fine needles from the sheathe she carried them in and washed them in the red wine Svein liked so much. She then slopped red wine over the site to be excised. She swiftly placed six of the needles around the periphery of the pustulant bulge. And four that tracked the meridian pathway from the site to the spine.

'Now, Captain Svein,' informed Ruth, 'we must wait about half an hour for the needles to do their work in dulling the meridians that govern the perception of pain. It is important that you remain where you are and not move about while we wait.'

'You mean I have to stay like this over the barrel?' blurted the captain.

'Oh, and what a pretty picture it is Cap'n,' chortled the first mate which brought a round of laughter from the assembled crew.

While we were waiting, Ruth placed some cheesecloth in a bowl of red wine to let it soak and take up the prophylactic properties within it.

After half an hour, Ruth gently jabbed the peripheral aspect of the boil with her scalpel.

'Did you feel that?' she asked the captain.

'Feel what?' came the reply.

'My turn to cut,' said Ruth to me, 'You take care of removing the detritus, the bleeds and packing with the cheese cloth. Okay?'

'Okay,' I replied.

And so it began, without so much a peep of discomfort from the captain. Ruth and I drifted into that amazing synchronicity of anticipating each other in the procedure and accomplished the task in half the usual time.

'Don't that look pretty,' commented the mate to those of the crew still observing, 'Your bum is all wrapped up like a gift for the king!'

Again, the crew laughed at the mate's wit and the captain's predicament.

'Hardee, Har, Har,' replied the captain slowly standing up and pulling his trews up around his waist, before securing the short and small rope that served as his belt.

'I will need to change the dressing and the wicks daily for a while,' explained Ruth, 'Depending on how well you heal, will decide how often you have to bare your backside like this again. Perhaps next time, Ippolito and I can attend you in your cabin.'

'Well, now I know there's no need to throw you overboard,' he said after examining the rancid products of his gluteal infection, 'My God, the goop in there absolutely stinks.'

'Not as bad as your breath,' quipped the mate again.

'Careful, Mr Mate, or you may find some of it on your dinner plate and, forced to eat it!' came the captain's reply. The look he gave the mate suggested he would indeed do it.

That shut the cheeky mate up. Well, for a little while at least.

The operation was successful and the captain seemed to be possessed of remarkable healing qualities. The cavity we left in his buttock rapidly closed with a layer of soft skin growing back within a week. The wicks were able to be removed earlier than I expected and he was up and moving around, and before long, sitting down without any discomfort.

The captain gave Ruth and I another cabin to share in appreciation of what we had done for him.

# 57

The captain wisely chose to circumnavigate the island of Sicily the long way around, rather than risking his bobbing tub through the straits of Scylla and Charybdis which had almost taken our lives on the way to Salerno. It was a longer route and, thanks to the prevailing winds set against us, was considerably slower as we were constantly having to tack the square sail into the wind. It also brought us back into the realms of the Muslim and Berber pirates that infested these waters.

I spoke with the captain about our earlier experiences with pirates in the location, but he seemed unconcerned, stating he had a "little trick" that would keep them at bay. Quite frankly, I could not see how any "little trick" in this bobbing tub would see us evade the sleek and fast corsairs who infested and patrolled the area, looking for easy prey. Prey just like our jolly little floating tub.

Our fat and bobbing cog had one advantage over the low and sleek corsairs and that was we sat much higher in the water and our deck was further above the water line. I supposed this was Svein's "little trick". It meant we would be able to shoot arrows, bolts and lead balls down onto the decks of any threatening vessel that approached us and got too close for comfort.

I was wrong and found out a few days later when the look-out called, 'Sail Ho off the port bow,' from where he clung to the junction of the spar and mast above the deck.

We turned and cast our eyes in that direction. Sure enough, a vessel was sitting on the horizon with only the bare minimum of sail showing and was hull down below the line of the horizon. It was difficult to see at first and the captain speculated he was laying far off to wait for a more opportune time to attack or, alternatively, waiting for reinforcements to arrive.

It turned out to be the latter. The next morning, there were three vessels, sail up and hull down below the horizon, sitting a league or two away. The look-out informed us they all had the same horizontal stripes running across their sails.

'Blow me down,' said the captain, 'looks like we have caught the attention of some of the Emir of Tunisia's raiding fleet. 'He is a right nuisance on this coast. It will be good to take some of the punch out of his sails.' He turned and called for the mate.

'I think a couple of dozen of our special surprises are in order, Mr Mate,'

'Aye, aye, Captain,' said the mate, unable to hide the glint of mischief in his eyes. He returned carrying a box of orange sized clay pots stoppered with corks.

'Take a third of them to the bow, leave a third here in the mid deck and the rest to the stern castle. Duncan and Thorgerd have good strong throwing arms. Leave the pots with them and tell them to wait for my command.

We had to wait yet another day, with the corsairs ghosting our progress from the horizon. Three days of being tailed by these pirates was beginning to take its toll on our nerves and patience but when we at last saw the ships come about on the third morning, they had been joined by a fourth vessel.

'Better bring up another dozen pots Mr Mate,' ordered the captain, 'and distribute them as before.'

'What is in the pots?' asked an inquisitive Raymond.

'You will see before too long,' the captain smiled enigmatically.

The extra pots came up and were distributed as ordered, as we watched the four striped sails ballooning their way towards us.

'I'm not sure I like this,' said Ruth, 'I will be in the cabin preparing my remaining knives, just in case. Shouldn't you gird yourselves as well?' she suggested.

We did so straight away as the corsairs seemed to be picking up speed and were making a heading directly toward our bobbing tub. When we returned to the deck, armed and ready for the fray, the corsairs were much closer and only a few hundred yards away. We could hear their yelling and blood curdling shrieks and ululations coming over the water. Individual pirates could be seen waving swords in our direction. The distance slowly closed until we could make out faces and clothing as well. The vast majority of the corsairs we could see on deck were dressed all in black, an indication that they were the Emir's men and not just ordinary freebooting seamen.

'Watch out for those fellows in black,' warned the captain, 'They are fierce and determined warriors.'

On and on they came, till they were a mere 50 yards away and coming up behind us. I was relieved that none of these corsairs had forward rams, being too light, the captain said, to carry the extra weight the larger galleys could.

'Artillery at the ready?' came the order from the captain.

'Ready,' came the two responses from stern and bow.

'They will try to grapple and board but those ropes hanging from the spar of the second vessel suggest they might use them to swing aboard,' cautioned the captain as the vessels drew even closer, the yelling of their crews ringing in our ears.

'Prepare to repel boarders,' yelled the captain as swords, knives and pikes were grabbed from the on-deck armoury by members of the crew.

'Duncan, be ready.'

'Ready, Sir,' came Duncan's reply as he held the pot in his hand with his arm crooked back to deliver a mighty throw.

'Fire from the stern,' called the captain.

Duncan's hurl of the clay pot fell short and crashed against the bow hull of the corsair, where it exploded and burst into flames, which quickly enveloped the front of the corsair, sending heat and black smoke back along the deck choking and blinding the crew on deck.

'Fire again.'

This time the pot smashed onto the foredeck and through the smoke I could see corsairs frantically trying to put out the flames. The corsair veered away to be replaced by the next vessel in the line of attack. This time the captain threw his pot as Duncan threw his. Both landed on the decks with catastrophic results. The explosion of flame ignited the sails and rigging, as well as many of the pirates, most of whom plunged overboard to quench the flames on their burning clothes. Our sailors picked them off with bows, arrows and sling shots.

It was enough of a demonstration of our fire power to deter the two remaining vessels and they veered away to assist their stricken companions in the other two boats before they went down and their entire crews disappeared below the water.

A few of the lads jumped on the stern castle, dropped their sailors' trews and bared their backsides to the retreating pirates.

'Job well done,' roared the captain, 'Extra rum all around this evening.'

It was Raymond who put it all together and said to the captain, 'How does a Danish skipper get access to Greek fire?'

'That! Is a secret,' smiled the captain, his face enigmatic once again.

<h1 style="text-align:center">58</h1>

We never did find out how Captain Svein came by his "flame pots". The Greeks had jealously held the secret of their "Greek fire" for hundreds of years. What really surprised us was, it was not a small armoury of flame pots but an entire section of the hold, carefully packed in straw, of over a hundred of the incendiary pots. The leftover ones from the raid were carefully replaced in their straw mattresses and packing by the mate.

'Well, that turned out easier than I thought it would,' commented the captain, once everything was stowed away in its proper place. 'Three pots to drive off four corsairs. If only every encounter on the high seas were as successful. Perhaps you three are bringing me some luck. You have certainly brought me some comfort,' he said gently tapping his backside.

And so, we bobbed along in our fat, little cog slowly making our way eastward, sometimes a little faster under a favourable wind, sometimes a little slower when it blew contrary to our intentions. We crossed the Ionian Sea with no further incidents and rounded the Peloponnese into the southern reaches of the Aegean Sea. Off Crete, we saw only the peak of Mount Ida, barely raising its tip above the horizon. And on we slowly sailed. Well actually, bobbed, upon the gentle swell.

We passed a few other vessels, all merchant traders going the other way, who, when we called out from the decks across the water, were unable to give us any news of what was happening in Outremer. The best advice we received was that it was all chaos as the Crusaders and Franks had given up Jerusalem and fled to fortify their coastal centres of Tyre, Ascalon, Jaffa and Acre against the might of Salah-al-Din's forces. Apparently, if we had made landfall at Cyprus, we may have encountered Richard the first of England and his cousin, Phillipe, the king of France, heading the second crusade to take Jerusalem back from the Muslims, who were busy preparing a besieging action against Acre as the next part of their campaign to hurl the accursed foreigners from their land and drive them into the sea.

'This news out of the east is not good for us,' said Raymond as we stood on the deck watching an evening sun sink beneath the horizon in a blaze of purples, pinks, reds and oranges, over a sea reflecting the potpourri of colour above it.

'The coastal towns are well defended now that the Franks have fallen back and consolidated their defences along the coast,' replied Ruth, 'Or so the captain of that trading dhow said. We can still make for Acre and get a sense of how things lie there and in the rest of Outremer. I won't give up on the dream of our hospital.'

'Nor will I,' I replied, 'especially now as we have the money Baldo stole from Cherubino and me to establish one.' I then paused, before adding, 'I can't help but wonder what has become of my father's house, his warehouses and emporia, let alone what has happened to my youngest brother Cherubino at sea, or otherwise.'

'After the disappointment and brutality of Baldo's attempt to take all from the both of you, I am not surprised. Acre must be gnawing at your desire and curiosity,' observed Raymond.

'You are not wrong in that assessment of my thoughts, at the moment,' I said as I placed my arm around Ruth in gratitude of the endless understanding she always managed to show me. She snuggled back up into my embrace and we stood there silently, taking in the colourful and changing vista of the sunset as we each pondered our fears and worries about what our futures might bring us.

We sailed on for another three weeks before we noticed a change in the light to the east and the swell of the sea. We were not far from Outremer, just further to the north of the eastern shore of the Mediterranean than the captain expected us to be. We were off the coast of the County of Tripoli and not far north from the city port of Tripoli. The captain was determined to put in to replenish supplies and carry out the necessary repairs after so many weeks bobbing across the Mediterranean Sea. At least our stay in Tripoli would give us some more accurate and detailed news of what was happening in Outremer and the Kingdom of Jerusalem.

The news was unsettling for all of us. We knew that the young King Baldwin had died of the leprosy we had sought a cure for in Hind and The Himalayas, some years back. There had been a lot of acrimonious dissent between the lords of the lands over who would assume the regency for Baldwin IV's young son, Baldwin V. Sadly, young Baldwin V ended this acrimony by dying the next year, which began a war of black words and black politics between Baldwin IV's sisters, Isabella and Sybilla and their respective husbands, Humphrey IV de Toron and Guy de Lusignon, as well as the young Baldwin V's regent Joscelin III of Courtenay.

Eventually, the throne had gone to Guy and Sybilla who, in an amazing feat of military incompetence, proceeded to lose, not only the army of the Kingdom of Jerusalem, but most of the Kingdom of Jerusalem, including the cities and territories of Tiberias, Acre,

Jaffa, Ceasarea, Haifa, Sidon and Ascalon to the armies of Salah-al-Din in a few short years.

Most shocking to the Christian world, was they also lost the Holy Cross upon which the Lord Jesus had died. Rubbing further salt into all these Frankish wounds, the Holy Roman Emperor, Frederick I, had drowned in a river enroute to relieve the crusaders. Most of his army had turned around and gone back to Europe but a small remnant had pushed on to the crusaders' camp currently besieging Acre under Frederick IV, Duke of Swabia. They were in such poor condition that the first thing they did on arrival was set up a field hospital to care for the wounded and emaciated. This was not seen as much help for a besieging army.

The world we were returning to had been turned on its head once again.

'There is good news,' said Ruth, 'Apparently, the pope has directed King Richard I of England and Phillip II of France to bring a force of crusaders to recover our losses. They are expected any time to arrive near Acre to support King Guy de Lusignon's siege of the Muslim-controlled city. Saladin is organising a naval blockade to prevent support arriving from the sea for the crusaders.'

'Should we still make Acre our first port of call?' asked Raymond.

'I'm hoping our captain, with his store of pottery jars down below, can be of assistance in getting us through to Acre's besiegers,' I replied, an idea forming in my mind, despite the looks of surprise on my friends' faces. I turned and sought out the captain.

# 59

'You ask a lot, young Ippolito. I, too, have heard about Guy's siege of Acre and you want me to run the Muslim naval blockade to get you there,' said the captain after I had put my proposal to sail there to him. 'But I am in debt to you and Ruth for the return of my comfort and the ability to sit down again. After so many years of pain and discomfort, I am indebted to you both.'

He smiled at this and then continued, 'I have no doubt the element of fiery surprises will get us through to a mooring depth near the crusader's shore but getting back out may prove a problem as the Muslim vessels will know what to expect and may provide some surprises of their own for me as I make my exit.'

'I know Acre. I was born there,' I said, 'At this time of year the setting sun is in the southwest. If we make our run to Acre under full sail and around sunset, the sun will be in their eyes, making us difficult to see at first. Then if they get close, we can toss a fire pot or two. After what I have seen, they will be much more cautious about getting too close even when you are making your exit.'

'Very well. I was going there anyway but changed my mind on the news coming from down south, but I can change my mind once again and unload my cargo and manifest there, make myself a tidy little profit for my worries and then make a speedy escape.'

The captain was another week affecting repairs and renovations to the inside and outside of The Mermaid before he was satisfied that she would do the job of running the Muslim blockade and making it to the Acre shore. With the rising sun, we left the port of

Tripoli on a swiftly running ebb tide and headed south with a good tail wind filling our sails fit to burst and make our bobbing progress all the more difficult for those getting about on deck.

The wind stayed that way all day and it was as the sun was setting that we spied the evening cooking fires and smoke rising from the city port of Tyre. We did not pull into the port for shelter but instead, anchored offshore some leagues past the city. Acre was only half a day's sail away and we did not wish to arrive too early the next day.

Around midday, the captain ordered the anchor to be hoisted aboard and the young cabin boy back up onto his precarious perch on the spar next to the mast with specific orders to keep his eyes peeled for any shipping. We set sail, the wind still blowing favourably for us and made good speed down the rest of the coast. The cabin boy tied himself to the mast as a precaution against being "bobbed" off the spar and into the sea.

It was as the sun was low in the water that we saw the first vessels of the Muslim naval blockade patrolling further out than the captain had expected. There were three of them and they barely constituted a fighting force as they were only medium-sized dhows with what looked like only the bare number of sailors aboard.

'Scouts,' said the captain, 'They will turn and run back to shore or their command vessel any moment now that they have taken our measure.'

But they didn't, they kept coming towards us.

'A dozen fire pots, Mr Mate. On deck and now!' ordered the captain.

The first mate ran to carry out his orders, grabbing another sailor along the way to help him carry the dangerous pottery as safely as possible back to the deck. Once this task was completed, we continued on our bobbing way and waited as the dhows drew nearer. They drew themselves into a line of three and, as a line of bowmen appeared on deck, we realised they intended to strafe us with arrows into surrender or death. We were higher in the water and, again it was to our advantage as by keeping ourselves low on the deck, the bowmen below us could not see any targets until the lone figure of Duncan suddenly stood up and launched his first pot.

The pot landed midships right by the mast and the sail, which were both set on fire with the initial explosion. The explosion also occurred beside coils of rope and other flammable material that added to the sudden conflagration and chaos that erupted on the deck of the dhow. Her timbers must have been old and dry as the flames quickly spread to the rest of the vessel. It was not long before men were jumping overboard rather than attempting to extinguish the fire. It was safer in the sea for those who could swim or had spied some flotsam or jetsam to cling to.

The second dhow was following closely behind the first and got a similar treatment from Duncan's strong arms and throwing ability. It was only moments before it, too, was a floating ball of flame and the crew were abandoning ship probably in the hope of being saved from drowning by the third dhow, which had turned away from its line of sail with the eruptions on the second dhow.

We sailed on, the captain drawing the sails to get as much speed out of the cog as the walls and towers of Acre became more visible on the horizon. As I had told the captain, the sun was directly behind us and we would have been difficult to see clearly. Unfortunately, the smoke from the burning dhows had alerted the nearby shore fleet that something was amiss and very quickly, seven large sails were turned and headed in our direction.

'All hands grab a pot and wait till my command,' roared the captain, 'You two as well,' he said indicating Raymond and me. We both hurried to comply, eager to have a go at this ancient form of weaponry.

The large war dhows made the same mistake the three smaller ones had and formed up in a line to strafe us with their arrows and javelins. The only problem this time was the larger dhows sat at about the same height above the water line as our bouncing Mermaid.

We could hear the shouts and yells of encouragement in eastern and western tongues from both the crusaders on the beach and the Muslims on the towers and walls of Acre.

We all kept low, with the exception of the captain, who kept up a steady stream of commands only occasionally ducking projectiles launched in his direction. He waited until two dhows were close beside us and then loudly yelled, 'Now.'

As one, we stood and launched a dozen incendiaries, six to each, onto both vessels with an even more intense fiery outcome. It was enough for those trailing war dhows to come about and alter their course to avoid what was happening to the first two. The men on the shore cheered loudly with encouragement.

The captain did not bother to slow The Mermaid, instead he pointed it at the shore and, with all the speed he could muster from his fat, little bobbing boat, ran it straight onto the shore where it wobbled a bit and then gently toppled to one side as it came to rest. The men onshore quickly surrounded us, cheering madly at the spectacular display they had just witnessed.

I was back home. Well, almost.

# 60

Unfortunately, the final topple of The Mermaid onto the beach as we ground ashore on the sand, dislodged some of the fire pots below decks and it was only a moment or two before fires erupted and overtook the beached little cog. We all jumped madly onto the beach or were assisted to get down by the men there.

Amidst all of this, the captain was running around and yelling at everyone, 'Get away from here. Run. Run.'

And we did. And not a moment too soon as, in one huge explosion, the cog was blown to pieces. Its scattered remains enveloping us in a blanket of flames, smoke and debris that kept us running away from the conflagration. The rest of the fire pots had blown off below decks all at once. The size of the explosion brought a cheer from the Muslim garrison upon the walls of Acre.

Into this chaos rode, what I thought was a noble commander by his dress, but in fact was King Philip II of France. He was accompanied by half a dozen nobles all richly adorned in fine clothes and jewellery, their horses similarly caparisoned and a small troop of mail clad royal guardsmen.

'Superb, superb,' called the king, 'Excellent work. Where is the captain? I must congratulate him on an excellent show of skill and tactics.'

Captain Svein had come up beside me.

'I'm no longer a captain as I no longer have a ship,' he said in that enigmatic way of his, 'This was your idea. You are coming with me to meet this gawdy-looking King of France.'

Svein and I moved through the crowd of sailors and soldiers, accepting claps on the back and cheers of praise as we did. We approached the king and his retinue, rather anxiously and awkwardly.

'Your Grace,' we said simultaneously and then bowed our deference as well.

'A fine show, a fine show indeed,' said King Phillip, 'What are your names?'

'Captain Svein Trollface of Copenhagen.'

'Ippolito of Acre,' came our replies one after the other.

'Tell me, good gentlemen, are there any more of those fabulous fire pots you were tossing about on your way in here?' asked the king.

'No, your Grace,' replied Svein, 'The last of them went up in that massive explosion and the fire you see before you.'

'A shame,' replied the king, 'Are you able to bring us anymore?'

'I am afraid not, your Grace. They were from an old Byzantine armoury stockpile on the island of Cos. Apparently, they were forgotten about by the Greeks who just left them behind after deserting the island for me to discover many years later. I'm afraid you will have to ask the Emperor of Byzantine if he has any left to give you.'

'Which he never has. He is a crafty and oily Greek only interested in what profits him and cares nought for westerners,' came an almost snarled reply, but not directed at the two of us, 'What has brought you here to this place?'

'Trade and passengers,' replied Svein.

'The latter to be one of those standing with you?'

'Yes sire. The whole idea for our foray came from him.'

'Well done, young man. Ippolito, was it?'

'Sire,' I replied in affirmation.

'And you were born here?'

'Yes, Sire.'

'He and his companions are physicians of considerable excellence as I can vouch for from personal experience,' interrupted Svein, not waiting to be spoken to first by the king. Phillip did not seem to mind the lapse in normal royal protocols.

'I should like to meet some prospective physicians. Perhaps your little team, yourself included Captain, might come to my pavilion tonight for supper? I can appraise you of how things stand here in Acre at the moment.'

'It would be an honour, Your Majesty,' I replied, 'Although I must admit that none of us would be suitably attired for such grand company.'

'There are no fashions in the circus we call the arena of war, Ippolito. Come as you are.'

And with that, the king and his entourage galloped off to closer inspect the remains of the disintegrated and still smoking Mermaid.

'Supper. With the king of France,' said a shocked Ruth when Svein and I arrived back to the remains of The Mermaid, 'But I have nothing to wear!'

'The king decried the need for any royal pomp or ceremony in what he called a circus of war and said to come as we are. A good wash to clean away the stink of so many weeks at sea should suffice.'

'As you can see,' said a fully replete Phillip lounging back in his camp chair holding a goblet of wine later that night at dinner, 'the situation here in the kingdom of Jerusalem and Outremer is grave, with Christendom in danger of losing all that she has won in the last century.

'We here, in this army, are currently the meat between the bread of two Muslim forces. Within the well-fortified city of Acre is a Muslim garrison of somewhere between 15,000 and 20,000 soldiers. Acre is a difficult city to storm. It is ringed by double walls and towers on the land side and strong dike walls protect the seaward side of the city. Besieging them are our forces of a little under 60,000, made up of crusaders from France, Anjou, Pisa, Sicily, the Papal States, Armenia, Cilicia, Denmark, The Holy Roman Empire and Genoa, amongst a number of other smaller freelance groups. That does not include the Knights of the Temple and The Hospital nor a large English contingent under King Richard that are expected any day.

'Unfortunately, we too, are under siege and encircled by Salah-al-Din's relief forces who conservatively number around 45,000. Both our navies are blockading and contesting Acre's harbour and the surrounding coast. Fortunately, our ships outnumber theirs two to one. Just as many of their ships, trying to run the blockade to the city, have been lost or taken, as have ours trying to run supplies to our troops on the coastal surrounds. Still, supplies are getting through to both sides and neither side has been able to invest the defences of the other, despite some desperate and bloody attempts to do so.'

I sat in some consternation at this summary of the situation surrounding Acre. I desperately wanted to enter the city and see what had become of my old family home and my father's warehouses and emporia.

'Do you think things might change when the English King Richard, his fleet and his army arrive,' I asked.

'I'm sure Richard thinks so,' came Philip's almost caustic sounding reply.

# 61

Philip had not been idly waiting for his brother king, Richard, to arrive in the kingdom. At various sites around the city's perimeter, great machines of war were being constructed and rising up to threaten the garrison within the city. Philip had constructed seven massive stone throwing machines that kept up a day and night bombardment of the city. Philip had also significantly strengthened the palisades around the crusaders' encampment, protecting them from Saladin's surrounding force and any forces from the garrison bursting forth to break the siege.

Archers and slingers kept up a steady night and day barrage that ensured heads behind the parapets of Acre stayed permanently lowered, thereby enabling attempts to fill in the dry moat surrounding the city with all manner of detritus from rocks and earth to dead horses and humans. There was even a story of a woman who, dying from a Saracen arrow, requested that her body be thrown into the moat so her passing might help the current crusaders.

To counter the filling of the moat, the defending garrison divided themselves into groups of three: those who broke and cut up the horses and corpses into portable sizes, those who carried the putrefying remains to the sea and those who defended the others against crusader attack. Philip was building a momentum within the corps of crusaders that only needed to be ignited.

That ignition would be the arrival of the English King Richard. He had the larger army, more ships and greater monetary resources than Philip and it was for this that Philip held off attempting his own assault on Acre's walls.

The King of England arrived in style, having sunk and burned a Muslim supply ship with all aboard, within sight of the Frankish camp. Before his royal ship had even beached itself, he had leapt from the bow into the shallows and, up to his chest in water, waded ashore, waving his sword ready to take battle to the foe.

'He is certainly very tall,' commented Ruth as the king emerged from the sea and stood on the shore dripping and issuing commands. 'Long legs and arms as well.'

'All the better for drawing and using the sword,' added Raymond.

'That red-gold beard and long hair certainly looks like a lion's mane. No surprise his nickname is "Lion Heart",' I added, not knowing the name was more for his prowess in battle than his leonine features.

And he roared like a lion, issuing commands and giving orders left, right and centre as his troops, horses and war machinery were disembarked and brought ashore. His voice could be heard above the crowds of soldiers on the shore and those looking on. He wasted no time in bringing all his men ashore, commandeering a campsite for his army to the north of the city and commencing reconnoitring activity around the city and along the camp's perimeter, assessing every possible weakness in the enemy's dispositions and opportunities for the crusader attack.

Just over a week later, King Richard was laid low with an illness that confined him to his tent. Or so his royal physicians had recommended. In a fit of frustrated belligerence, the king had his litter carried to a protected area near the walls of Acre and spent his time firing crossbow bolts at those on the wall. His lords and court sycophants applauding his many kills.

'He's a good shot,' said Raymond in admiration, during one of the breaks we were taking from our duties in the camp's field hospital, 'but with his teeth and hair all falling out, one can hardly call it a royal and heroic look.'

'I'll bet we could cure him,' said Ruth, 'but the king insists, for security's sake, to be tended only by his dung-ministering western quacks and physicians.'

'Perhaps you might have better luck with the French King,' laughed Raymond, 'They say he has the illness as well. Perhaps that welcoming kiss of peace they gave each other has spread something around.'

Whatever the cause of the royal malaises, siege activity continued on a daily basis. While teams of sappers were deployed, digging mines beneath the walls of Acre, intermittent attempts at storming the walls with ladders, firebombs and men, took place as others defended the rear of the camp from Saladin's surrounding army. Throughout all of this, there was the noise of trebuchets and catapults being cranked, the whip and crack of their release and the almighty crash of their munition against the walls of Acre. Some of these machines were so large and destructive that they had been given names such as "Bad Neighbour" or "Gods Catapult". And, of course, there were the screams of men being burned, crushed or pierced.

Along with the usual diseases and illnesses of siege encampment, all this military activity naturally kept the three of us busy in the field hospital treating the wounded and sick. The three of us worked together; Ruth and I using the needles to provide analgesia, in our almost telepathic synchronisation of surgical procedure and Raymond assisting in numerous useful ways around the clinic and wards.

We were well removed from the walls on either side of the encampment and unaware of much of what was happening immediately outside of Acre and at our rear. All we knew was the number of wounded being brought in for treatment was increasing and we feared the campaign was faltering. We kept working hour after hour, through our fatigue and weariness, somehow finding the energy to keep repairing the broken bodies brought before us. Every so often, Raymond would take one of us outside and douse us in a bucket of water as the amount of blood on our persons had become so sticky and cloying as to make holding instruments and needles impossible. The same applied to our clothing, which became stiff and uncomfortable due to the amount of drying blood on their surface and was restricting our movement and ability to operate. Blood and screaming were everywhere, both outside and inside our little field hospital, as well.

Our fatigue was so great that it was some time before we noticed the number of incoming wounded was decreasing in numbers and severity and the noises of battle were diminishing. All was made clear when a sergeant of the hospitallers entered the tent announcing, 'It is done. The heathen dogs have capitulated. Acre has fallen and is ours once again.'

# 62

It would be three days before we were allowed to enter the city of Acre. Negotiations between both sides had taken place concluding that: the city and all its contents were to be surrendered to the Franks, the lives of all Muslims, living within the city, were to be spared, the depleted captive garrison of 2,500 were to be held hostage as guarantors for a further 200,000 gold dinars to be paid to the crusaders as soon as Saladin could raise the enormous sum, the True Cross was to be returned and the release of over a thousand Frankish prisoners was to be immediate.

The city was saved from a sack and further feral death and destruction, as strict orders relating to this were disseminated amongst all the crusaders, no matter their nationality. During this time, the three of us existed in a state of bewildered exhaustion, the fire of endurance, brought on by an extremity of necessity, had died within each of us and we spent two days collapsed in our tent, drinking only water and sleeping.

Eventually, the city gates were thrown open and the defeated garrison of Acre marched out of the city to make their formal submission to the crusading forces. The three of us watched the procession and I could not help but admire the brave and noble face the garrison put on as it confronted its humiliation. The soldiers were disarmed and relieved of any armour they wore and then led back into an overcrowded imprisonment beneath the city's citadel. Some of them were in a dreadful state, sporting untreated wounds, the sores and infections of disease and the emaciation of malnutrition.

When Ruth, Raymond and I entered the city later in the day, we were struck by the hollow-eyed indifference the citizens of Acre seemed to show us. It was as if they were floating in a dream of their own making and that the cessation of the crusader bombardment was only a temporary respite. They did not exhibit any of the joy or appreciation that liberated people normally show to their heroes. Their city was basically in ruins and it was the crusader weapons that had brought the destruction.

The destruction had been random and showed no preference to any within the city. Mosques, synagogues and churches lay in desecrated ruins, the houses of rich and poor alike lay in rubble crushed by the enormous stones hurled by the giant mechanical beasts of siege warfare and marketplaces seemed like wastelands in miniature. The citadel and the port harbour were relatively untouched as they were furthest from the walls and the machines of destruction. Sadly, the house I had spent my childhood in was no more, a victim of fire and not heavy stones, as were the nearby warehouses and emporia that had belonged to my father.

Aside from the capture of the city, Saladin's prize Egyptian fleet had become trapped within the harbour by the enclosing blockade of European ships. Over 70 vessels changed hands with their capture and Saladin's dreams of challenging Christian control of the Mediterranean were dashed. It was with his tail between his legs that the sultan Saladin slinked off to the east to lick his wounds, try to rebuild his reputation and contemplate his revenge against the accursed Franks.

Saladin was not the only royal personage to depart Acre after its fall. King Philip of France also decided he had fulfilled his crusader's pledge in the fall of Acre and took the vast majority of his fleet and army with him back to France, leaving King Richard as sole commander of the crusading forces. It also meant a depletion in his forces.

Once we had recovered from our marathon surgery, we held a meeting to discuss our plans.

'Saladin still holds all the land between Acre and Jerusalem and he is allowing freelance and renegade Bedouin bands to raid and pillage any parties foolish enough to try and reach the Holy City,' reported Raymond.

'And with Philip having left for France, I doubt Richard will spare any troops just to get the three of us, or anyone else, back to Jerusalem,' I added.

'Apparently the king wishes to secure the coast before marching on Jerusalem to protect his rear. A reasonable and wise stratagem on the face of it but one that will delay us reaching our objective,' said Raymond.

'It would seem we must place our trust in Richard to eventually lead us home, albeit by an indirect means,' concluded Ruth.

Richard was keen to march south to take the coastal towns of Haifa, Caesarea, Arsuf, Jaffa and Ascalon and apparently was growing daily more impatient with Saladin's recalcitrant attitude in honouring his payment, returning the True Cross and releasing the Frankish prisoners he held in mostly dark and dank prisons.

Finally, he was prepared to wait no longer. One afternoon, five weeks after the surrender of Acre, Richard marched out of the town, beyond the trenches of what had been a besieging army to the plains of Acre and established a temporary camp within full view of the rear guard of Saladin's army posted on the nearby peak of Tell Kaisan. Richard then had the bulk of Acre's Muslim garrison marched out onto the plain, herded and bundled them to sit on the ground where they huddled in fear, uncertainty and confusion of what was going to happen to them. Was Richard planning to release the prisoners before moving down the coast?

The king raised his arm and then quickly brought it down in a signal to the troops awaiting his command. Immediately, hundreds of crusader knights and soldiers charged and fell on the undefended garrison, striking blows and stabbing in a frenzy of blood-letting, yells and agonised screams. Within a short while, the Franks and the ground around the massacre were drenched in blood. Heads, limbs and headless bodies littered the field.

We had been watching from what was left of one of Acre's walls along with most of the local population and members of the army. We held our breaths in absolute horror at Richard's ruthlessness. By carrying out this outrageous massacre, after having given his word of their eventual release, he had dishonoured himself for all time.

Richard turned and rode back into the city, leaving the bodies to rot where they fell. Unencumbered with prisoners to guard and feed, he was now free to travel south and carry out his plan to subjugate the southern coast before turning inland to retake Jerusalem.

# 63

Two days later, leaving a garrison behind him to rebuild and defend the city of Acre, Richard marched his army from the city and proceeded to head south, keeping as close as possible to the coast and his supply fleet that shadowed and supported us at sea as we trudged along over the sands of the Levant. Just as the supply fleet shadowed our army from the sea so did the Muslim forces from the low hills that ran parallel down to the beach, shadow our force from our landward side.

Richard organised an order that also saw three divisions marching in parallel to the sea and the fleet with its supplies and reinforcements, if needed, on the right. The column to the outer left of the march consisted of heavy infantry who had to rely on their shields, heavy armour and thick jerkins to take the bulk of the enemy attacks which were frequent and at least daily. They were periodically replaced and replenished by men from the right-hand column by the sea. In the middle, rode the cavalry, led by the Templars at the front and the Hospitallers bringing up the rear guard. It was the Knights of St John in the rear guard who took the brunt of much of the attacks. With their heavy armour and jerkins, the Muslim arrows were only able to lodge in the chainmail of their hauberks and seldom penetrated any further. This often resulted in the warriors appearing like porcupines with dozens of arrows sticking out of their mail.

The three of us travelled on the right by the sea, which was a blessing, as it was the middle of summer and the heat was stifling. The hot sun, along with the soft sand, made the going slow for horses and men alike, so much so that we rarely made more than five miles a day as we travelled south. At night, double and sometimes triple lines of pickets were set, but still the Muslim army kept gnawing away at our defences and our patience.

Richard rode up and down the lines constantly, keeping his men in check to prevent any breakout to charge the enemy, as it would dissolve the line of march and our defences, leaving us more vulnerable. Warriors, however, are made, if not trained, to fight and it was with great difficulty that Richard curbed their natural instincts to attack the superior and annoying forces with their slingshots, arrows and javelins to try to drive them away. It was the Hospitallers in the rear guard and the left-hand column who took the worst of the Muslim skirmishers and cavalry attacks upon the marching army. Richard would brook no stopping enroute and the wounded would either have to be carried or assisted until the evening halt, when Ruth and I and other surgeons and physicians would have an opportunity to treat them. Many died of blood loss in the wait till the evening triage could begin.

After four days of stifling heat and continuous attack, the column reached the outer environs of Haifa when a fog descended upon the seaside plain, throwing many in the crusader column into disarray, particularly the rear guard. The Muslims, wasting no time, launched an immediate attack under Saladin's brother, al-Adil, upon the rear guard. If it had not been for the courage of Richard, charging like a blood- crazed demon into their ranks, slaying left and right and almost driving the enemy off on his own, the outcome of the day could have been horribly different. It was such a close call that Richard had the army rest up for two days while he reorganised it. He reduced the amount of equipment and stores being carried, increased the defensive forces of the left-hand column and issued ultimatums about the need for discipline, if we were to survive the march under continuous attack from Saladin's forces.

For eight days we pushed on through heat so intolerable that there were several deaths from it and much debilitation from fatigue and stroke. Many of the dead were ferried to the shadowing supply ships for recuperation and recovery. Richard was aware of the effect the heat had on his men and he proceeded at an undemanding pace and rested them near rivers and water, before the heat of the day became extreme.

'I'm glad we get to march by the sea,' said Raymond after we observed a knight fall from his horse, half broiled alive in his heavy armour and jerkin.

We passed by the ruined fortress of Destroit and pushed on to Caesarea by which time, our army was beginning to falter. Food was beginning to lessen in quantity and quality, arguments and fights broke out amongst the troops over the carcasses of the dead horses. Richard was forced to ration out the horsemeat amongst those he considered worthy, based on their contribution to the column's defence that day.

Despite Richard's unswerving nerve and courage, he was not immune to assault and on one day, he took a crossbow bolt in the hip. The king managed to remain in the saddle as his armour had taken the brunt of the blow and he was not seriously hurt. Had he fallen from his horse in the thick of the fighting fracas he found himself in, the crusade may have collapsed then and there on the beaches of the Levant.

Saladin, like Richard, was a king who led from the front and, on several occasions, we observed him riding amongst the skirmishers and slingers ignoring the arrows, javelins and spears that flew about his head. He was, every time, accompanied by two fearful looking pages, each leading a spare horse as they followed their leader from one hot spot to another in danger of collapsing, all the time exhorting his troops to greater effort for the glory of Allah and Islam.

Occasionally, Saladin was accompanied by a giant Egyptian Mamluk, known as Ayas the Tall, a celebrated and ferocious warrior who was known by both sides to cut swathes of blood and body parts through the ranks of his enemies. One day, as he was riding with Saladin, a lucky stroke from a crusader brought his horse down and placed Ayas, in his heavy armour, on his back like an upended turtle. He was quickly fallen on and butchered, while Saladin's bodyguard effected a quick retreat, protecting their commander. There was a lot of cheering and celebration in the crusader camp that night with the death of this ferocious warrior. It was very much a morale boosting event.

But still, the next day, the march went on, the attacks went on, the heat went on, the poor food went on, the dying went on and Ruth, Raymond and I went on. It was the same arduous journey for many, many more days.

When would this accursed march ever end? I asked myself several times a day.

# 64

The march would end, we were told, when we reached Jaffa. Take Jaffa and the gateway to Jerusalem from the coast would be open. It was, again so camp rumour said, only 25 miles down the coast and from there the king would strike west for the Holy City. But Saladin had still not attacked our army en masse in pitched battle and we knew it must come if he wished to retain Jerusalem. He had been patiently waiting, reconnoitring and carefully selecting his ground and time for an offensive engagement. He also underestimated the cunning of the English king.

Ahead of us, our route ran through the forest of Arsuf before it reached the River Rochetaille, our planned campsite for that evening. On the other side of the river, the narrow sandy beach opened out into a wide sandy plain that stretched six miles before the small town of Arsuf. Our campsite was protected by marshes lying to the inland of the mouth of the River Rochetaille.

Richard did the rounds of the army that evening, stressing the importance of maintaining the cohesive positions we had maintained throughout the march. His spies in the Saladin's camp had reported that the sultan was planning to make a major offensive on our lines the next day.

And indeed, the Sultan was.

'Oh, Beelzebub's balls,' exclaimed Raymond as he looked south to the plain and the surrounding low hills the next morning, where hundreds of mounted warriors wheeled into position and drew their horses up in a line across the vast expanse.

263

'So much cavalry. Is it Saladin's entire army?' I asked, joining him.

'I don't see any heavy or light infantry, nor archers or slingers,' he replied.

'The archers will be those accursed Turkish horsemen that have plagued us every day.'

At a signal from their commander the horsemen wheeled their mounts again and rode off to disappear into the forest in an orderly manner.

'How many of Saladin's forces are hidden in that forest. We have no way of knowing where he is deploying his main force and where and when he will bring his hammer down on us. It will be hard and fast when he does,' said a sombre Raymond.

We returned to our tent, struck it, ate a small breakfast and joined the column in our allotted position, before moving off in a southerly direction toward Arsuf.

Saladin was crafty. He left us unmolested by skirmishers for the first part of the morning, no doubt deploying them within the hidden confines of the forest. Action dispels fear and the lack of it that morning allowed our fears to magnify and the tension within the marching and riding ranks was almost palpable.

And then it began. Line after line of mounted Turkish archers swept by our lines, firing great black clouds of arrows into our ranks. The heavily armoured left flank and the rear guard took the brunt of the barrage, but Richard's discipline held strong and the soldiers of the left and rear marched doggedly on, their shields and chain mail armour bristling with Saracen arrows. The enemy, in an attempt to further unsettle our men, included a cacophony of drums, cymbals, gongs, trumpets and wild ululating war cries in their assault. The sound vibrated upon my chest and my ears ached from the volume of it.

I kept casting my eyes back down the line to where the rear guard Hospitallers were taking the full brunt of the Saladin's assault as they could be attacked from both the rear and the left flank. As I had feared, a force of some dozen Turkish horsemen broke through to the right-hand side of the line and were slicing a bloody swathe through the less well defended arm of the column.

'Enemy to the rear,' I yelled to all who might hear me, 'Here they come.'

Raymond stepped up beside me, drew his sword as I did the discarded one, I had appropriated after the fall of Acre. Ruth moved out to waist deep in the sea where the enemy's horses would be hampered trying to reach her and unsheathed her knives. Quickly, we were joined by other soldiers of Richard's army and drew up in a line two ranks deep to face the oncoming Turks.

The clash of horse and a line of heavy infantry is an uncertain event. Some of the enemy horses baulked at the last moment, rather than face a line bristling with spear and sword points. Others, better trained, crashed on into the line of defenders, their riders reaping heads, arms and hands as they slashed and cut with their deadly scimitars and jabbed with their fiercely pointed javelins.

I have always hated harming and injuring horses in battle. Ultimately, their use in the wars and battles of mankind, is a betrayal of God's will that mankind should have dominion over the beasts of the earth. To me, dominion includes care and guardianship. It pulled on my heart strings every time I launched a slicing blow through the front legs of a charging horse to send its rider tumbling over the head of his screaming mount to splash in the water. Once in the water, the heavily armoured Turkish cavalrymen were quickly dispatched by being held down and drowned or pierced through the eye slits of their helmets by knives and swords.

Raymond and our line faced and withheld several similar attempts by Turkish cavalry that morning. Each time the number of horsemen, getting by the battling Hospitallers in the rear guard, increased, our struggles became more violent and bloody. I watched as one Turk managed to lean from his saddle as he tumbled from his horse to grapple Raymond around the neck and drag him under the water in the macabre embrace of a drowning death. I pushed my way through the sandy churned up waters and dying men and horses to where I could make out their struggling forms under the opaqued water and plunged my sword down into what I prayed was the Turk's back and not Raymond's. A wave distorted my vision of what was happening below but then Raymond's gasping head suddenly burst above the water. I helped his spluttering form to his feet as he coughed and spluttered sea water from his mouth and nose, before we turned and faced the next riders.

Raymond and I stood our ground side by side and fought together, bringing down rider after rider and then speedily dispatching them with a quick sword thrust, rather that inflict the horror of drowning upon them. Besides, drowning a man wastes precious time and leaves your back exposed, as many of our men found out.

During a brief lull in the fighting, I looked around for Ruth, who was still standing further out to sea with the wounded and other non-combatants. She held up her hands, one of them holding an empty knife sheath indicating she had expended her small supply of deadly projectiles. I was sure she had accounted for more than one or two horsemen.

As I turned back, I noticed that the disposition of the Hospitaller rear guard appeared to be falling apart.

# 65

The Hospitallers were not however falling apart. They were disobeying Richard's instructions to maintain the order of march and not to sheer off in wasteful heroics. Whilst the vanguard of Richard's army had reached the relative safety of Arsuf's walls, the beleaguered Hospitaller crossbowmen had been forced into a position of having to shoot and load whilst walking backwards, a necessary action but one which caused the lines to lose formation and the flights of bolts and arrows to lose cohesion. Gaps had opened up and into these charged mace and sword wielding cavalrymen, creating havoc amongst the rear guard.

To counter this, I could see the Hospitaller commander, Garnier de Nablis, rallying his cavalry in the centre file and his men at the rear. Richard rode up to Nablis and remonstrated with him, apparently refusing Nablis the opportunity of a charge. It was not Nablis who made the decision but the Marshall of the Knights, Baldwin le Carron, who moved through the desperate ranks of Hospitaller infantry and into the Saracen ranks with resounding cries of, 'St George, St George'.

This was all that was needed for order in the rear to fall apart and the battle suddenly hung in the balance as Richard's rear guard disintegrated in a concerted charge against the enemy. Raymond and I ran to join them, whilst others attempted to fill the gaps emerging in the defensive line of march and the rear guard. Richard raced back to his heavy cavalry in a desperate attempt to prevent his strategy unravelling.

Saladin had spied the weakness in our rear and finally launched his reserves of heavy infantry into the fray. Raymond and I had taken up defensive positions and stances at the rear, along with the remnant of the infantry that had not charged off with the Hospitaller cavalry. We were in a pathetically desperate situation; a thin line of hot, weary and desperately thirsty men against a reserve heavy infantry division of fresh, watered, well-armed and armoured warriors bearing down on us.

Raymond and I stood together, true brothers in arms, as the enemy came charging and screaming towards our pathetic line of defence. I felt Raymond's hand upon my shoulder in a gesture of reassurance. I turned and saw his perpetually smiling face as he thrust his hand over mine into the warrior's wrist grasp.

'Together,' he said.

'Together,' I replied.

And then all hell broke loose as the enemy infantry crashed against our line. The force of their charge pushed our line back. It was hell on earth. Opposing forces' shields locked together, helmets tried to bash the faces and helms of those opposite, arms were trying to reach up to grab faces and gouge eyeballs, teeth bit at noses and cheeks, knees were raised over and over again, seeking other's testicles and it was all so cramped and close quartered that no sword could be raised by either side. It was a wild and vicious brawl of grunts, cries, curses and the occasional agonised scream.

I still carried the stiletto my father had given me on my departure to Jerusalem so many years ago. I somehow managed to get my hand down to its hilt through the crush of my body against that of a foul-smelling Turk, pressed so closely against me, I could feel the warmth of his rank breath on my face as he tried to bite at my chin. I turned the blade in my hand and lunged it forward as hard as I could at waist level. I felt the blade break though his tunic to be briefly stalled by the resistance of his mail armour, but the blade was slim and quickly slipped through the metal rings to pierce his groin and open the great artery that ran down the leg. I twisted it left and right, severing as much as I could. The Turk's eyes widened in front of me as the horror of his impending death settled upon him. He stood staring at me, an utterable curse upon his lips, unable to move his dying body which was held upright against mine by the crush. I watched the light slowly die in his eyes as his soul fled his body.

Raymond was still beside me but the hands of a Turk were wrapped around his neck and he was clearly struggling with eyes bulging and a pale purplish pallor taking over his lips and face. Despite the crush, I managed to retract the stiletto from the dead Turk in front of me and twisted myself to a point where I could try a similar thrust into the Saracen attacking Raymond. The problem was, I was not directly facing the man and had to settle for a kidney stab, painful but not as immediately deadly as the groin thrust. I felt my stiletto pierce armour and skin and twisted the blade every which way I could. The warrior arched his back in agony as his hands fell away from Raymond's neck, returning the colour to his face. The two combatants were crushed almost face to face but the warrior's knees buckled and we were able to let him slump between us to the bloodied ground.

On the struggle went, each side pushing and shoving. My stiletto, probably one of the smallest blades on the field that day, took numerous Saracen lives and before too long, Raymond and I had a pile of dead bodies lying in front of our position. This acted as both a deterrent and a defence that allowed Raymond to draw his sword and wield it effectively increasing the height of the pile before us.

Time seems to flow slowly or, alternatively, fly quickly in battle. It is always difficult to know how much time has passed when every moment could be your last. I know not how long Raymond and I stood our ground "together" as we had pledged each other before the battle. At some point in the crash and crush, the yells and screams, the clang and clash, I heard the distant and faint sound of trumpet blasts, six of them and my heart sank as I envisaged the attack of Saladin's heavy cavalry.  I could feel the distant thump and rumble of charging horses coming nearer under my feet.

# 66

Suddenly and almost as one, the crush of the enemy fell back as Richard and his heavy cavalry rode into and quickly broke the back of Saladin's forces attacking our rear. The enemy broke and ran and Raymond and I almost collapsed into each other as we were released from the press that had been holding all the combatants upright. As best we could, we parted lines to let Richard and the cavalry through our defences and at the retreating enemy army.

I watched the king, with his long arms and massive broadsword, cut a wide path through the enemy, his long reach making him, in turn, almost unreachable by his foes. On he led his cavalry, slaughtering the enemy in a bloody and terrible revenge for the weeks of torment they had endured at the sultan's command on the march south. Richard pursued the retreating forces for half a mile, over which bodies lay heaped, dead or dying, groaning or silent but no longer fighting. It was at this point that Richard slowed and regrouped his charge, too aware of them becoming scattered and vulnerable to further attack.

As he led the cavalry troop back to our victorious lines, the Sultan's cavalry regrouped itself, turned once again, showing incredible courage and recharged our lines. Richard easily repulsed this last-ditch effort of Saladin's forces and scattered the remnant of his army to the woods and hills in every direction, with the exception of west and into a bloody sea already choking with drowned and dead bodies.

In the midst of the floating bodies, I saw Ruth wading through them, turning them over and inspecting them. She removed a knife from the body of one corpse and I realised she was trying to retrieve some of her throwing knives from the mass of possible bodies drifting around her. Raymond and I joined her and continued the search, between the three of us rescuing four knives of her original six.

'We can get some more made when Richard sets up his base and we find a blacksmith to make some more,' I offered in consolation for the loss of two of her precious knives.

The three of us turned away from the blood and carnage of the battle, unwilling to witness the frenzy of looting that had already begun on the bodies of the deceased Saracens. The fury of the crusaders was still evident over the trials they had endured over the past weeks as fingers were cut off to remove rings, bowels and rectums opened to find swallowed and secreted wealth, teeth prized out for their gold fillings, gems gouged from sword handles and body armour and any other object of wealth ripped from its previous owner.

'I'm not sure I want to stay with this army of Richard's,' said Ruth as we ambled south along the beach away from the final horrific scenes unfolding after the battle, 'His murderous annihilation of the Acre garrison disgusted me and now I see his army desecrating the bodies of the lifeless with no regard to the sanctity or dignity of a deceased human being.'

'Where would you have us go? What would you have us do?' asked a pragmatic Raymond, 'Jerusalem is still closed to us or at least any safe route to the city is closed. The desert between here and there will be full of renegade deserters, Bedouin brigands and disillusioned and disappointed warriors wanting revenge on any Frank they can lay their hands on.'

'Raymond is right, Ruth,' I said, 'It seems we must stay with this king if we are to stay alive in Outremer. Life is simply too dangerous in this land right now.'

'And it is not dangerous right now?! Look at the pair of you, covered in blood, bruises around your necks and faces and countless minor cuts and wounds on your hands and forearms, let alone what I can't see under your armour.'

Suddenly, Ruth broke down crying, tears streaming down her face and great gasping sobs heaving from her chest. I took her in my arms and held her, while she hid her head against my chest and sobbed. In the seven years since we had left Jerusalem, I had not seen Ruth cry like this and I felt somewhat disarmed by her breaking down in such a manner. Raymond looked awkwardly away and was lost for words as he too had become so used to a heroically strong Ruth, persevering in the face of all sorts of adversity.

Finally, Ruth pulled away from my embrace and cuffing her eyes, dried them before looking up at me.

'I'm sorry,' she apologised, 'It's not just me anymore. There is another person in this picture. Ippolito, you are going to be a father and I am not going to lose this one.'

I was speechless for a moment or two, as the gravity of what Ruth told me settled in. I was going to be a father. A new life was going to come into the world that was part me, part Ruth. I would do anything and everything to nurture and protect that life. Ruth was right. Staying with Richard's army was no longer an option and I said so.

Raymond was all congratulations but at the same time troubled by our dilemma of "where to now?".

We sat down on the beach, Ruth lying against my side, her head upon my shoulder.

'It seems to me,' said Raymond, 'that the nearest, safest place for us may be Acre, even though it is devastated and in ruins. The Templars and Hospitallers will be keen to rebuild it as the new capital of Outremer and increase its defences at the same time. Although your father's house and emporia and warehouses are gone, the property they stood on is yours and can be rebuilt into whatever you two so desire. Your inheritance will find its way to you through the Templars banking connections and, most importantly, you two can start raising the large family you are bound to have.'

He smiled broadly and then announced, 'To Acre.'

# 67

Richard wasted no time in organising his forces, readying them for the march onto Jaffa and then Ascalon, the gateway to Saladin's Egypt and his principal source: men and materiel. He also had well over a hundred injured and non-combatant men, including both nobles and common soldiers. Richard was not going to slow his march south, impeded by the needs of the wounded and lame. It was a simple matter for the three of us to volunteer for medical and surgical duty in the column of soldiery returning to Acre.

Our column left the day after Richard's army departed for Jaffa. Again, we traversed the coastal route sticking close to the sea and its cooling coastal breezes. We were accompanied by 30 mounted knight Hospitallers and 50 heavy and light infantries. Our progress was painfully slow, thanks to the sand of the beaches we traversed and the slow pace of the lame and wounded. There were no wagons or spare horses for them and many simply died of exhaustion trying to make it back to the safety of Acre's walls. We occasionally caught sight of Saladin's scouts but they were quickly deterred any further investigation by the incursions of the knights on their locations.

For the most part, they did not appear terribly interested in our progress, probably due to the massive deterioration in morale and esprit de corps that had infected Saladin's army since the battle of Arsuf. We had heard on route that many of Saladin's emirs had taken their armies home, leaving the Sultan distressed and depressed about the reversal of fortune he had wrought in seeking to drive the Franks from his homeland. He had lost a lot in terms of men, money and materiels, but in the Muslim world, he had lost the most valuable commodity of all – he had lost face.

Whist the route march home was slow, it was also a chance for all of us to recoup our energies and restore our bodies as much as possible. While many died of their wounds, many more made good recoveries and the atmosphere of the march almost took on a festive atmosphere. During the day, we trailed a fishing net through the shallows. The net had been left behind in one of the many nameless, small fishing hamlets along the coast, the residents not having yet returned to their huts after the army having passed through. Each evening, we hauled in a catch of small, but tasty, sardines and other sea creatures. Various springs in the nearby hinterland provided fresh, sweet water and the one or two archers and crossbowmen brought in a steady supply of game and bird.

Raymond took to experimenting with seaweeds and shellfish, trying to recreate the flavours that Darma had concocted for us around the mouth of the Indus in what seemed a lifetime ago, when we were still in Hind. His early attempts were either too salty and left us thirsting madly for water or had an overpowering bitter taste due to the wrong seaweeds being tossed into the pot. We did eventually determine the best seaweeds for flavour and were able to complement our diet with fresh vegetable matter, even if it was from the sea and raised a few eyebrows amongst our companions, at least until they tried some of the tasty fish stew.

Several weeks later, we spied the walls of Acre and were amazed at the state of its repairs. Richard had left two of his closest advisors, Bertrum de Verdun and Stephen Longchamp, to maintain the garrison and rebuild the city as much as possible. Naturally, they had started with the defensive walls and towers, that only a couple of months earlier they had been striving to batter down with their heavy siege machines and sapping operations. Astonishingly, the defensive works were nearly complete and repairs to city buildings, homes and infrastructure were commencing. As Stephen Longchamp explained to me, the Christian and Jewish residents of the city had no love for Muslim domination as, being non-Muslim, they paid the dhimmi tax at very high rates and had no desire to return to Muslim government. They had been willing workers and artisans in the rebuilding of the city.

After we had placed those still needing care with the Hospitallers in their hospital compound, I found myself drawn once again to visit the site of my childhood. The three of us wandered through the old city and down to the port. The fire damage to the warehouses and emporia that had been my father's, was now cleared of detritus and the fire blackened remains of the buildings. I could not help but stand there as a flood of memories, smells, sensations and sights from my childhood washed over me in a bittersweet wave of nostalgia. A great sadness overtook me as I realised these no longer belonged to my family as Baldo had sold everything off. I wondered who owned the land now.

I did not have long to wait to find out.

'No loitering now you lot. There is nothing here to steal any way. Move on,' came a gruff voice from behind us.

'Aye, Sir,' I replied to the infantry man posted on guard duty by the docks, 'Perhaps you might know who owns this dockside land now. It used to be in my family.'

The guard eyed me sceptically, looking me up and down, weighing up if what I spoke was the truth. Finally, he acquiesced and said, 'I am not sure who the owner is, but the de Flores family were leasing the warehouses up until recently. I doubt they will have the money to do anything with it now.'

I made a mental note of the "de Flores" family. I would find out where they lived later.

We made our way from the docks to the Pisan quarter where my father's house had once stood, next door to the battered but still standing Church of Saint Peter. The old stones and bricks had all been removed and no doubt had new homes in the defensive reconstruction. The land was basically a large patch of dirt amongst other patches of dirt and houses left undamaged by the stones from the great siege engines.

'I think my bedroom was about here,' I said, standing in the dirt to Ruth and Raymond.

'Oh really,' said a new voice coming up behind us, 'I thought it was mine.'

# 68

The face was bearded, heavily tanned and weathered with deep creases and wrinkles around the mouth and eyes. The nose looked like it might have been broken once and then poorly reset. As the face grinned, revealing a mouth of intact, but yellowed, dentition, it was the blonde forelock sweeping the forehead that gave the newcomer's identity away.

'Cherubino?' I asked tentatively of the man I suspected was my youngest brother and whom I had not seen in over seven years since he had gone to sea in the months prior to my own departure to Jerusalem.

'Ippolito. Is that you?' came the reply as the eyebrows slowly raised.

'Brother,' I laughed holding my arms out and stepping towards him.

'Brother,' came the reply as he too stepped toward me and into a great embrace that saw us rocking back and forth, clutching each other's face between both hands and laughing for sheer joy. How different to my reunion with Baldo.

Finally, and almost breathless with exertion and emotion, we parted and stood there staring at each other taking in the changes time and circumstances had wrought upon us since we had last seen each other.

Cherubino had been the youngest of my three half-brothers and the one I had been closest to, Baldo having been a deceitful and lying bully and Gaetano something of a brawling dullard. I found myself overcome and felt tears welling in my eyes at the same time I noticed my brother's eyes were glistening as well. We both started laughing at each other and fell into another embrace.

Ruth and Raymond both stood by quietly smiling at this reunion, taking joy from it.

'Cherubino,' I said remembering myself and my manners, 'May I introduce .... my, my ... wife Ruth de Jerusalem and our good companion and loyal friend Raymond de Toulouse.'

'Delighted,' replied Cherubino, 'but please, call me Bino. It is how I am known these days.'

'As you may choose Ipp, Ippy or Ippo,' I replied recalling our childhood names for each other.

'This calls for a celebration. I have some excellent wine aboard my ship,' he said turning to the harbour and pointing to a two masted trading galley bobbing away at its anchor, 'Or we could find a quiet and friendly tavern. What is your wish?'

'I would see your ship,' piped a curious Ruth.

'My ship it is,' replied Bino as he turned and led us to the mole that protected the harbour of Acre and down some steps to an awaiting dinghy, crewed by two sailors.

We spent the day aboard The Gull drinking well-watered wine and a range of delicacies that Bino ordered from the galley. Bino congratulated Ruth and I on our "marriage", much to Ruth's quiet amusement and was even more delighted to know that he was to become an uncle.

Condensing the tales of the last seven or more years of our lives took all day, the evening and half the night. Bino was unaware of all that had happened to my father, his trading empire, Gaetano's tragic death on the wheel and Baldo's treachery and theft of the family fortune and our recovery of it. He was even more pleased to learn I had set aside his share and that all we had to do was present the promissory note to the banking marshal of the Templars once their operations were re-established in Acre. We did not mention that Ruth had killed Baldo, simply that he had fallen overboard in the fight we had and drowned.

Ruth was keen to add our dream of building a hospital for the poor, an idea that Bino said had much merit and praised us for such noble ambition.

Bino for his part had spent the first four years of his apprenticeship at sea on one of my father's trading galleys, learning both seamanship and business. He described the numerous ports and nations he had visited. Ruth, Raymond and I were in awe of his tales of the white snow bound northern lands, where for months of the year the sun barely shone for an hour or more. He claimed he had made a small fortune in furs, walrus ivory and amber. He showed us a long scar down his arm given to him by an uncooperative walrus. Apparently, the wound had become infected and it looked like Bino would die from gangrene. He said he had little memory of this time as he was for the most part delirious and, as he said, 'in another place'. His men had given him over to a local shaman who over the period of a few weeks had treated him with herbal infusions, enemas and smoke inhalations derived from various dried substances. Ruth and I paid close attention to this part of his story.

He also spoke of his time in al-Andalusia, a place he said of remarkable tolerance, learning and understanding where Christians, Muslims and Jews were able to live, work and study peacefully side by side, despite the petty war mongering of the minor lords of the land. Their contestations were mostly over territory, not race or religion.

It had not all been good fortune for him, though. His profits from his northern expeditions, his ship and most of his crew had been taken, killed or captured by Barbary pirates on his way home three years ago. Unaware of what had happened within the family, he had been imprisoned with some of his men and held for ransom – a payment which would never come as Baldo was in control of the family fortune by then.

A palace coup and a change of emirs in the Barbery province presented Bino and his remaining men with an opportunity to break free from their prison of three years. Inciting the other prisoners to rebellion, they organised a mass breakout that further destabilised the city even more than it was already. Using the chaos within the city, Bino had led his men to the docks, chosen a suitable vessel for their escape and then set the docks and ships there on fire to make good their escape. As good fortune would have it, their escape vessel was loaded with luxury goods that would fetch a good price in any port of the Mediterranean.

Bino and his new ship, renamed The Gull, set sail for the east and for Acre, eager to unload his manifest and see his family after his time in prison. He also wanted to find the answers as to why no ransom had come for him and his men. He now had them, sad and bitter though they were.

The night got away from us with so much to tell and it was in the small hours of the morning that Bino offered Ruth and me his cabin. He and Raymond would bunk with the sailors.

Lying in our bunk that night, Ruth said something I was a little too drowsy to take in.

'Did you notice how Raymond and Bino kept looking at each other?'

'Not really,' I yawned, falling quickly to sleep.

# 69

We slept late the next morning, the cheer of my brotherly reunion the night before still warming my soul.

Bino and I greeted each other with another great brotherly hug on the deck and were joined by Ruth and Raymond for a leisurely breakfast on, what Bino called, the aftercastle of The Gull. A raised platform above the rear cabins, which served both defensive and offensive purposes.

'We should approach the Templars and city authorities as soon as possible to try and redeem your land and money,' said Ruth chewing on a slice of deliciously pink melon, 'We have the deeds of title to your family home and the warehouses and emporia as well as the promissory note from the Templars.'

'The Temple has not re-established itself here in Acre yet. There is nothing you could call a compound or citadel for any of the Holy Military Orders. The closest we might find a merchant banking branch of the Temple would be in Tyre,' replied Bino.

'And the nobles have not yet settled their disputes over who is the king, or the queen for that matter, of the kingdom of Jerusalem. I think they are waiting on King Richard to decide for them,' offered Raymond.

'The Templars will honour their pledge when they are in a position to, here in Acre. All we really need to do is make sure that the land we own by the docks remains in our hands, along with that of our family home. We can do that by rebuilding as quickly as possible. That will put our stamp on the land well and truly,' offered Bino before continuing, 'I believe the cargo sitting in The Gull's hold will go a long way to getting us started.'

'Don't forget we have a hospital to build,' reminded Ruth.

'I haven't,' said Bino, 'In fact I would very much like to be involved in this noble project of yours. There are many old and permanently injured sailors who would benefit from such an organisation, one that was both a hospital and a home.'

'No reason why it shouldn't be,' I replied.

'Well,' said Raymond, 'I think we have a place and a project to start working on.'

And so, we did.